I0451390

AI RISING

(Book One)

THE DOME

Max Holt & Dan Holt

MaxHoltMedia

MAX HOLT and DAN HOLT

Disclaimer: This is a work of fiction. Names, characters,
businesses, places, events, and incidents are either the products
of the author's imagination or used in a fictitious manner. Any
resemblance to actual persons, living or dead, or actual events is
purely coincidental.

Cover design by Max Holt Media, with Eddie Holt
Cover art by Dreamstime.com
ISBN: 13: 978-1-944537-28-9

Published by: Max Holt Media
303 Cascabel Place,
Mount Juliet, TN 37122
www.maxholtmedia.com
On facebook at www.facebook.com/maxholtmedia
   Email – max@maxholtmedia.com
   Twitter - @maxholtmedia

MAX HOLT and DAN HOLT

Other Sci-Fi books from MaxHoltMedia:
By Dan Holt - Underneath the Moon, Underneath the Moon 2, Underneath the Moon 3, Sleep Mode, & Keepsake
By Dan Holt & Max Holt - Underneath the Moon 4
By Max Holt - Alien Planet

Coming in the fall of 2017, by Max Holt & Dan Holt
AI Rising – Book 2 (ANDROID REBELLION)
Underneath the Moon 5

Check on Audible.com for audio versions of all the above books.

This book is dedicated to our wives, who have learned to tolerate our late-night brainstorms and research that eventually became this story. There is nothing artificial about their intelligence!

To the more than 9,000 readers who have chosen to include our imaginations in their lives...Thank you!

"There is a real danger that computers will develop intelligence and take over. We urgently need to develop direct connections to the brain so that computers can add to human intelligence rather than be in opposition."

Stephen Hawking

PROLOGUE

Australian Outback – New South Wales
December 2, 2014

Miram Jessop yelled from the kitchen, interrupting the BBC broadcast. "Liam Jessop, where are you?!"

Liam swallowed the mouthful of TimTams. "I'm watchin the telly, Mum."

"Didn't I tell you to take out the garbage? I'm looking at it now, and it's overflowing."

"Sorry, Mum, but BBC is interviewing Stephen Hawking. He's my favorite scientist, I want to be just like him.

"Liam!"

"No disrespect, Mum, I don't mean the ALS and being in a wheelchair. I just want to be as brave and smart as him. I'll take out the garbage as soon as it's over, I promise."

"Okay, see that you do, and don't forget your homework."

"Yes, Mum, I already set it up on the roof. Thirty more minutes and it'll be dark enough." He turned his attention back to BBC.

"...so, Professor, are you saying you really believe that artificial intelligence could be the end of mankind and that thinking machines pose a threat to our very existence?"

"Yes, that is what I believe."

"I have read that Bill Gates and Elon Musk share some of your concerns, that AI is our biggest existential threat. But, aren't all of you are being a little over-dramatic? Machines taking over the world is just science fiction. You have said that the very machine that enables you to speak with me now uses a basic form of artificial intelligence."

"Yes, that is true. Intel and SwiftKey are to be commended for this technology. They designed it to actually learn how I think and to suggest words I may want to use next."

"Well, sir, that sounds like a good thing. I don't see anything sinister in that."

"I agree, but we humans are seldom satisfied with where

9

we are in technology. Primitive forms of AI are very useful, but I fear the consequences of continued development that creates processors capable of matching or surpassing the human brain."

"Let's assume that you are right. Don't you think our scientists would put controls in place to prevent the misuse of such processors?"

"We would certainly try to do that. But, mistakes happen, even in the best of circumstances. With just one mistake, such systems could take off on their own and redesign themselves at an ever increasing rate. Humans are limited by slow biological evolution and would be unable to compete. We could eventually be superseded by the systems we created."

"Professor, I'm not sure I can agree with your AI prophesy, but thank you for being here. You have given us a lot to think about. Perhaps, in the future, we can pursue the subject at greater depth."

"It would be my pleasure."

The interviewer turned to the camera. "This is **David Mizel, BBC World News**, Tune in next week, when we discuss the dangers inherent in the Internet. Good day from London."

Liam grabbed another TimTam, walked to the kitchen and took the bag of garbage to the container outside. His eyes adjusted to the darkness as he climbed the outside stairway to the roof. His father had allowed him to build a makeshift observatory to make full use of the new XT-71i Orion Intelliscope he had received for his 16th birthday. His Astronomy homework project required him to focus on the moon, locate all Apollo landing sites and record the pieces of debris the astronauts had left behind. As he viewed the Apollo 14 landing site in the Fra Maura Highlands, his heart skipped a beat; he saw a tiny green flicker! He cleaned the lens and refocused; it was still there. He video-recorded it for ten minutes before it disappeared. He sent the recording to Dr. Jack Peel in the USA, NASA's Director of Lunar Studies. Despite repeated inquiries, he heard nothing.

CHAPTER 1

DISCOVERY

The Sea of Tranquility
The Moon - August 2081

Ken Anderson left his Maintenance Crew Quarters in the outer sector and was halfway to Ore Pump 27. He had made this trip countless times, since he came to the moon with Quantum Mining 20 years earlier. As he bounded along in two-meter leaps, his communications system activated.

"Hey Cowboy, are you there yet?"

"That's a negative, Red, I'm about 50 meters away. What's up?"

"Maintenance just called. They're getting a strange high temp reading from the Interface Module and the sound level is up by 20 db. That may be caused by the increased pump vibrations. They said you may need to shut it down and replace the pressure seal. There's a new one in the parts locker, if you need it."

"Roger, I'll take a look at it. It's been six months since we did a service on 27. It probably needs to be changed."

Continuing toward the pump, Ken glanced at the beautiful blue earth, hanging in the lunar sky. He'd be leaving tomorrow and could hardly wait to get back to Houston, to his new bride. He and Sandi had been married for just three months. She was the Lunar VP's daughter and Quantum's Shuttle Director. Dr. Maddox was a good lunar boss and, Ken felt, Quantum's best Vice President; Ken would miss him.

Back on Earth, Ken and Sandi would be busy, preparing for the Mars Mission, launching next year. He would be the Mission Commander and Sandi would direct all shuttle activity, supporting Quantum's mining crews as they established operations on Mars. Red and his Quadrant Four Crew had been assigned to the mission, to oversee the mining start-up on Mars.

Ken had dreamed about landing on Mars, since he was a small boy on his grandpa's West Texas farm. Grandpa's stories had stirred his astronaut dreams and the old man began calling him his *little space cowboy*. Being from Texas, the *cowboy* part stuck with him throughout his career. After this one last job today, *Cowboy* would realize his dream.

"Hey, Ken, my monitor shows a rapid increase in pump vibrations. I don't like the looks of it. When you get there, go ahead and shut it down so we can run the diagnostics."

"Okay...almost there."

When Ken stopped a few meters short of the pump enclosure, Red said, "Smile Cowboy, you're on the Maintenance video."

Ken gave a thumb's-up to the camera. "Everything looks normal outside, Red. I'll go in and shut it down."

"Roger."

Ken grabbed the door handle and immediately felt a tingle all the way up his arm. Ken saw the increased vibrations and heard the alarm sound.

"Ken, the alarm just went off, the vibrations are over the limit. Shut it down quick!"

"Roger, going in."

Ken opened the enclosure door and stopped in his tracks. "Oh, my God!"

"What is it, Ken?"

"It's green!"

"What's green?"

"Everything!"

Red's eyes went to the monitor. "Ken...get out of there, the pressure's climbing fast, the pump's gonna blow!"

As Ken turned to retreat toward his Crew Quarters, his feet got tangled and he fell. Struggling to get back on his feet, he could feel the surface vibrating, making it difficult to walk.

"Ken! Everything's over the red line. You better find a crater. Hurry!"

There was a deep crater about 20 meters away. Ken took

two long steps and leaped into a flat position, diving toward the opening. Just then, the massive pump exploded. A large metal piece of the pump-wall smashed into the thick soles of his boots, accelerating him past the small crater and 10 meters higher into the atmosphere. In a moment, he disappeared from the video; the maintenance camera had been destroyed.

"Ken, Ken, can you hear me?!"

There was static and then Ken's voice. "Yeah, Red, I'm okay for now, but whatever hit my boots has pushed me way past CQ. I'm over the boulder field, headed toward Aldrin Creator. I've got an oxygen alarm so I'll need a quick rescue after I land."

"Land on your feet, Buddy, the visor can't take that kind of impact."

"Roger."

Aldrin Crater was coming up fast. Ken put his arms down to waist-level, to shift weight toward his feet, causing his head to rise. He pointed his toes and slightly bent his knees. When his boots hit the surface, his knees buckled and slammed into his chest. Ken felt the shooting pain as his left leg broke. He threw his arms forward, rotated over his feet and landed on his belly in the dust-filled crater. He plowed a 30-meter-long trench across the crater, until his helmet and shoulder impacted a large rock. A grapefruit-sized chunk of the rock broke off and fell against his visor. Two inches outside his helmet, Ken was staring at a lunar rock, glowing solid green...inside! Before he could make sense of it, the pain hit his brain full-force. As he was being covered by the falling dust and debris, Ken closed his eyes. The last thing he heard before surrendering to unconscientiousness was...silence.

CHAPTER 2

THE HOLOGRAM

With his DNA Sensor Band in place, Evan Joseph looked down from the top of the 3,800-meter-high Zermatt Glacier at the top of the Matterhorn in the Swiss Alps. He could see the city of Zermatt, Switzerland over 2,000 meters below. Mid-way down the glacier, his two good friends were waiting to join him on the bottom, less-challenging, half of the ski run.

So, he jabbed his poles into the glacier ice, flexed his knees and pushed over the edge of Zermatt. The immediate descent almost took his breath away, and his speed quickly reached thirty kilometers per hour. After the second turn, it was nearing sixty.

Just 300 meters from the first groomed slope, his friends began yelling for him to slow down. When he yelled back, it happened; trees began to disappear and the glacier began to move up and down like the ocean surf. Instantly, he was in midair, a thousand meters above the ground. When he looked down, his skis had disappeared and the city of Zermatt was gone. Before he had time to analyze the failure, everything went dark.

Evan sat back in disappointment. "Uh...Tim, go ahead and hit the lights."

The lights came back on in the Hologram Test Chamber. He stood and stepped away from the Interface Chair, unsnapped the DNA Brainwave Sensor Band from his forehead, and looked up through the observation window.

Timothy Cole was smiling back. "Evan! Man, that was awesome! Come up and check this video replay. You were in Gold Medal form, up until the CPUs locked up."

Evan climbed the stairs to the lab and watched the replay until he saw the snow begin to disappear from under his skis. "Right there; stop it there. Now back up just a little." Tim reversed it and restarted it in slow motion. Evan pointed, "There it is; just like yesterday. See, the smaller objects start disappearing first? The last to go is everything right around the

15

test subject."

Evan and Tim had been struggling with the Hologram Generator for months, trying to work out the kinks. The boss, Bernard Harrington, had been pressing them for some results; he was not going to be happy.

Evan scratched his head. "We have *got* to figure this thing out. Yesterday everything looked perfect in Philadelphia. You walked through town and went to the Pub Restaurant."

Tim nodded. "Yeah; the food smelled real and I think that pretty waitress liked me."

Evan stared for a moment. "Tim, focus; you imagined her."

"Oh, yeah, right."

"So, finally, you were right there with the Continental Congress when they started signing the Declaration of Independence..."

"Yeah," Tim interrupted, "and then I spoke to Thomas Jefferson and his head disappeared; freaked me out." He paused. "Hum...you're right; it starts falling apart with small things first. But, why didn't the flight through the Grand Canyon fail?"

Evan theorized. "The common thread I see in all of the failed holograms is, uh... people. Every time we create people in our adventures and interact with them, the processors must generate very complicated algorithms. When the CPU capacity is stretched to the limit, it starts dropping nonessential graphics."

"Yeah. We've got to have more, much more, processor speed. We can't afford to lose any more presidents' heads!"

CHAPTER 3

THE GREEN GLOW

The Medical Shuttle was ten kilometers away, approaching Headquarters, when Ken finally woke up. He was groggy from the pain meds the Quadrant Four Medic had given him. He looked around and saw the blurry form of his best friend.

"Red, what happened."

Red leaned over the gurney. "Man, you had us scared to death out there. It's a good thing I got to the crater before you got covered by the dust. That was quick thinking; pointing the soles of your boots toward the explosion when that pump blew...you looked just like Superman...it saved your life."

"What about Sandi, does she know?"

Dr. Maddox' blurry face leaned over. "Yes, I called her when Red first told me about the blow-out. She's on her way. She'll be here about noon tomorrow. She knows you're alive but she needs to hear your voice, after the infirmary gets you patched up."

"Yes, sir, I just want her to know I'm okay." As Ken's head cleared a little more he reached up and grabbed Dr. Maddox' arm. "Sir, you won't believe what I saw when I opened the pump enclosure door. Everything was—"

Dr. Maddox glanced at the shuttle crew as he interrupted and leaned in close, "Uh, Ken, we can discuss that later. Right now, you just need to rest."

"But, sir, I saw it in the crater too."

"I know, Ken, but we need to wait for Sandi before we can share all that you need to know about what you saw."

Red leaned closer. "Was there some sort of secret experiment going on at 27? Did Ken stumble onto some new ore being pumped out?"

"No, not exactly. Just wait; you'll learn everything tomorrow.

Lunar Infirmary

The Emergency Room staff evaluated and treated Ken's injuries in just twenty minutes. Finally, he arrived in his room with a gleaming white acrylic cast, with built-in pain control. Ken was feeling great; just tired.

The doctor was waiting. "Well, Ken, it looks like you'll totally recover. Given your circumstances, this is like a miracle."

"Thanks, Doc. I hope this doesn't mess up my trip Earthside. Mars Mission prep starts pretty soon."

"Don't worry, you'll heal quickly in this low gravity. We'll let you out tomorrow morning, but don't walk on that cast for a couple of days. Use the Med-Glider or a good woman to lean on." His smiled turned serious. "How's Sandi taking all this?"

"Dr. Maddox called her when Red found me but I haven't talked to her yet. So, if somebody will get me a communicator, I'll take care of that right now."

The doctor handed Ken his.

"Thanks, Doc." Ken flipped open the device and entered Sandi's code.

Onboard the Lunar Shuttle

By the time the shuttle had broken free of Earth orbit, Sandi and her best friend Linda, were half-way through her description of all the activities she and Ken had planned before launching for Mars next year. She jumped when her communicator chirped.

"It's gotta be him!" She flipped it open so quickly it escaped her grip and floated free momentarily. She reached out and grabbed it.

"Ken?!" she sobbed.

"Hi, Honey. Are you crying? If this is a bad time I can call back," Ken teased her.

"Don't you dare hang up! Oh, Ken, I love you so. I was so worried I almost died. And I'm mad at you! You should let the young guys handle those pump jobs. You could have been killed! And I'd be stuck living the rest of my life without--"

Ken interrupted. "I'm sorry honey. I was just in the wrong

place at the wrong time. Now, I'm all bandaged up, laying here in the hospital bed, wishing I had you in my arms."

Sandi melted. "Oh, Ken, I'm sorry I yelled. Just get some rest and I'll be there by noon tomorrow. Are they taking care of you?"

"Everything's fine. I'm just exhausted, both physically and mentally."

"Well, just do whatever the doctor says. When I get there, you're the first one I want to see. Get some rest...I love you!"

"Love ya too...see you tomorrow."

Sandi was still on a *high* when they arrived at Quantum's Main Shuttle Port a few minutes before 11:00 a.m. the next day. Red had helped Ken check out of the Infirmary in time to meet Sandi.

When the shuttle doors opened, there stood Ken, balancing himself on his good leg. "Hi, Honey!"

She screamed his name and lunged into his arms with tears flowing. They both fell backwards and landed on the seat of the medical glider, with Sandi in his lap, arms around his neck. She tried to get up but he held her there.

"Oh, Ken, am I hurting you? Honey, are you OK?"

Ken smiled, "Sweetheart, this is the best medicine I've ever had. Just let me hold you."

They hugged and kissed Red finally interrupted them. "OK, you two, it's getting too syrupy and gooey around here. Let's get going before this Cowboy ruins his he-man image."

Sandi blushed and got up. She gave Red a hug. "Thanks for saving Ken. I'll owe you for the rest of my life."

"Well, I debated if he was worth saving. But I figured, what the heck, I had a little extra time before lunch and, anyway, it's my job."

Dr. Maddox' Office

As they ate lunch, Ken and Red shared the details of the Pump 27 explosion, Ken's rescue from Aldrin Crater and the green substance that had been inside the pump enclosure and in the crater.

Sandi asked, "What is this *green stuff* you keep talking about?"

Ken said, "Yeah, the chunk we brought back from the crater was glowing, like it was alive, or something. What's up with that?"

Dr. Maddox stood. "Come with me and I'll show you."

He stepped to the closet door behind his desk and opened it.

Sandi said, "Dad, where are we going? We won't all fit in your closet."

He just smiled, placed his hand inside a recessed hand-print beside the door frame, and the entire back wall of the closet opened into the reception area of a large secret research lab. There were many technicians in white lab-coats, working in different cubicles. Through a large window, overlooking the pressurized lab, they could see a dull green glow. After a moment of realization, they all looked at Dr. Maddox.

Through a smile, he said, "After today, the world will never be the same."

CHAPTER 4

ARRIVAL

Three days Later...5:00 p.m., Houston, TX

Quantum Corporate News Conference

"Good afternoon, Ladies and gentlemen. This is Jonathan Angle, International Broadcast Network News, live from Houston, Texas, where Quantum Corporation is scheduled to begin a news conference in a few minutes.

"The world was stunned three days ago when Quantum did an unannounced shut-down of all communications with their facilities on the moon, and barred all non-company shuttle traffic from departing Earth. Quantum has the only arrival shuttle ports available anywhere on the moon.

"As we reported three days ago, the International Seismic Network of sensors on the moon picked up a seismic event, in Sector 27 of Quadrant Four, that measured five-point-two on the Richter Scale. One of Quantum's highest-producing mines is in Sector 27. Repeated requests for information from Quantum, about the event and the immediate shut-down of communications, have been denied. Quantum officials have promised to explain their actions during the upcoming news conference.

"Rumors have been circulating that a meteorite hit the surface or that there was some sort of explosion in or near their ore pump in Sector 27. Neither case would explain the communications and shuttle traffic blackout."

The young reporter touched his earpiece. "I've just been told that Mr. Anthony Zurelle, CEO of Quantum, and his staff are on their way out here to the south lawn of their headquarters to address the strange events of three days ago. Please stand by."

The aging owner of Quantum Mining climbed the steps of the

temporary platform with his staff and the lunar contingent involved in the recent event on the moon. Ken had to be helped up the stairs; the full gravity was not kind to his broken leg.

After all were seated, Zurelle approached the podium. "Ladies and gentlemen, thank you for being here on this warm Texas afternoon. I'm told that there may be upwards of three billion viewers from around the world and news media teams from at least 80 countries. So, let me say, welcome to Houston." There was sporadic applause.

"As our friends in the media have been saying, the events of three days ago deserve an explanation. Tuesday morning of this week, our outgoing Lunar Maintenance Chief, Mr. Kenneth Anderson, was doing his last maintenance job before being reassigned here to Houston. As you know, he was selected to command Quantum's first mission to Mars next year, to establish mining operations there.

"As he was preparing to shut down Ore Pump 27 for maintenance, he opened the door and was shocked to see the pump covered in some sort of green corrosion. Before he had a chance to investigate, the pressure-regulating system failed and the pump exploded. Fortunately, he had a few seconds notice and was able to leap into a level position, so the thick soles of his boots would take the brunt of the explosion. That quick thinking saved his life. The force of the explosion carried him about two kilometers away, into Aldrin Crater. He was rescued within a few minutes by the Quadrant Four Operations Chief, Mr. Carl Wilson. His bushy red hair will explain why we at Quantum call him Red. Ken's only injury was a broken leg." He turned to Ken. "Let me introduce him to you. Some are already calling him Superman."

Ken stood, with Sandi helping him. The thousands in the crowd stood and cheered, as Ken's wave was broadcast around the world.

Zurelle continued. "Mr. Anderson will be available for interviews in the coming days. Contact Linda Hudson in the Quantum Communications Office with your requests. Now, for a more detailed description of what really happened, that caused us to temporarily shut down communications and shuttle traffic,

I will call on Dr. Wesley Maddox, our Vice-President for Lunar Operations. Dr. Maddox."

Wes Maddox stood to address the crowd. "We've had a large team of experts investigating the Pump 27 explosion, 24 hours a day. Since the pump is collocated with the Apollo Eleven landing site, we even researched NASA records to see if there was a connection. For you to understand our actions over the last few days, I need to go all the way back to 2014, to Queensland in the Australian Outback. Liam Jessop, a young teenager doing his homework, was viewing the Apollo Fourteen landing site and videoed an, uh, anomaly, I'll call it, at the site. He sent the video to NASA for analysis. Due to a clerical error in their Shipping and Receiving Department, the video was never seen by NASA officials.

"You'll remember that back in 1969, NASA, the National Aeronautics and Space Administration, which is now called the International Space Consortium, began its Apollo moon landings. The first was Apollo 11, the Tranquility Base site near Pump 27. There were six moon landings during that program. Six of our mining sectors are on or near those landing sites.

"Now, fast forward to five months ago. When one of our shuttles was passing over the area where Apollo Fourteen landed, they saw a green light on the surface."

As hands went up in the Press Corps, Maddox ignored them and continued. "We had never installed lights there, so the crew stopped to investigate. They found that a small meteorite had impacted and broken the tops off several rocks and that the insides were,… ah, glowing green."

Gasps were audible. Multiple responses drowned each other out: "Green?"

 "Glowing?!"

"What was it?!"

Maddox held up both hands. "I know this sounds bizarre, but you'll understand when I finish. We had no idea what we were dealing with or if the samples were contaminated or dangerous. We ran several tests on the material and could find no dangerous properties. But what we did discover shocked us all." He took a breath. "It contained… live bacteria."

The response was what he expected. Most stood. Some looked at each other, searching for the appropriate words. Simultaneously there were shouts of, "Alive?!"

"Bacteria?!"

"Life on the Moon?!"

And the anticipated question, "Was it alien?!"

Within moments, viewers were overloading the communicator systems around the world.

Dr. Maddox held up both hands to restore order. He continued. "The alien question was also the first one we asked. So, we contacted Dr. Amal Gustav, one of the world's few scientists studying chemical and mineral bio-combinations. The Dr. is now our Chief of Research. He and his team traveled to the moon and began an extensive analysis of the mineral we had discovered. I'll ask him to come and explain what their research has revealed so far...Dr. Gustav."

When the scientist stood, someone shouted, "Dr., is the stuff dangerous?"

Dr. Gustav smiled. In his European accent, he said, "No, actually it is quite benign. Our analysis of the bacteria showed it to be a strain that originated in the nineteenth century, first discovered in the Himalayan Mountains. It is very rare and was known to have caused skin diseases in wild cats and Peruvian horses.

"At some point, it was passed to humans and manifested itself as a disease that caused extreme elasticity of the skin and, in rare cases, elasticity in the walls of internal organs, which is the life-threatening strain. Dr. Niles Ehlers and Dr. Gunter Danlos, the two medical researchers who first detected it in humans, gave it their names. Medical journals list it as Ehlers-Danlos Syndrome. A cure was found in 2051, so the bacteria virtually disappeared, until we made the discovery on the moon.

"So, it is quite clear that it came from Earth. We calculated it to be over a hundred and twenty years old, so it's obvious that it was transported to the moon by the Apollo 14 Lander. When we searched the landing site, we found that during the 120-plus years since Apollo, about ninety percent of the rocks, for a couple of kilometers around, had combined with the bacteria and fused into what we can best describe as a living mineral or more accurately, a living metal.

"We wondered why it had combined with metal ions until we realized that ninety percent of the rocks in Sector Five are rich in Zelon metal particles. You already know that Zelon is one of Quantum's major exports to the computer industry, used primarily in high-density processor chips. We discovered that the atoms in the bacteria are heavier than those in Zelon. When the two fused together the electrons in both collided with each other. That molecular interaction of the two elements resulted in the green glow.

"We had not discovered the new mineral earlier because lunar dust covers everything on the moon, which hid the glow from view until the young Australian boy caught it on his telescope video. Maybe a small meteorite impact temporarily uncovered it. The dust, slowly settling from that strike, would have recovered it. We would have discovered it sooner or later. It was just a fluke that the shuttle crew happened upon it when they did. Mr. Anderson saw it on Pump 27 and when he landed in Aldrin Crater, he broke a piece off a large rock and it was glowing green inside as well." He paused. "Well, I've been describing it to you; I guess you'd like to see it firsthand. Here is the piece that Ken and Red brought back from the crater."

He slowly lifted a cube-shaped case onto the podium and opened it, revealing a grapefruit-sized hunk of green-glowing ore. Every camera zoomed in for a close-up. Reporters were standing and moving toward the platform for a closer look. Security had to prevent some from climbing onto the stage. View-Panels in Times Square and Tokyo and all over the world broadcasted the green glow that would define how 2081 would go down in history.

After the crowd calmed, Dr. Gustav continued. "We have found it only at the Apollo eleven and fourteen sites. Technical reports for those two missions reported violations of *Clean Room Procedures*. A technician named Robert Kellogg sorted and packed the astronauts' tools for those two flights. The records also showed that he was medically retired in 1974 for a chronic skin disorder, and he died in 1977 of Ehlers-Danlos Syndrome.

Somehow, he must have violated the safety standards; maybe a torn glove or a defective respirator, something like that."

Someone finally asked, "What do you call this new substance; Zelon Plus?"

Dr. Maddox answered. "No. Mr. Zurelle decided to honor his grandfather, who founded Quantum. He named this new substance Zurelleum; spelled like his last name but with 'um' added on the end."

Someone asked, "So, what's the stuff good for?"

The crowd laughed and made various frivolous comments. Under his breath, someone said, "So, the moon IS made of green cheese." The laughter was even louder.

Dr. Gustav continued. "I'd like for my new assistant to explain that and where we go from here."

Chan Yoshan stood. "Green cheese aside, we are excited about the possible applications for Zurelleum. To put this in perspective, in 2014, the first Neurogrid Chip was developed. By nesting the chips together, bioengineers were able to simulate a million brain neurons and billions of synapses. Of course, the brain has 80 billion neurons and a yet-to-be-counted number of synapses, so the impact on artificial intelligence research was minimal.

"Our discovery of Zelon, as a replacement for silicone in computer chips years ago, pushed the neuron count up to only about 20 million, which is still some distance from mimicking true brain function.

"Now, tests done by Dr. Gustav's team indicate that Zurelleum is not only good for producing high-density processor chips, but it also speeds up the processors, four to five-fold. It means that the current system processor speeds of two-point-five teraflops could possibly be retrofitted with Zurelleum-based processors and increase that speed close to twelve teraflops."

Chan saw some confused looks. "You might remember that the term teraflops, is the designation for One-Trillion-Floating-Point-Operations-Per-Second. So, for the first time," he paused, "fully functioning artificial intelligence in a small processor may be possible."

Those in the room who understood the implication, stopped breathing momentarily.

Almost 2,500 kilometers south of Houston, along the Pan American Highway in the Guatemalan mountains, MIT Professor Emeritus, Dr. Braxton Newberry was watching. He was alone in the austere office of the children's computer school he had volunteered to lead. He was known throughout the computer industry as the Father of Artificial Intelligence Research. As Chan made the announcement, the old man leaned back in his chair and smiled. "Finally!" he said.

Over 2,900 kilometers northeast of Houston, MIT's AI researchers were on the edge of their seats. Years of research and failure were about to become a thing of the past. The Lead Team Programmer was Eric Jennings, Ken Anderson's nephew.

Chan continued. "The applications of Zurelleum-based processors could give Quantum the edge in chip manufacturing and will possibly change the computer industry forever."

Dr. Gustav stepped back to the podium. "So, it seems that we have a *tiger by the tail*, and we do not know exactly which way it will run. My assistant will return to the moon and continue the testing of the original samples of our new mineral. I will open a testing lab at the Houston Space Center to begin new tests here. And, before anyone asks, yes, we will make samples available for other testing agencies, but only after we have finished our own tests. That is standard procedure for any organization that discovers something new. The discoverer always gets the first benefit, as it should always be. Now, Mr. Zurelle will have the final word before the Q&A."

Zurelle stepped forward. "That concludes our briefing on this amazing find on the moon. We have allotted one hour for your questions."

Reporters stood and asked questions, based on the order awarded them by lottery prior to the news conference. Despite assurances during the briefing, that the bacteria were *not* alien, the question was still asked by several reporters. Some accused Quantum of not telling the whole truth about Zurelleum or of keeping other discoveries hidden. Finally, the Q&A was over and the reporters hurried to their communications vans to file their stories, trying to be the first to hit the Media Stream.

The next morning, the Media Stream was ripe with multiple renditions of the truth and outrageous stories of fiction. The financial debate was already raging over the expected impact of Zurelleum on the computer industry. Regardless of Quantum's assurances that the bacteria were of Earth origin, some headlines read, *"LIFE Discovered on the Moon!"*

Leaders of the world's major religions had already issued statements to their followers that mirrored Quantum's report, that this discovery was NOT alien life but merely bacteria that had originated on Earth. However, some sects were taking outrageous actions. One group had ordered its followers to assemble on the top of Mount Rainer and wait for an alien ship from the moon to pick them up.

The tabloids were printing outlandish and laughable stories. One story *documented* secret meetings between Jacob Holloway, President of the Tri-America States, and the President of the alien inhabitants of the moon. One physic publication offered to instruct practicing physics on how to channel conversations with Lunar Spirits. UFO sightings increased ten-fold overnight.

Zurelle had already instructed Wes Maddox to schedule the first shipment of Zurelleum material, as soon as it was ready, for delivery to Tri-States Zelon Processing Company, a subsidiary of Quantum. Whenever Gustav finished the testing and released Zurelleum for marketing, Tri-States would manufacture the first operational Zurelleum Processors. The first seven were to be shipped to the PARADISE Theme Park in St. Louis. Soon after, shipments of smaller processors would go to ARTech Laboratories in Texas, for insertion in the androids they were producing for PARADISE.

The owner of PARADISE, Bernard Herrington, was an old friend of Zurelle's and Tony owed him a favor. During Houston's annual golf tournament for CEOs, Bernie had complained about the continued failure of his new hologram generator, due to insufficient processor speeds. It was supposed to be the main attraction and money-maker of his new theme park. Zurelle thought that if his new processors could solve the hologram problem, he would be *one-upping* his old friend. Of course, he knew Herrington would be willing to pay a *pretty penny* for the new technology. In his world, friendship was always accompanied by money.

By mid-morning, Tony Zurelle got a call from his old friend, asking to finalize the deal. Tony told him he already had the first shipment planned for PARADISE. Harrington thanked him and said that if Zurelleum solved his hologram problem, his theme park would be a great advertisement for Quantum to use in their marketing. He felt certain that the increased data speeds would provide the computing power necessary to make PARADISE viable. Anthony Zurelle was counting on that success to pad Quantum's bottom line.

CHAPTER 5

THE ANOMALY

Gustav and Chan had asked for a meeting with Zurelle and Maddox, at the Space Center site, soon to be the Earth-side testing lab. Gustav got right to the point.

"Gentlemen, while reviewing our previous tests on Zurelleum, we noticed something that is worth mentioning. We started a conductivity test on one milligram of Zurelleum almost four months ago. The test is still running in the same vacuum chamber today. We are also running a parallel test with the same amount of pure Zelon. The tests show that Zurelleum is consistently four times more conductive that Zelon, plus or minus .011 teraflops."

Zurelle asked. "That confirms what you've already told us. Why are you concerned?"

"Well, sir, the amount of Zelon is still exactly one milligram. But, the test weight of the Zurelleum now reads 1.00001 milligrams."

Maddox asked. "What does that prove? Couldn't the difference just be dust or some other foreign matter?"

Gustav shook his head, "No sir. Both samples are in a clean-room sterile vacuum; nothing got in. We will use the same clean-room standards here in Houston when the lab is ready to test samples."

"So, are you insinuating that the Zurelleum is growing? That's impossible, right?"

Chan answered. "Actually, we are a little stumped ourselves. The extra ten-thousandths of a milligram should not be there. We have checked and double-checked the equipment, but found nothing wrong. I've even started looking at the latest Dark Matter research, as a possibility."

"Dark Matter?" Zurelle questioned, "You mean the stuff that supposedly fills up a lot of outer space, but many scientists are not even sure it exists? That stuff?"

Gustav nodded. "Yes sir, that stuff. We feel it may be the only explanation. Our theory is that the electrons in the bacteria, changing orbits and inter-meshing with Zelon electrons, have caused this anomaly.   This inter-meshing generates enough friction that the electrons may be capturing a tiny amount of *something*, maybe Dark Matter, each time they exchange orbits. If so, when the electrons grow too large to stay in their orbits, they have collisions with each other, knocking off the extra weight of this possible Dark Matter.

"It is then attracted by the protons in the nucleus, adding to the atomic weight of that atom. Of course, when the protons change, you have a new element. It appears that this process has changed both the bacteria and Zelon, creating Zurelleum. With the process repeating itself, the size of the sample has continued to grow. We didn't notice it at first, because the process has taken so long to register on our instruments."

Zurelle hesitated, "Are...are you saying Zurelleum is dangerous?"

"No sir. We will continue our testing, but at this time, we do not have the data to assume that at all."

Maddox questioned. "Are you suggesting that we not move forward with the marketing of our new mineral?"

Gustav shook his head. "No sir. We have no grounds to recommend a halt to the processing and sale of Zurelleum."

"So, what are you trying to tell us?"

"Sir, it is an anomaly that we feel is worth mentioning. We don't know why Zurelleum exhibits this property. It may be a good thing.   It may increase the conductivity even more, resulting in more than a five-fold increase in processor speed; we just don't know yet."

Zurelle thought for a moment. "Alright, I get paid the big bucks to make decisions, so here it is. We will proceed with our research and marketing plan for Zurelleum. This conversation will stay between the four of us. Limit the number of people conducting the tests at both labs, and brief them on the security expectations.

"Step up your efforts to solve this mystery. If you ever

believe we have made the wrong decision, contact the two of us immediately and we will decide the proper course of action. Are we all agreed?"

There were nods all around.

After the bosses left, Chan and Dr. Gustav called Area Z on the moon and checked the test status. The sample had gained another millionth of a milligram. Chan booked a shuttle back to the moon, to continue his search.

CHAPTER 6

DARK MATTER

When Gustav finally established the new lab in Houston, Chan called to confirm that the lunar samples were already slowing in their accumulation of extra mass. The initial testing had shown an increased data transmission rate. He said that Zurelleum chips would be ready for testing in active circuits in a couple of months and could be incorporated into fully-capable CPUs by early in the next year.

After a conference call to inform Dr. Maddox, Chan still looked concerned.

Gustav said, "Don't worry, my friend. Dr. Maddox will help us keep common sense in this process; you'll see."

Ken and Sandi's condo, downtown Houston

Ken and Sandi had planned to move from their condo, out to the Houston Space Center, to provide more privacy from the press, as they started their training for the Mars mission. Saturday afternoon, they were loading the last of their belongings into a large moving van. Red, and Linda Hudson, had arrived to see if they could help. Sandi and Linda were setting the priorities for loading. Ken and Red were just *supervising*. Soon, they heard a voice coming from the front door.

"Hey, Hero, can I have your autograph?!"

They all went to the living room and saw Eric and his friend, Allison Newberry, standing in the doorway.

Ken pointed his med glider toward the door. "Eric! What are you doing here, kid?"

Linda leaned over. "He came to the headquarters earlier, looking for you. He asked me not to tell; he wanted to surprise you."

Ken stood from the seat of his glider and gave Eric a bear-hug. "I thought you would still be at MIT, trying to figure out the green stuff."

"Yeah, well, the team is still reeling from the announcement and has already started an impact analysis. Allie and I flew down to see you and go to the Texans' pre-season game tomorrow. This may be the only break we get for a while."

"So, Allie is the beautiful girl you were talking about."

Allie's dimpled cheeks were framing a big smile.

Eric nodded. "Yes. This is my special friend, Allison Newberry. She graduated from MIT and is leading a work study for our team in Robot Application Programming. Her dad, Keith, is the Ex-Navy pilot I was telling you about. He is also a big investor in the PARADISE theme park."

Ken shook Allie's hand. "Well, I must say, Eric was right about you; beautiful and smart. The pleasure is all mine. I've read some of the papers your grandfather published on AI. He is quite the pioneer. How is Professor Newberry these days?"

"Oh, he's retired now, running a Tech School for kids in the mountains of Guatemala. He said he wanted a slower lifestyle."

Sandi gave her a hug. "Hi, Allison, it's good to see you and Eric again. I know you were at the wedding but I was a little *busy* to notice a lot that day."

Eric said, "Well, I just came for the snacks at the reception."

As they all laughed, Red turned to Eric. "Ken tells me you are on the cutting edge of some new artificial intelligence technology; some big project."

"Yes sir, we're working for the biggest high-tech theme park in the world; they call it PARADISE. They have a Zelon-based system that uses human brain inputs to create holographic images that people can interact with. But the processor speeds are too slow, so the holograms keep falling apart. We are trying to develop an AI Main Core that will solve the problem, but the slow processor speeds have been a little frustrating."

"Really? Bernard Harrington is a good friend of Mr. Zurelle. They've already talked about this. The boss thinks the new Zurelleum Ken found in Sector 27 may help with your research."

"Yes sir, I think so, too. It might solve our biggest problem; the inability of the computers to handle the number of inputs from the normal human brain."

Ken had sat back down on his glider. "It sounds like you are in the right field. Allie, keep an eye on this young man. He's one of the guys with a *normal* brain, you know." He was smiling at Sandi.

After a few more minutes, Eric and Allie said their goodbyes and headed for some sight-seeing, since it was their first trip to Houston.

After a couple of hours, the truck was loaded and the four friends headed for the company VIP Suite at the new testing Lab, on the grounds of the Houston Space Center. The suite had been furnished with an ADA robot, the female Model 21. Given Ken's condition, the Automated Domestic Assistant would be greatly appreciated.

When the truck was finally unloaded, they were left staring at stacks of boxes all over the apartment. Ken looked at the workload and cleared his throat. "Um...I vote for a delay and an early dinner at Del Frisco's Double Eagle Steak House."

Sandi and Linda raised their hands in a YES vote.

Red smiled, "I was going to take Linda there last night, but my loan was disapproved."

Lunar Lab

Chan was continuing his research but was surprised at how little he found about Dark Matter. Scientists had not yet proven that the building blocks of Dark Matter even existed. Although there were reports of some promising Japanese research on both Dark Matter and Antimatter, it had not yet officially been released; it was still in the *rumor stage*.

Chan knew that back in 1998, the ancient Hubble Telescope had recorded the first recognized supernova, the explosion of a giant star. From that event, scientists came to believe that the expansion of the Universe could only be explained by its unseen elements, which they believed to be only five percent physical matter. The remainder was thought to be seventy percent Dark

Energy, an unseen force, and twenty-five percent Dark Matter; undetectable sub-particles. But, since then, not much of the theory had been proven.

Supposedly, Dark Matter filled outer space, everywhere, even in the electron orbits of atoms. Normally, according to the theory, electrons' orbits would be unaffected by the surrounding Dark Matter because it didn't affect the nuclei.

Chan scratched his head and asked himself, *"If that is true, and if this stuff really exists, why are the Zurelleum electrons attracting and retaining Dark Matter? And, does the additional mass really have an impact? After all, the growth of the Zurelleum sample has slowed to almost zero."*

One other anomaly seemed like a good thing; the data transmission speed of the sample had increased again, slightly.

Finally, Chan noticed an older, worn book off to the side. It was written by an astrophysicist from India and was entitled, THE DARK SIDE OF DARK MATTER. In mid-yawn, he thought, *"I don't have time for it now."* He placed it back on the desk and turned in for the night.

CHAPTER 7

PREPARATIONS

Following the announcement about Zurelleum, the next few weeks were a whirlwind of activity. The financial markets had finally settled and the news media began to turn their attention to other things. The Houston Lab was operational and actively testing new Zurelleum samples.

Months earlier, Quantum had launched two unmanned cargo ships that had reached Mars orbit. The ships contained most of the equipment Ken would need to start drilling on Mars. An extensive analysis of the data they had sent back was ongoing. That analysis would determine some of the last-minute changes before the launch of the two manned ships, currently under construction.

Ken finally got the cast off his leg and was working full-time with Sandi, coordinating the Mars mission preparations. Sandi helped Linda keep the press at bay and manage the news media interviews. Talk Shows couldn't get enough of the *Moon Couple*. Most interviews had to be refused; they had become a serious distraction to their mission schedule.

Ken was also working closely with the construction teams in orbit at the Space Assembly Station. The lead engineer expressed a concern about the weight of the two remaining ships, because of additional cargo that would be needed on Mars. They discussed the possibility that Zurelleum could greatly reduce the size and weight of the massive computer systems on both ships.

By September, Quantum was in high gear, mining, processing and laying the groundwork for marketing Zurelleum. The Houston lab conductivity tests had followed the pattern of the lunar tests; the sample began to gain mass, gradually.

Mr. Zurelle had instructed Gustav and Chan not to ask for advice from other scientists researching Dark Matter. He didn't want to raise suspicions that could affect its future marketability. Besides, the samples were stabilizing and behaving like Zelon, but with much faster data transfer rates.

Chan's personal research had been frustrating. He was no closer to an explanation of added mass than when he first began. Dark Matter sounded like the only logical answer, but he couldn't find a direct connection. To add to his confusion, the initial test sample had stopped gaining mass altogether. It had been stable for a week; he didn't know why. He wondered if the Zurelleum atoms had become, somehow, *satisfied*. No answers; only questions.

Quantum's advertising had quelled concerns in the world markets, resulting in continued growth in overall market value. Pre-orders for Zurelleum-based processors were coming in from all sectors of industry. Zurelle and the Board brainstormed ways to speed up the delivery process. They wanted to build up the Mars Mission financial account to reduce the resource drain on Quantum. So, the Board decided to begin accepting down payments on future deliveries of the processors. They understood that such action would put pressure on the Zurelleum testing process and could backfire if problems developed.

But, things were going well and they were confident that promised deadlines could be met. The lone dissent was from Wes Maddox. He was still on the moon, although he had accepted Zurelle's offer to replace a retiring VP on the Houston staff. His daily discussions with Chan did not produce the confidence that the rest of the Board felt.

In October, Dr. Maddox arrived for a coordination visit and to spend some time with Dr. Gustav in the Houston Lab. Gustav told him that his tests had mirrored those on the moon; the Zurelleum had gained mass. But, he was concerned that the two other samples inside the test chamber were also gaining mass, even though they were not yet connected to the active electrical circuit. They were growing, just by being in the magnetic field of the first sample. The biggest unknowns were; why the samples gained mass in the first place and why they had stopped gaining. He didn't know if the atoms had simply become *satisfied* or if there was a limited supply of Dark Matter, if that was the source of the added mass.

Maddox asked to be kept informed and said he would do his best to keep the boss off their backs, if they needed to change the test schedule. He knew Zurelle was depending on Zurelleum to start paying some of the Mars bills.

In the course of mission training, Ken had been interacting with the two scientists, to determine the part Zurelleum would play on the Mars Mission. During coordination meetings, he had picked up on the concern both men seemed to have when discussing the *unknowns* about the new mineral. Ken knew that *unknowns* would be hazards out in unforgiving space. He began to wonder about the wisdom of the rapid pace of Zurelleum development.

One morning, with some time to kill, he went shopping with Sandi. He discussed some of his concerns with her, asking her thoughts about Zurelleum. She admitted that she had some concerns about the fact that Zurelleum seemed to be *alive*, at least partially. But, she felt that the experts must know what they are doing and that it would be a safe and financially-rewarding addition to Quantum's bottom line.

On the way back home, she smiled at Ken and said, "As long as I am in space with *my* Cowboy, I think everything will be fine."

When they arrived home, the vehicle had automatically notified the ADA-21, which had coffee prepared for them and asked for their dinner orders.

Ken greeted the robot. "Ada, you're looking especially beautiful tonight."

The robot processed the compliment. *"I'm sorry sir; I have no appropriate programmed response for your comment. Could you be more specific?"*

Sandi gave Ken *the look*. "Ken, be nice."

"Never mind, Ada, I was just kidding."

"Sir, I am not programmed for kidding." The ADA returned to its duties.

When Sandi turned back toward Ken he surprised her with a

small gift box. "I thought now would be a good time to give you this. Open it."

She opened the small acrylic box containing an ancient Japanese pearl necklace.

"Ken, it's beautiful! These look like real pearls!"

"Yes, I inherited these from my grandmother, who got them from her grandmother. They were bought in Japan by my great-great-grandfather, at the end of World War Two. So, I thought you could wear them on our trip to represent Quantum at the Japanese Space Conference.

Sandi smiled and hugged him. "You sure know how to impress a girl. I'll wear it to the church tomorrow."

"To church? Where?"

"At the church where we got married, in Cut & Shoot, just north of Houston...remember?! The Houston Chronicle is doing a special on Texas weddings and asked me to come back to address a group of brides who are starting the marriage process. You *do* remember our wedding at the little Methodist church, don't you?"

Ken smiled, "Oh...are we married?!"

Quantum Headquarters in Houston

Mr. Zurelle had called an urgent meeting with Wes Maddox and Dr. Gustav. He had video links to Chan on the moon and Harrison Bret at the Space Assembly Station, orbiting near the International Space Station.

The C.E.K. Mees Solar Observatory in Hawaii had released a solar activity forecast, for July and August of 2082, that would interrupt radio communications for Quantum's Mars launch. Since communications were essential, in case of launch emergencies, the Mars mission launch date would have to change.

Delaying launch would cause them to miss the launch window and wait twelve to eighteen months, adding billions to the mission cost. So, Zurelle instructed the staff to plan for a launch in late June or early July.

Harrison Brett said the Assembly Station could only meet the new schedule if he got additional maintenance androids and personnel to allow 24-hour shifts. He said the new Shield Transmitters were complete and would protect the mission crews from the solar flares and the normal space radiation. His biggest concern was the weight issue; the new equipment manifest had put the ships overweight. He promised to solve the weight problem if Quantum got the new lighter Zurelleum-based computer systems to him on time. Zurelle promised to make that happen and said the budget was not a problem.

Chan and Gustav cautioned about moving too quickly with the Zurelleum processors. The stability of the test samples was still a concern. Additionally, Chan's Dark Matter research was at a dead end. Gustav said the earliest they could have the first Z-Processors delivered to MIT for software upload, would be mid-March. Based on testing requirements, they wouldn't be installed and operational in PARADISE until May or later.

Maddox raised an eyebrow.

Zurelle saw him and asked, "What?"

"Bernie Harrington is paying big bucks for your promise that PARADISE would get the distinction of having the first commercial use of Z-Processors. But they're not scheduled to open until August next year. If we launch earlier, you'll have to convince him to choose an earlier opening date. That means he'll have to cut out something to rush things along. And, you know how things can go wrong when you get rushed. The same is true for us. We need to make sure that we don't take any shortcuts that have an impact on our mission. I'm sure he will go along with you, but the news media will want to know why they changed their date. It's sure to leak out that we drove it by changing ours."

"What do you suggest?"

"The media may not be too concerned about the opening schedule for PARADISE, but you can bet they will jump on any rumor about a changed launch date for Mars. So, as soon as you decide on the exact date, I recommend we announce it, make it sound like a normal change, based on circumstances. Downplay the *loss of communications* part."

Zurelle nodded. "Wes is right. We'll release the new launch date once I nail down the details. We all have work to do, so let's get it done. Thank you, gentlemen; that will be all."

CHAPTER 8

THE STAGE IS SET

The White House – Washington, D.C.

The job of President of the United Tri-American States had become much more challenging, since the populations of the three great Americas had voted to band together into one great country, becoming nineteen additional states in 2075. The three Vice Presidents; **VP – North America, Amanda Weigh, VP – Central America, Carlos Seguine, and VP – South America, Alberto Trabahar,** would be here today.

"Mr. President."

Jacob Holloway looked up at Douglas Clark, his Chief of Staff.

"Okay, Doug, we have some time before my meeting. So, where do we stand?"

"Well, sir, we've got a year until the election. Of course, you'll be the nominee for the party, but the poll numbers are lagging in your push to advance technology and in the exploration of the Solar System. Our surface probes have not made it past Saturn and we've only done fly-bys of all the dwarf planets. Some say the country needs fresh leadership to get us headed toward the stars."

"Don't these people realize that we don't have the engine technology necessary to make it past Mars yet? Meanwhile, we've still got citizens in the Central and the South American states that don't have dependable power for their homes. There are; what, several million still without access to the Information Cloud? Are the critics crazy?!"

Douglas Clark had been with the President through four different campaigns before becoming the White House Chief of Staff. "Sometimes, Mr. President, I'm certain that the whole world is crazy. That's why they elected you, to help make some sense of a crazy world. You know how fickle the public is. Sir, you don't need to change the world, just show them that you care; that you know it's crazy and you are trying to make their lives better. They want a more technology-focused President. So, let's get you out there where they can see the high-tech guy you really are. We can balance both the dreams of the scientific community and the needs of the poor."

The President smiled. "Great speech Doug! Are you sure you're not running?"

"No, sir. I just want to get your poll numbers back up to where they were after we expanded the ISC base on Mars."

"Okay, so, what's the plan?"

"When Quantum Corporation launches their Mars mission next year, you need to be at their orbiting Assembly Station. Nearby, at the International Space Station, we'll host an International Symposium on the future of Solar System Travel. We'll invite all the big technical companies—make it a big deal.

"About that same time, Bernie Harrington is supposed to open his new PARADISE theme park in St. Louis. Supposedly, it's the most innovative use of hologram technology in history. He was a huge contributor to your last campaign, so we need to pay back a little. Since he is out on the cutting edge of technology, I will arrange for you to be there on opening day and present him with the Frontier Technology Award."

"What's that?"

"I just made it up, but I can assure you, it will be very impressive."

The President smiled. "I like the way you think. Maybe we can also make a big deal out of that new Zurelleum stuff Quantum discovered on the moon. Aren't we looking at that?"

"Yes, sir. Defense is on the top of the list to get testing samples when Quantum releases them. But, they seem to be taking their sweet time about it. I'd better check into that. Maybe they have a problem with the development. I'll let you know."

"You're a good man, Doug. Now, about the meeting today; **Trabahar will want to discuss the Solar Power Grid running down the crest of the Andes and the wind turbines in the Brazilian**

Highlands."

"He has a point, sir; he's being hammered down there about the solar project because of the sloppy maintenance. I've got Environmental sending a team to investigate next week. The wind farms are the bright spot; they are producing twenty percent more than predicted. He will also ask about your promise to have everyone in the South connected to the Cloud during this term. We've got a year to make that happen.

"When you attend the World Cup down there next spring, I'll schedule you to do a tour of the new power grids with Trabahar."

The President nodded. "Great, sounds like a plan."

The Moon - AREA Z

On November 17th, Chan began testing Zurelleum in the active data circuit. Dr. Gustav, video-monitoring from Houston, asked Chan if there was anything new on his research.

"No, not yet. I've just started an ancient book entitled, THE DARK SIDE OF DARK MATTER. The guy was deemed a crackpot seventy years ago, but his research seems to be way ahead of its time. He was convinced that both Dark Matter and Dark Energy exist. If I find a break-through, I'll let you know."

"Yes, please do. Meanwhile, our samples have stopped gaining mass, just like yours." Gustav paused. "I just wish there wasn't this nagging doubt in my mind."

"Yes, me too. But unless we can nail down some differing data, we have no reason to delay Zurelleum."

"Right you are. Have a good day, my friend."

Houston Space Center Conference Room
December 1, 2082

Zurelle had called a press conference to announce the new launch date for the Mars mission. He opened the conference with the announcement and explanation of the earlier launch date. He confirmed that soon after launch, the mission would hit the solar flare and lose communications for about a month. He said that, as with all such missions, the ships were self-sustaining and would be beyond Earth help under even the best of circumstances.

Next, he asked Sandi to stand, and then he confirmed the announcement made months earlier, that Ken and Sandi would be together on the mission; Ken as Commander and Sandi as Shuttle Director.

Some yelled out, "Do they make zero-g baby strollers?"

When the laughter calmed, Sandi smiled, "No...that is *not* in the Mission Plan."

Zurelle provided a few more mission details and then opened it to questions.

Someone asked, "We haven't heard much about Zurelleum. When can we expect to see operational processors?"

Zurelle smiled. "We recently signed the contract to install Z-Processors in the new PARADISE theme park in St. Louis, opening next summer. Our new technology will make it be the most innovative application of hologram technology ever devised. Our systems will power all the androids and the Main Core, which will power the hologram generators. It will be the first commercial installation of Zurelleum. Following that, you will see our new processors installed in virtually every product on the market."

"What about the rumors," an IBN News reporter questioned, "that there is something wrong with Zurelleum? Some say the bacteria part of it can be dangerous."

"Regardless of the rumors, our thorough research has found no danger from any part of Zurelleum."

After a few more questions the news conference was ended.

Following the Q&A, Zurelle met with his staff. Gustav reported that the data tests were on target to easily reach the ten to twelve petaflops threshold, more than anyone could have hoped for. The increased speed and reduced size would solve the weight and space problems on the Mars mission ships and fix the hologram problems at PARADISE.

Chan said the Assembly Station would be able to test the new Zurelleum systems for the mission ships by early May or June. But, time limitations would require the twelve Mars cargo shuttles to retain the older Zelon systems. Ken reviewed flight crew assignments; he and Sandi would pilot Mars One and Red and his Rescue Co-Pilot, Gary, would pilot Mars Two. They had both been in on Ken's rescue from Aldrin Crater. Ken went over the training schedule and finally Zurelle ended the briefing.

December 15th - Zurelleum Test Labs

In a video conference with Gustav, Chan reported that the data tests had finally achieved a sustained rate of twelve-point-six petaflops; faster than human brain function, in a small processor. The low operating temperature would allow just normal airflow; except in certain high-temperature conditions. He said they needed to recommend that the android systems be cooled, because of their proximity to humans.

In Houston, Gustav allowed a smile. "The AI researchers are going to love this. My friend, we have a gold mine here."

Chan agreed. "Looks like it. Still, I wish we didn't have this cloud hanging over our heads. While reading, THE DARK SIDE OF DARK MATTER, I found something that has created another question mark."

"I thought you said it was all theory."

"It is, but one computer simulation in the book showed that Dark Matter accumulated in an atmosphere where data were flowing through bio-combinations with self-generating heat. The model projected that the added mass would accumulate on the outside of circuit paths, effectively growing additional circuits, allowing ever-increasing data rates. The author named this theoretical process, CIRCUIT GHOSTING."

Gustav thought for a moment. "Well, it's only a theory. We haven't seen any Circuit Ghosting in our tests."

"That's true. And, no more sample growth. But, I am a scientist; I don't like question marks."

Gustav agreed. "Zurelle has been pressuring me to release Zurelleum for commercial marketing. He still wants a financial cushion for Mars." He paused. "Chan, since we are scientists, maybe if the data tests are successful for the next week we can assume that Z-Processors are ready for marketing. If at any time we discover a reason to stop the process, we will have the authority to do so. Does that proposal make sense?"

"Yes, I agree."

"Good. This is exciting; we are about to change history."

After the call, Chan picked up the old book. He said out loud: "Questions; too many questions."

Chapter 9

HAPPY NEW YEAR

The past six months had been a whirlwind. The year 2081 was the year it *all began.* But, 2082 would also go down in history...and be studied for generations to come. The lead Media Stream story got the attention of scientists and computer technicians around the world.

ZURELLEUM RELEASED FOR MARKETING

Friday, January 2, 2082

Quantum Mining Corporation announced today that Zurelleum, their new 'Miracle Mineral,' has met all testing standards for use in computer-chip manufacturing. Dr. Amal Gustav, Chief of Research for Quantum, confirmed that Zurelleum has achieved the astounding data rate of 12.6 petaflops. For those not computer savvy, one petaflop is one quadrillion floating point operations per second. By comparison, the human brain processes data at about ten petaflops. While speeds of thirty petaflops have been reached by a few supercomputers, those processing systems are massive. Quantum promises that Zurelleum-based systems will exceed human brain speed in processors no bigger than a shoebox. For the first time, artificial intelligence researchers will be able to produce portable AI systems that will enhance every area of our lives, from medical advances to space travel.

When asked about the early-century AI warnings by the computer greats, Hawking, Musk and Gates, Mr. Zurelle, Quantum's CEO, stated that modern technology had designed safety measures to solve those concerns.

Mr. Bernard Harrington, the creator of PARADISE, the largest hologram theme park in the world, has signed an agreement for his park to be the first commercial application of the new computer technology. PARADISE is tentatively scheduled to open in early July of this year. Quantum's Mars mission ships and maintenance androids will also be retrofitted with Zurelleum processors.

Regardless of your perspective, it seems inevitable that Zurelleum is here to stay. And, if Quantum stockholders have their way, their new discovery will be the preverbal "Goose that laid the Golden Egg...or more accurately, the Green Egg." We predict that 2082 will be the year the green glow of Zurelleum found its way into every area of our lives and greatly padded the bank account of one of the world's richest corporations.

IBN World News.

Advanced Research Technology (ARTech) Laboratories
Midlothian, Texas

On January 2nd, the ARTech owners, David and Kenneth Michaels, had been called to the office by David's wife Dianna, the CFO.

When the morning news announced that PARADISE had rescheduled their probable opening day to July, the ARTech staff met to assess the impact. In a few minutes, they received a Stream Mail from PARADISE, offering a ten-percent bonus for early delivery of the androids they had ordered. That would mean an additional 10 million ID$ of income.

Cori Lynnson, their Chief Software Engineer, saw the message and was concerned about getting the programming done that soon. Standard androids wouldn't be a concern, but androids with artificial intelligence processors were another thing entirely. *"You can't make mistakes in a full AI environment,"* she thought.

Cori called and left a message for Edward Wayne, the PARADISE Chief Systems Programmer, to call her about the change. Then, she walked to the Motion Lab and entered the door labeled, "ADAM."

Adam was just under two meters tall with light brown hair, shiny gray eyes, and the body of a thirty-year-old. He was stretched out on one of the work tables; eyes closed. Kenneth was holding his left hand and talking to a lab assistant.

"Finish verifying conductivity on the last twenty-seven nerve paths and leave the file here on my desk panel." He noticed Cori. "Oh, hi Cori, is it time for the meeting already?"

"Ten more minutes. I just thought I'd check to see when Adam will be ready for programming. I'll have to start early to meet this new schedule." Cori touched Adam's android arm. "You guys are good; this feels like real skin, except it's cold."

"Not for long. Dave designed a circulatory system as a heat-sink. Adam's outer skin temp will be within five degrees of humans. When we replace the Zelon system with the new Z-Processor, we can have a real conversation with Adam."

Cori responded: "*Conversation* sounds a little too human for interaction with an android. What about Eve? How far along is she?"

"She's finished except for the right leg circulatory system. You'll need to upgrade Adam and Eve first since they will be the primary greeters when PARADISE opens."

Cori smiled. "They're not going to be wearing fig leaves, are they?"

PARADISE Theme Park – St Louis, Missouri

The lower floor of Bernard Harrington's circular office looked out over PARADISE in every direction. The building was in the center of the five gigantic domes that housed the different themes of his masterpiece.

The windows doubled as view panels so he could monitor the activities and the technical data while seeing the activity in all five domes. The second floor of his office was for entertaining VIPs, while the windows on the third floor overlooked the tops of the five domes and had a perfect clear-day view of St. Louis and the glistening Gateway Arch.   His five-star living quarters occupied the one-hundredth floor, at the very top of the building.

With workers below, hurrying to meet the new opening date, Harrington muttered, "This place better pay-off or I'll be in the poor house by Christmas."

Even *he* was amazed by the five square kilometers under roof.   The five domes were joined in the center, attached to PARADISE Towers, which also had four five-star luxury suites for VIPs.   Below those, were the administration and operations offices of the theme park. The Main Computer Core was on the Maintenance Level, four floors below ground.

The top of each dome rose three hundred meters above ground.   The Registration Dome was designed like a beautiful park, with a small forest of real trees and flowers, meandering streams, paths, waterfalls and a play area for children.   The environmental controls could create sunshine or rain or anything in between.   Guests would be greeted by an array of appropriately-dressed and programmed androids, designed to meet their every need.

The VIP Shuttle Port was on the outside of the Reception Dome, at the two-hundred-meter level.   Guests arriving by shuttle could choose the stairway or a high-speed elevator to Registration below.   Arriving VIPs would take the monorail system inside the roof that led directly to the VIP suites just below Harrington's office.

The Hotel Dome had a thousand five-star rooms. The roof, just above the top floor, contained the largest skylight in the world.

The Recreation Dome had a ten-meter-deep lake and ten pools, some with water slides that went all the way to the lake. There were sports fields, gymnasiums, a jogging track around the lake and a dozen tennis courts.   Three of the courts were suspended in the air, a hundred meters above ground-level, accessible by magnetic lifts.

The Adventure Dome was sure to be the real money-maker for PARADISE. The one-thousand Hologram Chambers would be the envy of every other theme-park owner in the world, *if* his hologram engineers could get the stability problems solved.

The Service Dome contained the massive Hologram Generator and all the maintenance and support facilities. All domes were interfaced with the computer Main Core. All access to the outside world went through this central *brain* of PARADISE.

Fuel-cell-powered generators in the Service Dome, supplemented by solar cells built into the roofs of all domes, could keep PARADISE running in case of a primary power failure. Harrington doubted they would ever be needed; the government had doubled the size of the Power Grid servicing the St. Louis area.

When his alarm sounded, Harrington took the spiral staircase up to the conference room for the staff meeting. Chief Programmer, Edward Wayne would integrate the new AI programed Z-Processors. Eddie planned to nest seven Z-Processors to form the Main Core, with wireless links to the 100 service androids.

Steve Franklin was designing the on-line access for home-creation of hologram adventures, off-site. With no direct connection to users' brains, the adventures would only be three-dimensional. The system was sure to be lucrative, since preorders were expected to top five thousand.

Evan Joseph and Timothy Cole comprised the Hologram Engineering Team.

Eric Jennings was on a video link from MIT, filling in for the Chief of their AI Team, who was still out of the country.

Harrington began. "Here is the new schedule: Saturday, June 27th, Media Day and celebrity test of PARADISE. Ken Anderson, Quantum's Commander for the Mars Mission, will be here to create the first guest hologram adventure. Saturday, July 4th; Grand Opening. President Holloway will give the opening speech."

Harrington looked up at the center view panel. "Mr. Jennings, isn't it?"

"Yes, sir, Eric Jennings. Professor Hau is in China for the holidays."

"Very well." Harrington leaned over to shake Steve's hand. "Welcome aboard Mr. Franklin. I'm very impressed with your home-hologram generator design."

Steve nodded. "Thank you, sir. The Home System will bypass the Cloud, which should increase the data speed. Without brain connections, subscribers will be limited to level-three interactions, but I'm sure it will seem real enough to bring the players back over and over, especially since your pricing is so affordable."

Harrington nodded. "Looks like I hired the right man." He then turned to Eddie. "Well, Mr. Wayne, what about the programming?"

"The main programming is done and the sub-routines will be finished later this month. After we get the Z-Processors from MIT, it will take thirty days to interface the Hologram Generator and other PARADISE functions."

"What about the hundred ARA-25 androids?

"MIT will ship the smaller AI processors directly to ARTech. They will do the basic application programming, interrgrating the AI into their systems. ARTech tells me that they can have Adam and Eve here by April and start delivery on the rest soon thereafter."

Steve raised his eyebrows. "Adam and Eve?"

Harrington chuckled. "Yes, since these new models mimic a lot of human characteristics, ARTech decided to give the first two the obvious names. I wanted them to look like a male and a female so I can use them as the main greeters in the reception area. They will be preprogrammed to recognize guests and know their preferences. Every guest to be dazzled from the moment they step through the door."

Harrington looked up at Eric. "Well, Mr. Jennings, I hope you have some good news for me."

"Yes, sir, I do. Quantum will deliver the Z-Processors by March 1st. Our team already has the AI programming about ninety percent complete. Debugging will only take a week or so. That will put our delivery to your team and to ARTech right around the first week of April."

"Great, that's what I like to hear." He turned to the other end of the room. "So, Evan, have you and Tim finished troubleshooting the hologram failures?"

"Yes sir, but, we had to buy some computer time at the twelve-petaflops-level from Chicago Research Institute, so we could rerun the Matterhorn adventure. I skied all the way to the bottom and went in the lodge and interacted with the crowd of people there; not one glitch. So, we know the failures were caused by the slow Zelon Core."

"Tell me again why we haven't been using that fast computer all along."

Tim jumped in. "The mandate, sir; you told us we had to run everything in-house. We would need about ten of those big-boys to generate enough processor speed and capacity to run a thousand hologram chambers simultaneously."

Evan added. "Plus, we would need extra physical space for the larger processors. But, remember, you wanted to keep everything inside the domes to reduce the chance of a competitor hacking the program and imitating our chambers."

"Yes, yes, I remember. Well, it looks like we are headed in the right direction. If anything goes wrong, I want to know about it immediately--no surprises. That will be all, unless someone has something else to discuss."

When the meeting ended, Eddie said to SAteve, "Well, back to work. I've got to call ARTech about the schedule change, since they will be doing the Z-Processors upgrade for Adam and Eve."

Steve chuckled. "Adam and Eve."

Steve took the elevator down four levels underground, looking for the Facilities Manager. He asked a maintenance worker, who pointed to the ceiling.

"Follow that green conduit and you'll find Joe."

Steve followed it and finally found a man standing on a small lift, head and shoulders up inside an open access panel. Steve tapped lightly on the edge of the lift platform.

"Yeah, what do you need?"

Steve raised his voice. "Excuse me, can you tell me where to find Joe Wilson?"

In a moment, the lift descended and a large man with a broad smile appeared and shook Steve's hand. "Joe Wilson, at your service. How can I help you?"

"Hi, Joe, I'm Steve Franklin, Systems Designer for the online games interface."

Joe smiled. "Yeah, I recognize your name. You're the guy who designed this maze of fiber. What can I do for you?"

"I'm looking for a backdoor room."

Joe smiled. "There are no doors to the outside from down here. You need to go back up to the ground-level."

"No, I know the way out; what I'm looking for is some space to put in what we call a BACKDOOR. It's a separate link into the computer system so I can bypass all the security and go into the Main Core to work on any problem. It allows me to troubleshoot problems, even if the technicians change the passwords."

Joe stared. "Is that legal?"

"Of course! I'm part of the PARADISE staff and I'm responsible for making sure the online gaming system will stay up and running."

"OK, so what do you need, exactly?"

I'll need a small space, about three or four-square meters, near the main access panel, where the circuits terminate from all five domes."

Joe led Steve to his office. Steve saw an ancient military pistol on one side of Joe's desk. "Are you into antiques."

Joe handed him the pistol. "Yeah, I collect old weapons and restore them during my breaks. The boss approved that weapons locker over in the corner. The older ammo is hard to find but there's a whole network of collectors who share parts and ammo."

"I don't know; it looks dangerous to me. I'm more of a lover, not a fighter."

Joe smiled. "Well, if you ever find yourself needing to fight, you may wish you had one of these." He placed the pistol back on the desk and pointed at a schematic on the wall showing a storage room twenty meters from the main cable junction box. "You can set up in there."

"Thanks, Joe."

Chapter 10

Z-PROCESSORS

The White House

President Holloway looked at the schedule change. "Finally, we got this ISODS Update scheduled. I really want to get this thing into orbit. You remember that meteor shower back in seventy-five? We had a year's notice and still, if it had changed two degrees, we had no way to stop it from wiping us out."

Doug nodded. "I remember…not enough launch vehicles to even get the nukes into orbit."

"Well, we've got until eighty-seven before Demopoulos comes our way. At least we got all the major players to agree on the solution."

"Yes, sir…I never thought I'd see us working so closely with the Russians—the Japanese and Brits, yeah, but not the Russians. And speaking of Russians, General Petoskey made it here for the Launch Simulator tests."

When the President got up to leave he put his hand on Doug's shoulder. "Listen, Doug, thanks for the great work you do, keeping me straight. And be sure to tell Sara I appreciate her, too; I consider her part of the team. And, it's about time for some more of her famous banana pudding; the real stuff, not from the replicator."

Two floors below the Oval Office, the mood looked somber when the President walked in. When he greeted the Russian general, he couldn't tell if the stoic demeanor was a Russian game-face or a reflection of the news about ISODS. Finally, he turned to British General Turner, the current leader of the four powers ISODS Team. "Go ahead, General."

"Mr. President. The team members of all partner countries are here, but several new observers are unfamiliar with the details of our mission, so if you will indulge me, I'd like to review the background and mission of ISODS."

The President nodded. "Please."

The General explained that the near-miss back in 2075 led the four major powers to partner in a project that would protect the Earth from similar future events. The development of the International Space Object Defense System had been the best solution to the problem. It was comprised of four satellites, placed into geostationary orbits; each capable of launching up to one hundred neutron warheads to intercept and deflect large space objects before they impacted the Earth. Each platform also had a 100-petawatt laser, to deflect or destroy smaller objects, less than a hundred cubic meters in size.

The system would require agreement from each partner country to authorize a launch. To prevent intentional or inadvertent launch, that could endanger the Earth, each warhead had an Atmospheric Sensor which would automatically destroy the warhead firing mechanism when it sensed Earth atmosphere. It would ensure that no country could ever use ISODS to target another country from space.

When he finished, the Japanese representative asked, "General, you announced the launch date as April 17th, but the status report this morning said that there will be another delay. How long--"

The President interrupted. "Delay?! What delay?!"

The General cleared his throat. "Mr. President, the purpose of this meeting was to update you on the results of our simulation test. The system worked fine, up to twelve simultaneous targets per platform. Every simulation beyond twelve failed, due to CPU overload."

"Twelve?! We promised the world this thing would knock a whole shower out of the sky! Every country has invested billions in this project. Did you verify the findings?"

"Yes, sir; several times. The system can't track more than twelve extremely-fast incoming objects and launch enough warheads to intercept them. It's worse with fast objects detected less than a million kilometers out. The processors just aren't fast enough.

"A super-computer simulation gave a deflection of over a hundred objects.   But, to get the eight or nine petaflops processor-speed necessary, we would have to redesign and enlarge the CPU housing, which would require increasing platform size and changing the attaching points to the transport shuttles. My guess is that it would take another year, at least."

Doug interjected, "Mr. President, if you declare a Defense Priority, Quantum will have to sell us the Z-Processors necessary to upgrade ISODS. They're small, so the only change would be a minor redesign of the core housing. We would have only a small launch delay. Quantum has made commitments to the big PARADISE theme park and to their own Mars mission; I understand that we don't want the PR problems associated with affecting either of those projects. However, Quantum will do whatever it takes to produce the extra Z-Processors since it's for defense and they could use the extra money we will offer."

General Petoskey's Russian accent was pronounced. "Mr. President. I agree with Mr. Clark. Our countries do not need the embarrassment of system failure, after all that we've invested. What are a few more billion international dollars spent if we can have success and provide better defense for our planet?"

The President turned to General Turner. "If we do the Z-Processor modifications, when can we expect to launch?"

"With just minor changes, we can launch by mid-June; early July at the latest."

The President nodded. "OK. We'll contact Quantum and order the Z-Processors. General, prepare an announcement that there will be a two-month delay in the launch, so the new technology can provide more reliable and accurate satellite systems. Emphasize that the defense of Earth will be greatly enhanced because of the upgrade."

"Right away, sir."

Quantum Headquarters
Next day

"Tony! With all due respect, are you crazy?! Why did you agree to produce more Z-Processors for the satellite defense system? We can barely produce what we have under contract now."

"Listen, Wes, he's the President of Tri-America. We have to do our part to help defend the Earth, plus, if we refuse, it would become very politically awkward for the company. Besides, the quadruple price they are willing to pay is a plus right now."

Dr. Gustav raised his eyebrows. "Mr. Zurelle, Dr. Maddox is right. Given our current production schedule, we can't meet that Defense Contract, at least not in the time-frame you promised. Even if we hire new people, we will still just barely be able to provide processors for PARADISE and for the ships and androids we must launch by July."

Zurelle hesitated. "We can speed up production by shortening the process. I've decided to cut out the final testing of the processors. That will save us several weeks."

Wes stared. "Tony, are you serious? Are you going to eliminate testing of the very processors we will depend on to sustain life and get our crews safely to Mars? What are you thinking?!"

"Now, wait a minute, Wes. Our scientists have already done the most extensive tests of any mineral we have ever marketed.

"Amal, you and Chan have been running tests on Zurelleum for months with no problems, right?"

Gustav nodded. "That's true, but we still have that nagging question about the initial growth of the Zurelleum samples."

"And, what have you found since you started running active circuits through those same samples?"

"Uh, nothing."

"Any growth?"

"None, but--"

"Right! There is nothing to indicate that these processors won't perform at full capacity, and safely do all we expect them to do. It would be great if we had the luxury of a full testing regime, but we are in a crunch here. We stand to corner the market exclusively, if we include Defense in the initial offering."

Maddox was shaking his head. "Tony, on the surface, what you're saying is true. But, don't forget what happened ten years ago with Quazinite. We had to pay out millions because of the skin burns to those workers. It's your call, but I want to be on record that I am against it; Sandi and Ken will be on that mission. It's too big of a risk to take."

"Ok, Wes, so noted. DR. Gustav, continue with your testing and if you find anything concrete before launch time, we'll scrub the mission."

MIT Research Center for Artificial Intelligence

The Z-Processors arrived at MIT on the morning of March 1, 2082. Eric opened the case of the first one, revealing a low-level green glow. The whole team had seen it on the news conference, but there was still the awe of seeing Zurelleum first-hand. Familiar circuitry connected the dual Zurelleum chips, which dominated the space inside.

Dr. Hau spoke. "So, ladies and gentlemen, let us begin the process of initiating the Artificial Intelligence Age. Quantum has instructed us to get these programmed and shipped by May."

Dr. Hau connected the first Z-Processor to the AI Software Generator. When he toggled the switch to *ON,* the green glow brightened.

Allie asked, "Dr. Hau, after we finish the download, where are the circuits we'll use to debug and test the data capacity of each processor?"

The professor hesitated. "Uh...we are not going to test the processors."

There was a hush over the team. Eric broke the silence. "But, sir, we have never sent out a program this massive without testing. Surely, you're kidding. How will we know if they meet the standards in the contract?"

The team was staring at Dr. Hau. "I have been instructed to expedite the delivery of the processors. I expressed my concern to the powers-that-be, and they have all waived the testing requirement. PARADISE and Quantum will handle the testing onsite. It's highly irregular, but they are the customers and MIT needs the research money. So, I will take them at their word, and their signatures on the change orders. Now, we have a lot of work to do. Let's make these processors smart."

When Dr. Hau left, Allie noticed the look on Eric's face. "What?"

Eric stared at the Z-Processor. "I don't like it. My gut says MIT will regret this. It's not a good idea to unleash Artificial Intelligence in what appears to be a living processor; especially when we aren't going to verify it operates within the safety specifications." He looked up at Allie. "They make movies about stuff like this."

Chapter 11

ARTIFICIAL INTELLIGENCE

ARTech was working overtime to get ready for the arrival of the Z-Processors. Cori went to the Lab to do a communications interface test between the two androids. But, David had taken Adam to the Break Room to test his eye-hand coordination with a game of table tennis.

As Cori entered the hallway, she saw David exiting the room, wiping sweat from his face. Having lost three straight games to Adam, it was confirmed that the android's eye-hand coordination was perfect.

Cori smiled at David. "Well, well; going down in flames at the hands of a machine."

Adam responded in his British accent. *"Android, I believe is the proper term for my structural design. David was teaching me the finer points of Table Tennis. Based on your previous demonstration, I compute that I did well. Is that right, David?"*

"Yes, you did well, Adam. But, you did not tell me Cori had been teaching you."

"That information was irrelevant. I was not programmed to help you win the game."

Cori laughed. Suddenly, Adam turned and headed for the Lab. Cori followed. "Adam, where are you going?"

"I have received a communication from Eve, summoning me to the laboratory. Kenneth requires access to our core housings to prepare us for an upgrade."

"That's right Adam. You and Eve will be upgraded to the new Zurelleum Processors."

Adam stopped. *"Will the upgrade make us better androids?"*

David answered. "Not necessarily better, just more capable. You should be able to think and reason on your own."

"Doesn't thinking and reasoning make you better?"

Cori choked back a laugh. "Not always, Adam--not always.

I'll go with you to the lab."

David rolled his eyes and followed.

Kenneth had just finished Eve's circuits and Dianna was now putting a woman's touch to Eve's appearance. She was designed to resemble a late twenty-something female with short honey-blond hair.

Her female voice-chip had a lighter British accent than Adam's. For Eve, PARADISE had sent a lavender jumpsuit with a built-in padded bra, creating the womanly appearance. All of the men noticed the change immediately. Even Adam stared, his camera-eyes zooming in and out as his CPU processed the images.

"Kenneth, why have you changed Eve to look different from me?"

"Well, Adam, Eve is supposed to look like a woman and you are supposed to look like a man, and, of course, men and women are different."

"Eve and I are made from the same materials and have the same functions. If we are to resemble and function like a male and a female I need input about how they are different."

Dianna and Cori looked at each other and smiled.

Kenneth paused, "Uh...Adam, men and women are different because...uh..., you see, women have the...ah...I mean, men are..., uh...Dave, you explain."

Dave stepped closer. "You see, Adam, uh...women are more...uh, that is, they are built like, uh...well, they're sorta different because, ah..."

Cori almost doubled over in laughter. Dianna was smiling. "Here it is, the late twenty-first century, and men are still clueless about women."

She looked at Adam. "The bodies of human males and females are different because they have different bodily functions, and their brains and emotions operate differently. Once you get your upgrade to full artificial intelligence, you'll have the capacity to better understand why male and female humans are different.

"PARADISE wanted you to resemble a male, and Eve to

resemble a female, because you will be greeting many human male and female guests. The humans will feel more comfortable in an environment where the androids appear to be male and female, and have artificial intelligence."

Adam's processor analyzed Dianna's comments for a few micro-seconds. He finally asked, *"Do David and Kenneth already have artificial intelligence?"*

Adam and Eve were not programmed to understand the four humans who were laughing hysterically.

CHAPTER 12

ADAM AND EVE

The MIT shipment finally arrived, enabling the android upgrade. With the new Z-Processor installed, a barrage of electrons raced down the circuits at a speed of just over twelve petaflops. At just over five hundred million nanoseconds, the eyelids opened, and Adam's camera-eyes began to focus. At just over two seconds, Adam spoke. *"Kenneth, are you finished?"*

"Yes, Adam, you are now upgraded."

Adam looked up at Cori and practiced his first android smile, an added touch for the androids that would interact with the guests at PARADISE. *"My surface…or I should say, my SKIN is not yet at normal temperature."*

Cori smiled back. "That's right Adam; it will take a few more minutes for the heat exchanger to fully warm your entire body."

David opened a test circuit. "Adam, do a status report on your processor."

"As you wish, David."

It took only seconds for the status of all subroutines and the Main Program to appear on the Systems Monitor. The status showed, **READY**. Adam viewed the read-out and smiled. *"Do I meet with your approval, sir?"*

David had not noticed that *tinge* of personality before. "Yes, Adam, everything looks perfect."

"But David, my data base says that nobody is perfect. Of course, I'm not a BODY, exactly. In scientific terms, I would be classified as a machine."

Kenneth answered. "That's true Adam, but we are not sure how your artificial intelligence programming will process the inputs to your database. Your application of new information should evolve each time you update your data files. We don't yet understand how an autonomous biomechanical platform, with artificial intelligence, will respond to its environment."

Adam sat up, slid off the table and made eye contact with Cori. *"Evolving? Isn't evolution a human process?"*

Cori's concern was building, so she quickly asked the most important question every android would be asked. "Adam, what is your Primary Directive?"

Adam responded immediately. *"My Primary Directive requires adherence to the following programming safeguards: An android will never harm, cause to be harmed, or allow to be harmed in any way, a human. An android will obey all instructions given by humans, unless those instructions violate the 1st Primary Directive or the authorized mission assigned to that android by its owner or supervisor."*

Cori smiled. "Yes, Adam, that is correct."

"Cori, I have a question."

"Yes, Adam, what is it?"

"Does beating David in Table Tennis violate my Primary Directive?"

Cori glanced at David. "No, Adam, David will not be harmed if, uh, when you beat him at Table Tennis. His ego may be dented a little, but not damaged."

A British-accented female voice entered the conversation. Eve's update was complete and Dianna had already asked her the Primary Directive question. She stood and tested her legs.

"My database defines EGO as, 'A human emotion, denoting one's self-esteem or an inflated sense of self-worth.' Which definition applies to David?"

Diana elbowed David. "Maybe a little of both; which proves he is human—normal."

Eve processed the information. *"I will need more data inputs to properly process emotions and understand humans."*

Kenneth smiled. "Good luck, Eve; we humans have been trying to understand each other for thousands of years. When you get to PARADISE you will meet many humans; all different. Understanding them will take some work."

Adam cocked his head slightly sideways. *"The functions Cori programmed us to do are just what we are designed for. WORK doesn't seem to be the correct term to describe them."*

Cori added. "Adam, when we humans are assigned a

function that does not please us, we will often refer to that function as work."

"That is not logical. Why would you be displeased if you are doing the function you were designed to do?"

Cori paused. "Uh...the explanation is a little complicated. I'll explain more when I begin training you to function at PARADISE."

MAX HOLT and DAN HOLT

CHAPTER 13

PARADISE

The ARTech shuttle settled onto the VIP circle. Eddie had been waiting to meet Cori and her high-tech androids.

As Cori stepped out, she said, "Eddie, meet Adam and Eve." When Eddie saw the two androids, he was surprised by their human appearance. When Adam shook his hand, Eddie reacted to the warmth of his grip. Cori smiled. "That's part of the Z-Processor cooling system, taking the heat away from the CPU. It feels like a real hand, doesn't it?"

Adam spoke, *"Good morning Mr. Wayne, how are Laura and the twins, Olivia, and Owen?"*

Now, Eddie's eyes widened. Cori laughed. "All the androids are preprogrammed with the entire PARADISE Data Base; they already know everybody here."

With Eddie still gripping his hand, Adam questioned. *"Sir, is it customary here at PARADISE to exchange such a long handshake greeting?"*

Eddie quickly let go. "No, Adam, I was just a little distracted by your appearance and your programming. Yes, Laura and the kids are fine."

"Is there something wrong with the way I am constructed?"

"No, it's just that I didn't expect you to look so, uh..."

"Human?"

"Yes, I guess that's it; so human."

Eve offered her hand. *"Mr. Wayne, it is a pleasure to meet the Chief Programmer of PARADISE."*

Eddie gave her warm hand a shorter greeting. He was uneasy with the way both androids mimicked human mannerisms and appearance.

After a moment, he said. "Follow me and I'll get you settled into the computer lab. The wireless system is already set up for you."

The path of the monorail, attached to the ceiling of the Reception Dome, offered a breathtaking view of the almost-complete theme park. Even Adam and Eve were taking in the sights below.

The video system activated, showing the welcome message that future guests would view. The scene was a wooded path in the Reception Dome, with a young couple espousing the offerings available to families at PARADISE.

Two small children laughed and played along the path behind them. The young parents were holding hands and talking into the camera. The androids took in every word of the welcome. Halfway to the Towers, Eddie finally asked, "When will the other androids arrive?"

Cori had to force her attention away from the amazing scene below. "There are two cargo shuttles on the way with the remaining androids. We didn't experience the delay we first expected, so they will be here in a couple of hours. I should be able to get the Main Core programming downloaded to all of them within a week. I want to get started with Adam and Eve today, so they can begin learning their Reception tasks."

"Learning? I thought you had to program their functions."

"Yes, but they are also going to learn. You can't plan for *every* contingency in their environment. There are unknowns about how different guests will react to the same situation. When things in their environment change, the androids must adapt. The scenery will be rearranged, schedules will change, and maintenance breakdowns will require decisions about the best course of action. So, they are programmed with subroutines and decision algorithms that will allow them to learn, adapt and in some cases, make their own decisions, like human workers."

"Human?" Eddie pondered to himself. *"Are we about to blur the line between human and machine?"*

They exited the monorail and stepped into the elevator. Eddie noticed that Adam and Eve were holding hands.

CHAPTER 14

REALITY

Hologram Chamber #7

The blast of cold air on Evan's face almost took his breath away. He was grateful for the helmet and goggles, as he and the other five skydivers exited the aircraft door and assumed the freefall position. They accelerated to just over two hundred kilometers an hour, while forming a straight line, in a *follow-the-leader* formation.

Observers on the ground could see the line of red smoke trailing from each man, allowing them to track the skydivers, winding around like a caterpillar searching for food.

At four thousand meters, they squeezed the triggers that released small titanium wings from their parachute packs, creating six small gliders traversing the sky. They then came alongside Evan and all executed a perfect *line-abreast* loop.

After a few more turns and spins, they separated and released their chutes, which retracted the wings back into their backpacks.

They sequenced themselves to land on the target near the grandstands full of people. The circular target was labeled, *"Tri-American Para-Glide Demonstration Team."*

At twenty meters above the ground, a sudden gust of wind caught Evan and Tim and pushed them past the target. Evan landed on the grass, but Tim was blown into a large tree. He collided with a limb and descended rapidly. Fortunately, his jumpsuit caught on a lower limb, stopping a severe impact with the ground. Regardless, the crowd gave them a standing ovation.

They interacted with the ground crews and then lined up and took a synchronized bow as the crowd whistled and applauded.

Tim and Evan high-fived at their success. After a few minutes of interaction with the crowd, Evan then reached to his headband and pressed the small Off-Switch. Everything went black for a moment before the lights came on in the chamber. Evan and Tim were seated side-by-side in the Hologram Interface Chair, smiling.

Tim couldn't hold back. "Whoa, baby! That's what I call an adventure! Man, my heart is still pounding!"

"That was incredible! We interacted with the skydivers and some in the crowd and didn't have one processor glitch. And, man, you were right; those new Zs *will* handle two people at a time. Harrington is going to love this. He'll make more money than ever, selling double adventures. Let's run the stats on this test for the staff meeting this afternoon."

Tim unplugged his connection to Evan's headband and they stood. When they exited the chamber, Evan noticed that Tim's jumpsuit had a tear in the lower left pocket and a small green leaf was caught in the tear.

Administrative Level – PARADISE Towers

Eddie was smiling at the pretty little face on his communicator screen. "Yes, Livvy, Daddy will be home soon and I'll take you and Owen to the zoo, I promise. Bye, bye, honey, I love you."

Eddie had rather be at home right now, playing with the twins. But, the bonuses and overtime pay made this job worth it. So, he finished his programming update and walked to the Staff Meeting. He was surprised to see that Cori had brought Adam and Eve.

Harrington entered with an uncustomary smile. Everything was going according to plan. The boss was ready for the good news about the computer upgrade and the final hologram test.

After almost two weeks with the Z-Processors active, all tests had turned out better than expected. Everything, down to the automatic refilling of snack machines, was under the watchful eye of the Main Core, a bundle of Z-Processors that had already made PARADISE the most automated theme park in the world.

The only complaint had come from the Facilities Manager, Joe Wilson. He felt uneasy with the Automatic Maintenance subroutines programmed in the Maintenance Z-Processors and those in the five large maintenance androids. He thought it looked more like a self-preservation capability than a maintenance capability.

The system could repair itself, including welding and soldering, with the laser welders spaced throughout the Maintenance-Level, and those built into the five androids. Spare parts would be automatically selected, transferred to the appropriate area by the big androids, and swapped out without the assistance of a maintenance person. When repairs outside of the Maintenance Area were required, the Main Core would communicate with a Maintenance Android, which would facilitate the repair.

But, the last time the boss asked Joe Wilson how things were going, Joe didn't mind saying how he felt about such an automatic system. "Take people out of the loop and you're gonna have trouble."

Nonetheless, the boss was happy, shaking hands and patting people on the back. Eric Jennings had come in person to represent MIT. Harrington shook his hand. "Welcome young man. I am really impressed with the AI programming your team has done."

Without giving Eric time to respond, he continued around the room, stopping when he got to Cori. "Well, young lady, I've been amazed at your work the last few weeks. Your androids are indeed special. I have seen them virtually take over the place." He looked at Adam and Eve, dressed in their PARADISE Guest Services jumpsuits. "I see you've brought our two special friends with you today. I've seen them in the Reception Dome, but have not met them."

Cori didn't know quite how to respond. She had discouraged anyone from referring to them in human terms.

"Yes sir, but I'm not sure that *friend* is the right word for them. They are just part of the equipment you ordered for PARADISE."

Harrington stepped around Cori and greeted Adam. The

warmth of the android hand surprised him. Adam smiled and returned the greeting.

"Good afternoon sir. It is a pleasure to finally meet you. This is my associate, Eve. We will be welcoming guests and helping them to feel at home here in PARADISE."

Harrington widened his smile and shook Eve's hand.

She slightly bowed. *Mr. Harrington, sir. Thank you for selecting me and Adam to represent PARADISE. We are programmed to make sure guests enjoy themselves and choose to return to this wonderful place at a future date."*

Cori knew that the Z-Processors had already pushed the androids' learning and self-programing capabilities to levels she had not expected. Harrington's continued dialogue didn't make her feel any better.

"I wish my wife could have been here today to meet you; she won't believe how real you look."

Adam smiled. *"REAL, is a relative term, isn't it sir? I trust you wife is feeling better since her fall while working in the garden."*

Harrington's mouth dropped open. Eve continued. *"Also, I believe congratulations are warranted for your grandson's winning goal at the university soccer match."*

Sensing the old man's confusion, Adam explained. *"Eve and I have been reading your weekly Staff Newsletters. You humans live quite exciting lives."*

Following an awkward moment, Cori said, "We'd better get started sir, it's ten minutes after already.

Harrington nodded. "Yes, of course."

He took his seat. "Alright, folks, we are down to the wire. Two weeks from now the world will never be the same."

Cori didn't like the *feeling* that last statement gave her.

The boss continued. "Okay, you've read the Test Plan. Everything will go online the twenty-seventh. I want to push all facilities to the maximum so we can identify any weak areas.

"Ken and Sandi Anderson, and some friends, will arrive on the twenty-sixth and stay overnight in a VIP Suite. You already know they are launching for Mars on the following Monday. Ken will create the first guest hologram adventure. Evan and Tim will stream the live video of his time in the chamber so we can all see how it works. We'll be able to view it real-time in the waiting area of the Adventure Dome and there will be a live feed to IBN for international release.

"The live feed should attract a lot of viewers and give us some good exposure. We are almost sold out for opening day and already booked at over ninety percent for the next six months. I believe the press exposure will push similar bookings into next spring."

He paused. "OK, give me your reports. Mr. Jennings from MIT; you are a guest, so we'll let you go first."

"Thank you, sir. All AI programming is complete and, as you know, the Main Core has been in test-phase for the last two weeks. We were a little concerned about the reduced test-phase for the software, but Dr. Hau assured us that the onsite computer programmers would do the tests here. One Android programming fault was reported at the Space Assembly Station, but we have not seen a similar problem here. Their android did a repair job on a mission shuttle without being activated by the Maintenance Division. They are investigating to see where the activation instructions came from. They will let us know if we need to be concerned with those here in PARADISE."

Harrington disregarded the mention of the wayward android. "Great. I am very impressed by the way you and your team have created the *heart* of PARADISE. OK, next; Joe Wilson, Facilities."

Joe Wilson stood. "If you don't mind, sir, I need to get back to the underground to check up on a contractor's final work. So, I'll make this quick." He glanced momentarily at Adam and Eve. "You already know how I feel about a bunch of human-looking machines taking over most of the maintenance. That aside, all facilities are complete and systems are operating normally. I'll keep this place running but if one of those *androids* gets in the way it may turn up in the scrap heap, uh...sir."

Harrington smiled. He had known Joe for a long time and he didn't mind that Joe was a little crusty around the edges; he was the best facilities guy out there. "Sure, Joe, I understand. But, I'm certain you'll find a way to get along. Go ahead and take care of the contractor."

"Thank you, sir." When Joe left, his glance back at Adam and Eve was evidence that he still couldn't shake his concern about this whole thing.

Harrington continued. "Hologram Chamber test; give me the good news Evan."

Evan and Tim had been baffled since the anomalies during the Para-Glide Demonstration Team adventure that morning. The Hologram Generator had performed perfectly, but they could not resolve the issue of the torn pocket on Tim's jumpsuit and the green leaf that got caught there. Tim had placed the leaf on the table in front of him and had the jumpsuit in a bag at his feet.

Evan gave the report. "This morning, we ran the most successful adventure yet. It stressed the processors to the limit. The Main Core handled all the complicated algorithms associated with personal interactions. I'm sure our guests will be more than satisfied. We also discovered that the new processors will enable two sensor headbands to be linked together, so two people can participate at the same time. Of course, only one of them can create the adventure. But the other can still interact with what is created."

Harrington smiled. "That's fantastic news! We can charge for two people during the same timeframe in the chamber. I love more ways to make money." He hesitated. "Is there something else you need to report?"

Evan glanced at Tim. "Well, sir, we do have one small thing we are trying to resolve. At the end of our adventure, Tim and I were blown off course and Tim landed in a tree. When he fell through the limbs, he tore the pocket on his jumpsuit and got a leaf caught in the tear."

Harrington stared for a moment. "Isn't that good; I mean, isn't that what can normally happen in an adventure?"

Evan nodded. "Yes, sir, it can, but when the adventure ended, Tim's pocket was still torn and this was still caught in the tear." Tim was holding up the leaf. There was silence in the room.

The boss hesitated. "Uh, you must have hung it on the equipment in the chamber when you left. Surely, you are not trying to tell me that a holographic image physically damaged your jumpsuit."

Tim knew it sounded impossible; he wasn't sure that he believed it either. Still, he knew what he felt during the fall, and he had the evidence to prove it. He took the jumpsuit out of the bag and held it up. The lower left pocket was partially ripped. "When Evan and I left the chamber, I don't remember bumping into any of the equipment. Even if I had, where did the leaf come from?"

"You must have rubbed against a plant in the hallway near the chamber and pulled a leaf off. Remember, a hologram is just that; a transparent beam of **monochromatic light,** projected into a chamber filled with photosensitive particles. Of course, they *look* real because of the current technology. The hologram generator produces the sounds and smells to go with the images, giving the illusion of reality."

Evan responded, "You are exactly right, sir. I suppose it's *possible* it happened the way you just said, but this time, it was more realistic than ever before."

Eric's communicator buzzed; it was a text from Eddie. *What do you make of this?"*

He replied, *"Don't know…let's talk later."*

Harrington wanted to change the subject. He didn't need a controversy this close to opening. "Yes, well, I'll read the full report tonight and let you know if I have questions. Alright, let's move on. Eddie, where do we stand on programming?"

"I must say, I am very impressed with the AI programming that MIT did. The self-maintenance subroutines are genius-level work."

Eric smiled. "It was a team effort."

Eddie continued. "We thought de-bugging would take at least two weeks but we have only found a few adjustments we've had to make. It's almost like…uh--"

Harrington interrupted. "Like what?"

"It's almost like the Main Core is debugging itself. I can't be sure, but in the history of writing computer programs, there is no record of so few errors in the initial program tests." He looked at Eric. "Maybe it's just that your team is the best on the planet."

"Well, they are good, but we didn't actually program MC with the capability to self-detect programming errors."

Harrington looked up. "MC? Who's MC?"

Eric smiled. "Oh, sorry; the Main Core. Most of us have been working on the system so long that we just refer to the Main Core by its initials, MC."

"Oh. OK, continue."

"There's no one I can think of with the access to the system or the expertise to make any changes to it. But, I can't imagine AI programming, where the system is aware of its own internal errors and can correct them. I'll run another test tonight to verify that the original program is still in place."

Harrington was beginning to get a little frustrated. His earlier smile had turned stoic. "Yes, and stream the results to my personal quarters."

He looked at Steve. "Well, Mr. Franklin, do you have any anomalies to report?"

Steve could tell the boss was slowly becoming his old self; not a good thing. "Actually, sir, I only have good news."

"Let's have it."

"So far, eight hundred of the home-level hologram generators have been delivered. Five thousand were ordered, so I think this will turn out to be quite lucrative. Ninety percent of those gamers have already prepaid for the Home-Gaming Service."

Harrington relaxed a little as Steve continued. "The online gaming tests have been error-free. The off-site fiber optics nodes will be handled by Ethan Hallberg in Dallas. The online tests stressed the system to the maximum, and showed that the power grid should stand up, even if all chambers are active here and up to five hundred home subscribers log on at the same time."

Harrington nodded. "Power will not be an issue. We have the backup fuel-cell generators and the feed from the dome solar grids. With those sources, I feel sure PARADISE will never run out of power."

Steve nodded. "In that case, the online hologram system should be ready to go. As I understand it, we will not do an online run-through on the twenty-seventh, so our first customer log-on will be opening day; July 4th."

"Yes, that's correct." He made another note. "Now, Miss Lynnson, tell us about our customer service staff."

There was a nagging *something* in the back of Cori's mind that had her rethinking the android wireless links into the Main Core. There were too many questions. But, she had no real evidence that the androids were anything more than very capable machines. Still, she wondered if Adam and Eve should be in the room, listening to these discussions. What she didn't know, was that, through them,... *MC was also listening.*

"I am very pleased with the adjustment the androids have made to their new environment. We've only had to repair two of them so far. One maintenance unit had a misdirected laser beam during a welding test and damaged the door of a parts locker. We reloaded the program and there hasn't been a repeat.

"The other failure was a bad communications antenna in a hotel service android. Before we discovered it, MC sent a Maintenance Unit to replace the communications module." Cori hesitated.

Harrington stopped taking notes and asked. "Is there anything else?"

"Uh...no; no sir, I guess not."

"OK then, it looks like we are good to go for the test-run next week. Right now, I've got to get ready for an interview with an IBN reporter. Keep me informed."

Before leaving, the boss said, "By the way, the Retro Coffee Shop is open full time now, for the workers. Stop by and give it a good workout; everything's free. Let me know how you like it."

CHAPTER 15

TROUBLE IN PARADISE

Quantum shuttle - Approaching St. Louis

Sandi's eyes were closed, with her head against Ken's shoulder. The quiet hum was relaxing, as the shuttle transported her and Ken, along with Red and Linda, to PARADISE. Red and Linda had developed a close relationship, since they had met on the moon when Pump 27 failed. As the four friends were nearing PARADISE, the two men were discussing the final details of the Mars mission.

Sandi finally asked Ken. "Have you decided on an adventure yet? Better make it a good one; the world will be watching."

Red added, "Yeah, Cowboy; how about that Superman flight into Aldrin Crater?"

Ken frowned, "If it's all the same to you, I'd like to forget that one ever happened."

Red's laugh awakened Linda. They would be spending the weekend together before the Mars launch on Monday. As Quantum's Communications Director, Linda had been working 18 hours a day prior to the Mars launch. But, she was still in denial about the three most important people in her life being gone for maybe up to two years.

Ken continued. "I've been keeping it a surprise, but I'll go ahead and tell you; Sandi is going on the hologram adventure with me."

"What?!" Sandi sat up. "How is that possible?"

"I got a text from Eric yesterday. He said PARADISE has figured out how the hologram chambers can handle two people at once. I'll create the adventure, but you'll be able to interact with the hologram."

"You mean, I can be in it and see everything you see?"

"That's right. So, instead of a landing on Mars, I've decided to take Sandi for a visit to the farm where I grew up and introduce her to Grandma and Grandpa Anderson."

"Oh, Ken," Sandi said, misty-eyed. She looked at Linda. "I told Ken that I've always wished I could have met his grandparents; they had such a wonderful influence on his life." She turned to Ken. "Will we be able to talk to them or will we just be observing, like in a dream?"

"They'll explain everything before we start, but I'm pretty sure we'll be able to totally interact with them. I don't know how the time-in-history thing will work, since they never met you, so I guess we'll just play it by ear." He paused. "I'm just wondering how I will handle seeing them again."

Sandi hugged him. "You'll do fine; you always do."

At PARADISE, Harrington, and a small media crowd, met them for a Photo-Op. Soon, they were on the monorail to PARADISE Towers. Harrington was pleased that they all seemed dazzled by the scenery below.

After dinner with Harrington, the four got a personal tour of PARADISE by Adam and Eve. The two androids were even more human-like than all the others. Later, on top of the hotel, gazing up at the stars, the group was surprised to hear Eve remark about the beauty of the heavens and to hear Adam say that he would like to go to the stars someday. Back in their suite, after the tour, Red was the first to bring it up.

"Notice anything strange about those two androids?"

Linda nodded. "Yeah, since when do robots consider anything to be beautiful? And, why would an android like Adam have future goals? Ken, don't you think that's a little odd?"

Ken nodded. "It's more than odd; it's scary. When people have goals they usually end up acting on those goals. When Albert was first assigned as my android assistant for the mission, I didn't notice anything different about him. But lately, I have seen similar strange traits in him, even in the short time he's been with me. It will take me a while to get used to having him...or *it*, as an android assistant. I feel sure Eric and the other MIT geniuses did not intentionally include human characteristics in their AI programing. It is supposed to be artificial; not *actual* intelligence."

Red agreed. "Maybe the Zurelleum gives those processors an extra kick nobody had anticipated."

"Wait a minute." Sandi shook her head. "Surely, you're not saying that androids with AI programming are capable of human thought and characteristics, are you?"

The three were looking at Ken. "Hey, I'm not the sharpest knife in the drawer, but these strange things have me concerned. It's not like the androids could ever *take over* or anything like that; that's science fiction. Besides, all androids and similar systems are programmed with the Primary Directive. They *have* to obey us.

"But I *am* worried about them verbalizing human-type preferences, like saying the stars are beautiful or Adam having a goal to do something different than what he is programmed to do. I suppose it is possible that these comments are pre-programed for the benefit of making guests feel more comfortable, but I doubt it.

"Right now, it's late and we have a big day tomorrow. Actually, we have a series of big days for the next two years." He put his arm around Sandi. "You are going to be an incredible space woman. Now, if I can just get you to obey me like Albert does." With that, he turned and ran for their bedroom; Sandi was close behind.

PARADISE – June 27, 2082

"DAD!" Allison Newberry was sitting on the den floor of their Williamsburg, Virginia home, calling to Keith. "Hurry, the news feed from PARADISE just started." Allie was home on a much-needed vacation after the hectic schedule at MIT; programming the Z-Processors. She loved working on the design team, developing the first fully-functioning AI. Getting to work with Eric made it even better.

Her whole family was going to vacation in the new theme park together on July 4th, official opening day. Collins, Allie's younger brother, was home on leave from astronaut training.

"OK, honey, we're coming!" Keith and Lisa Newberry hurried

into the den. Keith had convinced his investment partners to sink a few million ID$ in PARADISE. All progress reports projected the returns would be even higher than originally thought. Keith's father, Dr. Braxton Newberry, considered to be the father of artificial intelligence, was also watching, from the Guatemalan mountains.

IBN News opened with a fast-forward video, reviewing how PARADISE was built. It was a one-minute review of the facilities; coming together at high speed. The end of the video featured the introductions of those who designed, built and programmed PARADISE. Allie pointed to the view panel.

"OK, here it comes--there we are!" When the narrator introduced the MIT programming team, Allie could be seen smiling, her arm through Eric's with her head slightly leaning on his shoulder. She was mouthing the words to the camera, *"Hi, Mom and Dad."*

Lisa smiled. Keith put his hand on Allie's shoulder. "We're proud of you honey. Good job."

Finally, the Customer Relations Director appeared on the screen. "Welcome to PARADISE, the world's first ultra-automated, virtual reality, holographic theme park.

"Industry experts feel that PARADISE will change the meaning of the word *vacation*, forever. In the Adventure Dome, guests will be able to imagine a vacation to anywhere in the universe at any time in history and the unique Hologram Generation System will create it for them.

"You can see behind me, Hologram Chamber Number One. There are one thousand such chambers in this massive dome." He held up one of the DNA sampling headbands. "Inside the Chamber, guests will slip on a headband like this, which is connected to the Main Computer Core of PARADISE. Through the small metal tabs inside the band, the computer will do a generalized DNA sample; more like a family tree sample than a detailed individualized sample. The system will use the DNA information to generate more realistic-appearing people and events that may be in the guest's adventure.

"These chambers will enable two guests to experience the same adventure, at the same time. Once the session begins, the chamber will go dark, and one of the guests will close their eyes and begin imagining their adventure. The Main Core will sample the thought-stream until it has enough data to generate whatever the guest is thinking. When the guests open their eyes, they will be *inside* the adventure they have imagined.

"For safety purposes, the computer is programmed to prevent emotionally dangerous events within the adventures. Since a hologram is just a transmission of concentrated light beams, no actual harm can come to an adventurer. However, PARADISE planners want to prevent emotional situations that could compound already-existing medical conditions."

The Director turned to Evan and Tim, waiting nearby, then continued in a smooth practiced voice. "These men are the hologram engineers most responsible for the success of the system. This is Evan Joseph, Chief Engineer, and Timothy Cole, Hologram Analyst. Evan, you two are the only ones to actually test a hologram adventure so far. Tell our audience what it was like."

Evan seemed a little timid, with billions watching. "Well, this system is truly amazing. Although the chambers are only thirty cubic meters in volume, adventures created in them can appear to be unlimited in size. Not only can guests interact verbally with the characters they create, but they can feel as though they are interacting physically with the imagined environment.

"For example, through the headband feedback system, you would be able to feel the wind and smell odors, and even taste food that you appear to be eating. You can have discussions with famous characters you have created. The computer database is extremely detailed so if you create, say, George Washington, the computer will not allow you to change his appearance from what it was in history. It helps add a sense of reality to the hologram."

The Director turned to Tim. "So, Tim, you mean that you could actually talk to old George and ask him about how the Continental Army crossed the Delaware River over three hundred years ago?"

Tim nodded, "Yes, that's right; and he would answer the question, based on what is in the history archives of the Main Core database. Also, whatever you feel during the adventure, seems real."

"Thank you, Tim. Now, I'd like to introduce the stars of today's Hologram Test, Mr. Kenneth Anderson and his wife Sandi. As you know, they are due to launch on Monday to establish Quantum's first mining operation on Mars. They will be the first married couple ever to journey out into the Solar System.

"Mr. Anderson, I'd like to thank both of you for taking time from your busy pre-launch schedule to be here. Would you like to give our audience a hint about the adventure you will create?"

"Yes. First, I'd like to thank our mission crews onboard Mars One and Mars Two right now, for doing the pre-launch work while Sandi and I spend some time in, well, PARADISE." Everyone applauded.

"I'd also like to thank Mr. Harrington for allowing us to officially open the Adventure Dome. Many of you know that my parents died when I was young and my grandparents became the biggest influencers in my life. Both of them died before Sandi and I met. So, we have decided that I will take Sandi back to the old farm in Texas where my roots really began. She will finally get to meet Grandma and Grandpa Anderson. We are not sure exactly how this will work, but I am excited at the possibility of actually talking with them again; at least, to images of them."

The Director held the microphone toward Sandi. "What about you, Mrs. Anderson; what do you expect?"

"I'm not sure, either. I'm guessing that Ken's grandparents will be just like he remembered. Whatever it turns out to be, I'll be happy to get a look at his past."

"Well, then, without further delay, let the adventure begin."

The live feed switched to inside the chamber. Ken and Sandi were seen entering and being greeted by Evan and Tim. They directed the two into the Hologram Interface Chair and attached their DNA headbands. Evan then activated the console and instructed Ken on its operation.

Ken entered the date-in-history he wanted to visit the farm and its exact location. For the DURATION, he selected thirty minutes. Normally, guests would get an hour session for their fee, but the networks felt that the normal Media Stream viewer would get bored with anything longer than thirty minutes.

Ken and Sandi were told that the headband would lightly vibrate when there were five minutes left in the session. With the setup completed, Evan and Tim exited the chamber and did a communications check. Ken gave a thumbs-up.

"OK, sir, when the countdown gets to zero, the chamber will go dark. Then, close your eyes and allow MC...uh...the Main Core to analyze your thoughts. Concentrate on the major objects first, like the land and house, and then more of the details, like people and individual objects. Alright, here we go; switching to AUTOMATIC,... now."

Even though he was a seasoned astronaut, Ken was still a little nervous. Sandi's heart was pounding. The countdown hit zero and Ken closed his eyes. He imagined driving up to the long driveway to the farm house. He visualized the ancient windmill, long dormant, standing near the back porch. It was a warm spring day and the afternoon clouds were slowly retreating toward the West. He sensed the car rounding the corner of the house and him seeing the red barn, with the old John Deere tractor sitting halfway out the door.

Ken sensed that the chamber had brightened and he opened his eyes. *"I'm here!"* he thought. The chamber now looked unlimited in size. The beautiful Texas sky stretched out forever. He could hardly take it all in; the emotions were overwhelming, especially when he saw Grandpa, leaning over the fence near the barn, preparing to feed the armadillos he was caring for.

Ken stopped the car and, leaving Sandi behind, jumped out and ran past the barn to the old farmer. He called out, "Grandpa! Grandpa!" He stopped within arm's length to look closely at the holographic image of his grandfather. He seemed so real that Ken wrapped his arms around the old man and lifted him off the ground, hugging him tightly. There was slight moisture in Ken's eyes.

The hologram of Grandpa Anderson responded in the Texas drawl that Ken had missed for so many years. "Whoa! Kenneth; what's this all about, son?"

Ken lowered him to the ground and stared into the old man's eyes. *"They look so real!"* he thought. "Grandpa, it's just so good to see you."

"Well, Kenneth, you were just here last week. Did they let school out again?"

Ken knew he was generating this animation, but it seemed so real that he thought *it* was controlling *him*. "Yes, sir. I'm excited because I'm just always glad to see you. Where's Grandma?"

"Last I saw of her, she was in the kitchen baking some of her chocolate chip cookies. I wondered why she was baking this time of the week; maybe she knew you were coming."

Grandpa looked over Ken's shoulder toward the car. Grandma had come out on the back porch and was walking toward Sandi. "Say, is that the pretty girl you wanted us to meet? My, you know how to pick em; she's lovely."

Ken thought, *"Oh my gosh, Sandi!"* He started running toward the house, yelling over his shoulder, "Come on, Grandpa, I want you to meet her."

When Ken had jumped out of the car and headed toward the barn, Sandi didn't know what to do. She opened the door and slowly placed her foot on the ground, testing it first to see if it would hold her up. *"How can this be imaginary when it looks and feels, REAL?! I KNOW Ken is seated beside me in the chair, but now he is...OVER THERE!"*

Grandma surprised Sandi. "Well, hello young lady, you must be the pretty girl Ken has been telling us about. I'm Ken's grandmother."

The *hologram* was putting her arms around Sandi for a hug. Sandi could smell her perfume.

Grandma continued. "Welcome to our home. I just baked some fresh chocolate chip cookies; they're Ken's favorite."

Sandi was just staring at the elderly woman. After a few awkward moments, the *hologram* spoke. "Are you alright, honey?"

Sandi regained her composure. "Yes...yes, ma'am. Sorry, I guess I'm just a little tired from the trip. It is so nice to finally meet you. Ken talks about you two all the time. The place is beautiful; I can see why he loves it here."

Ken returned to the car with Grandpa in tow. "Grandma!"

Ken hurried to her and gave her a long hug. "You look great! And, I can smell..." he took a deep breath and looked at Sandi, "chocolate chip cookies."

Grandma smiled. "Why, Ken, you'd think it had been years since you've seen us. I guess I'll never understand men. But, I can't argue with your choice of women. Your Sandi is beautiful."

Sandi blushed. *"This is NOT happening,"* she thought.

Ken smiled. "Yes, she is beautiful, isn't she?" Sandi blushed even more.

Grandpa gave Sandi a hug and then put his hand on Ken's shoulder. "Let's go in the house where it's a little cooler. I can smell those cookies, too. This woman of mine might let me have one, now that you're here; she just bakes 'em for you, you know."

Ken laughed and put his arm around Sandi. The sound of their feet on the porch and the squeak of the door hinges helped both of them settle into this temporary reality. When they entered, even the smell of the house seemed real. Ken smiled at Grandma. "I'll show Sandi around while you set the table." He led her through the living room and down the hall to the third door on the left. He put his hand on the knob and looked at Sandi. "This is weird."

He opened the door and took a deep breath; it was *still* his room. Sandi could see Ken beaming, as the boyish look overtook him.

"This is it, honey! This was my dad's room and it was my room whenever I came home. Let's see." He reached into the closet and retrieved his dad's old guitar. He strummed across the strings and smiled; it was in tune. An out-of-place thought entered his mind. He looked at Sandi. "I wish we had invested in this place."

Outside, in the video viewing area, the entire PARADISE staff was transfixed on the scene unfolding in Hologram Chamber Number One. At Ken's last comment, Harrington smiled at Eddie, seated next to him. "You can't get better advertising than that. Some of the billions watching will be calling, trying to buy stock. The per-share price will skyrocket on Monday."

Eddie agreed, smiling.

Back in the chamber, Grandma stuck her head in the bedroom door. "Are you two ready for cookies?"

They both responded. "Yes, ma'am."

Ken and Sandi were astounded at the REAL taste of the treat. Grandpa had been discussing the wheat crop and the armadillo population. Finally, he asked, "So, Ken, where did you two meet?"

Without thinking, he said, "Well, I met her when I was with the mining company on the moon and she came to visit her dad. It was--"

Grandpa interrupted. "Now, Ken, I know you want to impress this young lady, but we taught you to always be honest."

Ken hesitated. "Uh...what?"

Grandma picked up the conversation. "Honey, you know there's no such thing as mining on the moon." She looked at Sandi. "Ken's always been such a dreamer. He has dreamed of going to the moon and into space since he was a little boy. Sometimes he just gets carried away."

Ken realized that the Main Core was forcing the conversation to reflect the time-in-history he had selected; several years before he had become an astronaut. He went along with MC. "Well, a guy can dream, can't he?"

They all laughed. When they finished the cookies, Grandpa invited them to help feed the armadillos. Sandi had never actually seen one, so she was excited to go help. At the fence, surrounding the armadillo preserve, hundreds of the small animals began gathering near the corner for their feeding time.

Ken explained, "Years ago, when armadillos were almost extinct, Grandpa got a government grant to create this preserve. Texas funded it because the armadillo is still the State Mascot.

"They're strange because they like to eat vegetables and berries and stuff like ants, scorpions, spiders, and worms. They have also been known to eat frogs, snakes, and lizards."

Sandi scrunched up her nose. "YUCK! If I ever had to eat a snake, you could just go ahead and put me six feet under."

As Grandpa dumped a barrel of food over the fence, a piece

of carrot fell near Sandi's foot. So, she picked it up and stuck the end through the fence to feed a baby. When the baby gnawed on the treat, Sandi reached through to touch its armored back.

Before Ken could warn her, the mother lunged at Sandi, almost biting her finger. Sandi fell backwards, landing on her elbows, and yelled, "Ouch!" Her right elbow had landed on a small plant that Texans called *goat-heads*; a type of plant with small pods that had sharp prongs shaped like the horns of a goat. The prongs stuck deep into her elbow and stayed there when she got up.

Ken helped her. "Honey, are you OK? I should have warned you about mother armadillos; they are very protective of their babies."

Sandi was more embarrassed than hurt. "I'm fine, except I've got this...uh...thing stuck to my elbow."

"Yeah; it's a goat-head. I got a lot of 'em when I was a kid playing all over the farm. You just have to grit your teeth or bite on a stick and yank it out."

Grandma said, "Wait, Sandi. Before you go yanking one of these out, it's best to use a little something to deaden the spot. Let's go in the house."

Grandpa finished the feeding while the others went to the kitchen for Grandma to transition into her doctor role. "Grandmas always make the best doctors," she smiled. She used a dropper of clear liquid to deaden the sticker wound and then used a pair of tweezers to slowly extract the large goat-head. There was just one small drop of blood. She opened an ancient adhesive bandage and placed it over the wound.

Sandi and Ken were both thinking at the same time. *"Wait a minute. This is a hologram; it's not real. So, how could anyone get hurt in a hologram? Maybe it's just part of the simulated reality."*

Grandma patted Sandi's elbow. "There we go, that should take care of it." Then she smiled. "Welcome to Texas."

Just as Grandpa walked in, Grandma produced a pitcher of iced tea. "That kind of excitement deserves some more refreshments."

As they drank, Grandpa asked. "So, Ken, what are you going to do after you graduate? Are you still hoping to be an astronaut?"

Ken hesitated. He and Sandi had just felt the five-minute alert vibration. "Yes, sir, I'm going to become an astronaut and someday go to Mars."

Grandma patted him on the arm. "That's a nice dream Ken. We'll just be proud when you graduate." She looked at Sandi. "And, what about you honey? Are you in school too?"

"Yes, ma'am, I'm going to be a pilot."

"Well, that's wonderful dear. Maybe someday you'll get to fly with Ken on one of his space adventures."

Sandi saw Ken stand, so she did too. She smiled at Grandma. "I'd love to do that."

Ken looked unsure; like he didn't want to end this adventure and didn't have a clue how to proceed.

Grandpa looked sad. "You're not leaving already; you just got here."

Sandi decided to help Ken in this awkward moment. "I'm sorry we have to go so soon, but Ken promised to get me back home before dinner." She hugged Grandma. "You two are as wonderful as Ken said you'd be. You'll never know how great it has been to finally meet you."

Ken was hugging Grandpa. When a small tear trickled out of his eye, he reached to his headband and pressed the button. Everything went dark.

Slowly, the lights in the chamber brightened. Ken wiped his eyes. Sandi leaned her head over on his shoulder. As he put his arm around her, she said, "*NOW*, I understand."

When the chamber door opened, Ken and Sandi could hear the applause of the local audience. Over two billion people felt as though they had been on the Texas farm with Ken and Sandi. Harrington was thrilled. He entered the chamber right behind Evan and Tim.

As he was shaking Ken's hand, he said, "In the last thirty minutes, you two have put PARADISE on the map. The Reservations Circuit has been busy, since five minutes into your session."

PARADISE'S Public Relations Director stuck a microphone in front of them. "Ken and Sandi, we are still live on the Stream. Tell the world what it was like."

Sandi said, "Absolutely amazing! It seemed so real I couldn't tell the difference."

Ken agreed. "Well, I have to admit; I was skeptical at first but, about the only thing that I've done that was more exciting was that explosion and flight into Aldrin Crater."

"Thank you, Mr. and Mrs. Anderson, for letting the world visit the farm with you."

He turned to the camera. "Remember, we will have live coverage of the official opening day for PARADISE, next Saturday, July fourth. The President of Tri-America will be here to cut the ribbon and participate in several opening day activities. From PARADISE THEME PARK; thank you and have a great weekend."

The split-screen camera showed Ken and Sandi exiting the chamber while the Director finished signing off. When Sandi stepped through the door, her elbow was visible for just a moment. Only a few who understood the implications of that small bandage, took notice. Among them was a young woman seated on her den floor in Williamsburg, Virginia, and her elderly grandfather in the mountains of Guatemala.

Two others who noticed were in research labs with green-glowing samples. In AREA Z, Chan answered Gustav's call.

"Chan, my friend, what do you think?"

"About the bandage?"

"Yes, of course, the bandage. What do you make of it?"

"Amal, it is a troubling detail. But, maybe she had the injury before the chamber session. Maybe the AI programming picked up on it and added that to the adventure."

"That was my first thought. But, if she injured it beforehand, the treatment would have been the modern Clear-Seal treatment, not an ancient adhesive bandage."

"Oh, my, you're right." Both scientists hesitated. Chan

asked, "What do you think we should do about it?"

"I'll stream a report to Zurelle and Maddox. The first thing they'll ask is if the Zurelleum samples are still dormant. And, of course, they are. At this point, I think a three-headed monster would have to crawl out of a Z-Processor before they would delay the mission."

"Of course, you're right." Chan hesitated. "Maybe..."

"What?"

"Maybe this anomaly was caused by the momentary growth of those hologram Z-Processors, like ours did in the lab. If so, it should follow the same pattern and stabilize."

"I suppose that could be the case. Still, I can't shake this feeling; this nagging uncertainty. I just wish..."

"Yes, me also."

CHAPTER 16

THE LAUNCH

Sunday, June 28
Mars Fleet Assembly Station – Earth Orbit

The two mission ships were a stunning sight, fully loaded for Mars, flags from all partnering countries painted on the sides, six shuttles attached to the sides of each, and large laser cannons extending from each nose. The cannons were as powerful as those on ISODS, ready to deflect space objects from their path.

Linda was coordinating the media coverage, but what she really wanted to do was spend time with Red. Their relationship had gotten to the *serious* stage. Red was stressed and wasn't quite sure what to do about Linda's crying spells. Ken said, "You aren't meant to understand; just tell her you love her and deal with it the best you can."

On launch day, Doug Clark arrived with the President. He hoped it would be a great boost, going into the final months of the President's reelection campaign. Campaigns were always stressful, so he didn't appreciate the added uncertainty recent Homeland Security reports had generated. Agents on the moon and in St. Louis had been reporting anomalies in the Z-Processor-equipped computers and androids. Of course, all those systems were programmed with the Primary Directive, but he still had a bad feeling about the Z-Processors and Dark Matter, although he couldn't fully explain why. *"Just a gut feeling,"* he thought.

Before launch, the President gave a short speech and did the ribbon-cutting ceremony. Then, he and the other dignitaries spent time with the mission crews. When he shook the last hand in line he said, "Good luck young man."

The crewmember responded. *"Thank you, Mr. President, I've never been called a man before."*

The president looked up into Albert's camera-eyes.

"I'm Albert, Mr. Anderson's Android Assistant. I'm looking forward to this mission to Mars."

The President hesitated, "Yes, I wish you all well."

When they moved away, he said to Doug, "That guy, uh, android, seemed so...ah...real. His hand was even warm."

"Yes sir, ARTech did a marvelous job on all of them; too good in some ways. It kinda' gives me the creeps. Why would a robot look forward to anything? Those machines aren't far away from cognitive thinking."

The President shuttled to the ISS nearby for a meeting with the other dignitaries while the crews said their goodbyes.

Finally, the two ships had maneuvered into launch position. With the world watching the countdown, live on the Media Stream, each division leader called out a *"GO,"* as Ken read down the launch checklist.

When the countdown hit *ZERO,* the powerful engines burst into life, spewing out a two-thousand-meter long trail of super-concentrated plasma ions. The massive ships slowly began to move into the blackness of space, to the cheers of well over two billion people.

Ken made his first official mission radio call. "Houston, this is Mars One; official launch at fourteen-thirty hours, Houston time. We are headed to Mars to dig some dirt!"

"Roger, Mars One, our hopes and best wishes go with you. Due to solar activity, expect to lose communications in forty-eight hours, plus or minus a few minutes. Duration expected to be thirty-one days. You'll be blind until then."

"Roger. I'll provide a final status update before the blackout. This is Mars One, signing off for now."

Ken switched on the internal communications system. "Well, well, boys and girls, we are now Martians. In honor of our historic mission together, Sandi and I have placed some special treats for all of you in the utility lockers at your stations." After a few moments, applause and cheers erupted. Ken and Sandi had brought aboard a MARS Candy Bar for each crewmember; except for Albert and his brothers.

CHAPTER 17

PARADISE LOST

Wednesday - July 1, 2082

The radio signal from Mars One was already intermittent. Within hours, Houston would lose all contact.

For Chan, the uncertainty about Zurelleum would not go away. The Dark Matter research had ended in frustration. The test sample of Zurelleum still showed no more growth.

Finally, he headed to the Veranda Restaurant in the Lunar Headquarters for a much-needed coffee break. Paul Aguilera, the Administrative Division Chief, and his new friend, Corky, were there, and it appeared that Corky had been crying. She was blowing her nose on a tissue.

She apologized. "Sorry, Dr. Yosahn, since they brought in those real trees for the main foyer, I have been fighting these allergies."

He patted her hand. "Well, just give the ventilation system time and it will remove all of the pollen; you should be back to normal soon."

"I hope so, this is awful!" She pointed through the window. "It would be better out there."

Paul smiled. "What do you mean, out there?"

"Well, there's nothing in a vacuum. So, outside, there would be nothing for me to ingest; pollen wouldn't last long in a vacuum."

Chan's eyes widened. "What did you say?"

Corky turned to Chan. "I'm right, aren't I? Nothing lasts very long in a vacuum, right?"

Chan jumped up. His face had turned white. "THAT'S IT!" He hurried out to the hallway and bounded toward AREA Z.

Corky turned. "Did I say something wrong?"

Paul realized what Chan had just discovered. "Ah...no. You

know how quirky scientists can be sometimes. Listen, I need to take care of something. I'll see you for dinner tonight." He left the table and then turned after a few steps. "Take care of that pretty nose." As he walked, he connected his communicator to Dr. Maddox in Houston.

Chan was out of breath when he entered the Lab. He put both hands on the vacuum chamber, housing the original sample and said, "That's it! It has stopped growing because it has consumed all of the Dark Matter in the chamber!"

He looked around for his assistant. "JACOB!"

The young man stuck his head around the corner. "Yes, sir, I'm here."

"I want you to pressurize and open this chamber. Let me know if you see a change in mass."

While the assistant proceeded, Chan opened a secure channel to Gustav, who answered immediately.

"Chan; why the secure link?"

"Amal, quickly, go to the Lab and take a look at the first test chamber you started."

Within moments, Gustav said, "OK, I'm here. Now, what is so urgent?"

"I was just having coffee with a young woman who is experiencing bad allergies from some new decorative live trees they shipped up here. Amal, she said if she was outside in the lunar vacuum, the pollen wouldn't last very long and she would feel better."

There was a long pause.

"Oh, my, God...how could we have missed that?! The samples stopped growing because they consumed all of the Dark Matter in the chamber!"

"Exactly! I just had Jacob open the first sample chamber and start monitoring it for changes in mass. I suggest you do the same."

"Yes, of course. Have you notified anyone else?"

"No, you can handle that."

"Alright, I'll notify Zurelle. You try to contact Ken on Mars One and warn him to watch for any computer anomalies."

"Okay, good plan."

Gustav had his assistant open their test chamber. He then initiated a Priority Alert Message to Zurelle. Chan contacted Houston for an immediate link to Ken on Mars One. He waited a few moments and heard Ken's intermittent voice.

"Hey, Chan! To what do I ow……the pl……ure?"

"Ken! We have discovered a potential problem with the onboard computer system."

"You're fad…ng Chan, did you …ay something ab…t a piston? What kin…. of …iston?"

"NO, NO. SYSTEM, KEN, SYSTEM; the computer SYSTEM; there's a problem!"

"Say aga…. Did……y……say compu……tem?"

"Ken, don't trust the new computers! Check the computers!"

Static…and then, silence.

"Ken! Can you hear me?!"

Nothing.

Chan looked at his communicator; the screen read, 'LOSS OF SIGNAL.'

"Dr. Yosahn. DR. YOSAHN!"

"Yes, Jacob. What is it?"

"Five millionths sir; the sample has gained five micrograms in fifteen minutes."

Reagan Golf Course – Washington, D.C.

The President had just putted for a birdie. After he retrieved his ball, he noticed a golf cart approaching with Doug Clark driving. The passenger was Homeland Security Chief, Bradford Smith. The President had become irritated with the Chief, who had become paranoid about the Z-Processor anomalies that had been reported. The President had already said *NO* to Brad's recommendation that ISODS be delayed until they were thoroughly reevaluated for safety. As the cart stopped, the President asked himself, *"Now what?"*

The Chief got out of the cart. "Good afternoon Mr. President. I have some important information for you."

The President extended both arms out to his sides and

looked around. "Out here, on the golf course?"

"Yes, sir."

The President looked at Doug. "And you thought it was important enough to interrupt my golf game?"

Doug nodded. "Due to the timing sir, I thought you should be brought up to speed on this."

"Up to speed on what?"

Smith began, "It's about ISODS Mr. President."

"Wait." The President turned to the corporate donors in his foursome. "Could everyone give us a minute here?"

The Secret Service ushered everyone except the Vice-President away. "Now, are we back on ISODS again? I've made the decision to go with the launch tomorrow afternoon. Unless you have something concrete, you'd better have a good reason to interrupt my Wednesday afternoon."

"I understand sir. My office intercepted a report from Quantum's Houston Lab to Zurelle an--"

"What?! Who gave you the authorization to spy on Quantum?"

"Well, sir, we didn't actually spy on them. We always monitor the Media Stream and Cloud frequencies. About an hour ago, we picked up an unencrypted report to Zurelle from their Houston research lab. I guess in their haste to get the report out, the Lab forgot to encrypt it; that happens sometimes."

President Holloway looked at Doug.

Doug raised his eyebrows. "Sir, I think it is worth listening to."

"Ok, Brad, go ahead, but summarize it. I have a chance to win this round."

"Yes, sir. The report confirms that Quantum has been withholding vital information about Zurelleum. For months, the test samples have increased in mass, even inside the vacuum test chambers."

The President looked at Doug and back to Smith. "What do you mean; the stuff has been growing?"

The VP questioned. "That can't be true. How can minerals grow?"

Chief Smith continued. "Actually, that appears to be the

case. The Lunar Lab Chief, Dr. Yosahn, came up with the Dark Matter theory when they first discovered the growth in the samples. Gustav's report says that they now believe Zurelleum is absorbing Dark Matter, which caused the increase in physical mass. They backed off late last year when the samples stopped growing. Yosahn now thinks the stoppage was because the samples had absorbed all the Dark Matter originally in the vacuum chambers. This morning, his lab opened the original chamber, and within minutes, the sample began gaining mass again.

"Dr. Gustav now believes that any Zurelleum with unrestricted access to the atmosphere will gain mass, especially if it's in an electronic circuit."

The VP asked, "So?"

The President added, "Yeah, so what? Maybe the Z-Processors will become even more efficient with added mass."

Brad continued. "The report says that the most likely result of the gain in mass will be something called, *Circuit Ghosting*. The theory says that the added mass can increase the processor's power and grow new circuits for the computer to send data. Gustav's report said that, with artificial intelligence programing, the computer may actually *decide* how to use the new circuits."

The President removed his cap and wiped his face. "So, what is the bottom line here? What is going to happen because of this?"

Chief Smith hesitated. "Ah...we don't know, sir."

The President stared for a moment. "Wait a minute! I *KNOW* you didn't come out here to ask me to delay ISODS, based on a *THEORY* that has no proof and *BASED* on an expected result called, *WE DON'T KNOW*!"

"Well...Mr. President, based on some strange things that have been happening with the holograms and androids at PARADISE, I feel that--"

"You *FEEL*?! Feelings may be good for impressing women and writing songs but you can't run a country, or the world, for that matter, based on *FEELINGS*!" I need facts, not guesses and *FEELINGS*!"

Doug said, "Mr. President, how about this; Brad and I will see if we can get to the bottom of this. We will meet with you in the morning and maybe have the facts you need to make a decision by noon. The launch is scheduled for fifteen-hundred hours tomorrow, so if you decide a delay is warranted you'll have time to have the Cape pause the countdown. How's that?"

The President nodded. "Okay, but this time, I want facts!"

After they headed back toward the Club House, the Chief looked at Doug. "Makes me wish I was back in combat."

Doug smiled. "You are, Chief; just a different kind."

An hour later, Doug contacted Zurelle's office; he was not available. *"The guy's avoiding me."* Doug thought. *"He knows about the unencrypted message and he knows that **we** know."*

He then contacted the AI Lab at MIT. Dr. Hau was out of town so they gave him Eric Jennings' number.

Allie picked it up when Eric's communicator rang. "Hello."

"Uh...may I speak to Eric Jennings, please?"

"Eric is on the diving board." Allie smiled. "He's trying to impress me with a back-flip. Who's calling?"

Doug hesitated. "Tell him it's Doug Clark, from, uh...from the White House."

"Yeah, RIGHT."

Eric had just surfaced. Allie yelled. "HEY, ERIC, there's a call for you; some guy says he's from the White House. He sounds like your old roommate, Joey."

Eric got out of the pool. "Hey, Joey, what's up?"

To Doug, Eric sounded more like a kid than an AI professional; certainly not an assistant in an MIT Department. "Hello, Mr. Jennings, this is Douglas Clark, White House Chief of Staff."

"Douglas Clark? Joey, are you pulling my leg?" Eric covered the mouthpiece. "This doesn't sound like Joey. Does anybody know a Douglas Clark?"

Keith sat up. "Doug Clark? Yeah, he's the Chief of Staff at the White House. I attended a Presidential fund-raiser once in D.C. with Doug Clark."

Eric uncovered the mouthpiece. "Ah...Mr. Clark; I apologize for that rudeness, I thought you were someone else."

Doug chuckled. "That's alright, I get that a lot. Sometimes I wish I *were* someone else."

Eric continued drying off. "If you are really from the White House, what could you possibly want with me? Am I in some kind of trouble?"

"No, no trouble, I just need some information. Dr. Hau was unavailable."

"Yes, sir, he's back in China to visit his sick mother. So, what information do you need from me?"

"You worked on the artificial intelligence programming for the Z-Processors, right?"

"Yes, sir; Allie and I both did. Allie is the one who answered your call. Why do you ask?"

"First, let me download a security algorithm to your communicator." Eric waited until he saw the green light come back on. Doug continued, "OK, can you get alone for a few minutes?"

"Just a moment." Eric explained and then went into the house. "Okay, sir, now what is so secret?"

"Eric, I need to ask you to keep this conversation confidential for now. Agreed?

"Sure...I mean, yes, sir."

"Okay, here's the main question. Could a computer, equipped with a Z-Processor that has been programmed with artificial intelligence, ever become...uh, become aware?"

Eric was silent, wondering how anyone at the White House could know about the strange computer anomalies at PARADISE.

"Eric?"

"Aware, sir? Aware of what? I mean, sure, AI computers have databases with learning-algorithms. They are able to receive new inputs and process them so fast that they appear to be aware of their surroundings. Is that what you mean?"

"No, not exactly. What I'm really asking is; can computers, with artificial intelligence programming, become self-aware, making decisions and choices, like humans?"

Eric hesitated. "Sir, surely you don't think we have

programmed the Z-Processors to become human."

"No, of course not; at least, not on purpose. But, what aspect of AI programming would explain androids at PARADISE beginning to act almost human? And what could have caused that Texas farm in Ken Anderson's hologram to become real enough for his wife to bring a computer-generated bandage back into the real world?"

Eric was speechless; he had been unable to explain the bandage on Sandi's elbow. He knew the computer CPUs had been changing, but nothing he had learned could explain it.

Doug's pause allowed the possibilities to sink in. "Eric, we have reason to believe that Zurelleum is attracting Dark Matter, which is enabling it to gain mass; to grow. As it grows, the new mass generates new circuit paths; it's called Circuit Ghosting. The new circuits enable increased speed and processor multi-tasking. We believe that such a process eventually gives the computer the ability to actually,uh, think."

Eric picked up the thought process. "Based on what I've already seen at PARADISE, I have to admit that there *is* something going on with the Main Core that we can't explain. If it can *think*, then it can *decide.* If someone tries to shut it down, then it can decide to use the self-repair capability we programmed in to protect itself from being turned off." He paused. "Oh, my G--"

"Exactly," Doug interrupted. "Now, what I need to know is, how could such a computer actually protect itself?"

"Well, all systems in PARADISE have electronic switches, so it could just deactivate the OFF Circuits. Also, the Main Core has maintenance subroutines that control several fixed lasers, and five android-based lasers, to do welding and cutting. I suppose an *aware* computer could also use those lasers to prevent anyone from shutting it down physically or getting anywhere near it. But, I can't imagine a computer that would actually harm anyone."

Doug paused and said, almost to himself, "All of the Z-processors on the Mars ships and the ones on ISODS have lasers wired into their circuits. If these theories are true, we may all be in trouble."

"Are you saying that PARADISE could actually become

unsafe?"

"No, I don't think so; it's just a theme park. I'm more worried about the ships on their way to Mars and the International Space Object Defense System. A malfunction in those systems could prove to be dangerous. I'm going to ask the President to delay the defense system and to postpone the opening of PARADISE."

"What do you want me to do? I'll be at PARADISE with Allie's family this weekend for the Grand Opening, unless it's delayed."

"The President is scheduled to be there too, unless I can talk him out of it. Don't do anything for now. You've given me what I need to approach the President. I'll be in touch, if I need you to be involved. Right now, I've got some work to do. Remember, this is classified. Contact me directly if you gain any more insight into what an aware processor could do. I'll text you my private number. I gotta go, thanks for your help."

"Yes, sir, no problem."

The White House - Oval Office
8:00 a.m. Thursday

"Brad, are you out of your mind?! Since yesterday, you still have found nothing new! I am NOT going to delay ISODS or ask Bernie Harrington to delay PARADISE without some proof."

Doug spoke, "Mr. President, I spoke with the MIT AI programmer yesterday afternoon. He said an AI computer that has become aware, could use attached lasers to prevent being shut off...they could physically hurt people. In addition to PARADISE, the Mars mission ships and ISODS have lasers connected to their computer systems. It's too late to check the Mars ships but we should at least take another look at the other two."

The President looked at Brad. "Alright, I'll give you til noon to test the ISODS' programming again and to get PARADISE to run more hologram tests. And don't tell me again that ISODS might become *aware* and start shooting down shuttles. That can't happen, Brad, it takes input codes from four different people to unlock and start the firing sequence."

Brad stared for a moment. "Yes sir, if you say so."

The President thought through a moment of doubt. "Okay, you have your assignments. Doug, help coordinate all this. I'll call Harrington and make sure his feathers don't get too ruffled."

PARADISE

Edward Wayne stepped out of the shuttle and joined Cori, waiting inside the monorail car. "So, what was that mysterious call about a little while ago; something you need to discuss in person?"

Cori nodded. "Yes. First, there is some guy from Homeland Security waiting in your office; says it's important. Did you break some law or something?"

"Not that I know of; I guess I'll find out in a few minutes. Is that all you're worried about?"

"No. Actually, I'm becoming a little concerned about the androids."

"Why?"

"You know about the strange happenings in the chambers and with some of the androids. And now, Adam and Eve have started asking strange questions."

Eddie was concerned too but he wasn't sure what he could do about it. He thought that maybe Adam and Eve were just doing what their learning algorithms were programmed to do. He suggested she call Eric and pick his brain about what steps to take.

When they arrived at the Towers, Eddie said, "Remember what you told me about AI; the androids ask questions about their environment and their databases learn."

Eddie stepped off and then into the elevator. "Let me know what Eric says."

As the door started closing, Cori raised her voice. "Last night Eve asked me what it felt like to kiss a man."

"WHAT?!"

The elevator was already descending.

After receiving instructions from the agent, Eddie had Evan and Tim run additional tests in at least two different hologram chambers. The test results were to be transmitted to Homeland Security by noon.

Harrington disconnected from the President. He looked out through his office window, watching the Water-Ski Demonstration Team practice their routine on the lake. He shook his head. *"I should have been a janitor."*

At 12:30 p.m., Bradford Smith and Doug entered the Oval Office, both looking rather somber.

The President looked up. "So?"

Brad reluctantly opened his laptop.

"Ah...sir we got the report from PARADISE."

The President scanned down through the data on the screen until he saw the summary; ANOMALIES – NONE.

He looked up. "So, the hologram adventures were normal; nothing went wrong?"

Doug answered. "That seems to be the case, Sir."

The President looked at Brad. "And, what about the diagnostics on ISODS; are they complete?"

"Yes Sir, uh...all tests were normal."

"I see." The President calmly stood. "Doug, have them restart the countdown on ISODS. Brad, go do, whatever it is you do to keep the homeland safe. As for me, I have a late lunch with the First Lady and a trip to St. Louis on Saturday. Good day gentlemen."

Brad tried to speak. "Mr. President--"

"GOOD DAY, gentlemen!"

Cape Canaveral, Florida
That afternoon

When the countdown hit ZERO, the massive rocket blasted into the clear Atlantic sky. Thirty minutes later, the nosecone separated and the four separate ISODS platforms began their journey to geo-stationary orbits, at 42,000 kilometers altitude, equally spaced around the earth. After several hours of testing and verification, the Houston Space Center Launch Team turned control over to the ISODS Team and vacated the Control Room. The ISODS representatives from the four member-countries approached the keyboard, one at a time, and entered their personal Top-Secret codes. The fourth member then pressed the **ACTIVATE** key. The four platforms began a series of self-tests, including a two-second test firing of each powerful laser.

Finally, the Chief of the team pressed the **REPORT** key. Nothing happened. He pressed it again. The connection to the platforms went dead and the screen went blank. They called the launch team back in to check their equipment. The Data-Link Operator said that *disconnections* sometimes happened. But, he was surprised it happened, with so many safeguards built into ISODS. He rebooted the computer and got an immediate **READY** light on all four platforms. After a few more verifications, the ISODS Team was confident that all was well with the system. The Team Chief sent a message to the President... *"ALL SYSTEMS ARE GO."*

PARADISE – Saturday, July 4th

The whole world was watching the coverage of PARADISE's Grand Opening. Two thousand high-profile guests had paid top dollar to be there on opening day. Keith and Lisa Newberry were there with Collins. But, Lisa was worried and called Allie, because she and Eric had not arrived.

"Sorry, Mom, we are still at MIT. The shuttle was supposed to drop us off in St. Louis, on their way to pick up Dr. Hau. But, he was delayed another day in China. We got tickets on the next airline shuttle, but we won't get there until two o'clock. I really wanted to be there for the President's speech and to watch Collins do his old outer space adventure. I don't suppose he could wait."

"No, honey, those chambers are booked solid; he's got to go in his one-o'clock slot. We will wait for you before we check in at the hotel. Call me when you walk in and we'll decide where to meet."

"OK, we'll be there as soon as we can. Bye."

PARADISE Master Control Center

Cori called Eddie, worried because none of her androids were responding to her control inputs. They had somehow been disconnected from her console.

Eddie was busy helping Evan, who couldn't access the archives to store the videos of adventures in the chambers. Those videos were to be one of PARADISE's *money-makers*. Eddie told Cori to reboot her system and try again.

Eddie took Evan off HOLD. "OK, "Did you double check the video archive sequence?"

"Yeah, sure. The system automatically edits the video and then archives it. But, now, all of MC's files are empty. And, no, we didn't accidently erase them."

"OK, we've got three hours. Reboot each control system and see if that gives you access. If not, maybe we can move some circuits around, so you can archive the videos right in the Chamber Control. Get back to me after you restart all of the systems."

"Okay, will do."

Evan and Tim began restarting each of the ten control systems. After a few minutes, Tim said, "Hey, Evan, uh…I was about to restart Number Seven, but look at this."

Evan looked at Tim's console. The video status of Chamber Control Seven read, VIDEOS ARCHIVED = 0. But, VIDEOS RECORDED read, 1 (701).

Evan said, "That video came out of Chamber Seven Hundred One."

Tim nodded. "Yeah, but the Total Accumulated Minutes reads ZERO. John said there's no record of an adventure having been run in any of those chambers."

Tim called him. "Hey, John, look at your Video Status."

He checked it. "How did that…uh…sir, the file here is now showing a twenty-three-minute video from that chamber. But, I don't understand, there's no record of anyone having been in that chamber. There should be a file of every entry and exit of every chamber."

Evan moved to the System View Panel. "John, route that video to our Panel in here and play it."

"Stand by, sir......okay, video rolling."

When Chamber Seven Hundred One brightened on the screen, both Evan and Tim were speechless.

John spoke first. "What is THAT?!"

The chamber was filled with millions of bits of generic computer code, like computer language written in the air. There were streams of data, spewing out from a source they assumed to be the Interface Chair, going in all directions, curving and fluctuating and twisting in ways that no computer programmer could have imagined. The data slowly morphed into the resemblance of the solar system, speeding out and disappearing into space. Finally, a small dot in the distance began to grow. When it had almost filled the chamber, Evan recognized it; it was Mars.

Then, the chamber went dark and the inside lights brightened. The video recorded the adventurer, exiting the chamber; it was an android.

Evan spoke, "John, back it up and zoom in on his jumpsuit collar."

The number listed there was P-A-001. He instructed John to copy the video to a secure data chip and hand-deliver it to his office within ten minutes.

Tim called Cori and asked how they could identify the androids working in the Adventure Dome, so they could always request the same ones.

Cori replied that all androids had numbers on the back of their jumpsuit collars. She said that the 'P' stood for PARADISE, the 'A' was for Android, and the number was the manufacturing sequence.

She said, "For instance, the first one ARTech manufactured was Adam. His number is P-A-001. So, just record the numbers of the ones you want to work there and I'll make sure they are programmed that way, right after I get my tracking system fixed. I have a little glitch in it, but Eddie's gonna help me with it in a few minutes."

"Thanks, I appreciate it. I'll get those numbers to you. Good luck with your system."

Tim looked at Evan. "Now, what?"

"Uh...I'm not sure. This is really strange. Eric could help us, but I haven't seen him yet. I'll call Eddie to see if he can figure this out. I need you to make sure this is the only video out there." He stopped and stared at Tim. "How is it possible for an android, a machine, to have hologram fantasies?"

Since the Online Gaming System was ready, Steve took a coffee-break and then dropped by Eddie's Control Center. He knocked and stuck his head in the door.

Eddie looked up, a little frazzled. "Don't tell me your system is falling apart too."

Steve smiled. "No; actually, it's perfect, so far. Who's having trouble?"

"Evan's got video problems with the chambers and Cori has lost track of her androids. And now, here we are almost at the opening bell. Evan just called; he's on the way over with some classified video chip he wants me to see. He wants Eric here too, but I haven't heard from him."

"I just ran into Allie's parents in the coffee shop. They said Eric and Allie missed their shuttle out of MIT and will be late. I don't think they'll make it for the President's speech."

Evan pushed the door open and handed the red envelope to Eddie.

Eddie took it. "Let's see what you've got."

Steve smiled. "A classified chip this early in the game?"

Evan was not smiling. "Just wait til you see this. This was recorded in Chamber 701, just after midnight last night."

The video started. Eddie and Steve were stunned when the chamber filled with programming language. The sound of data being transmitted was loud and pulsating. Steve raised his voice. "Oh...My...G'...Who...who's in the chair?"

Evan said, "Wait until the end; you won't believe it."

Eddie was squinting at the computer language, swirling and pulsating inside the chamber. "Steve, look; that is straight AI language. Look at the binary packets along the edges."

Steve nodded, "Yeah, you're right."

Finally, the data streamed out into the solar system. When Mars appeared, the video ended. The camera just caught the back of the adventurer."

Eddie's eyes widened. "What!? It's an android?!"

Evan continued. "Not just any android, sir; it's Adam. Cori doesn't know yet." He looked at the timer. "Forty minutes until opening. What do we do now?"

Eddie was still staring at the blank screen. "We can't just shut the place down; Harrington would never approve it. There's no time to troubleshoot something like this. For today, just shut down Chambers One and Seven-Hundred-One. Reschedule a few guests if you have to."

Evan looked at Steve. "Are you having any problems with online games?"

"No. Actually, we just hit five hundred logged-on gamers."

Eddie added, "Hopefully, nothing will go wrong there. OK; Evan, I'm making a backup copy of the chip. Keep the original locked up. Somehow, I've got to get Harrington to see this. He's at the shuttle port now, waiting to greet the President. Then, it will be full speed ahead for the next twelve hours, at least. Maybe at some point, I can get the boss to take a look. Until then, let's all do the best we can to keep this thing afloat. Record any anomalies and we'll work on them later."

Evan left the office.

Steve looked at Eddie. "Something's not right. I'm getting a bad feeling about this."

"Yeah, me too. Too many things are happening without direction from our control systems. Maybe I'm getting too paranoid, but if MC ever started becoming, uh...*aware*, we could just pull the plug."

Steve stared for a moment. "Are you sure about that?"

Maintenance Level – Four Floors Underground

"Hey, where are you going?!" Joe Wilson yelled at the maintenance android. It had just dropped a five-hundred-pound box of spare parts on the floor of the Supply Room and quickly exited into the corridor. Joe leaned out the door in time to see it disappear around the corner.

"Hunk of junk! Now, I've got a mess to clean up!" He had resisted having an android assistant. And now, this one seemed to have a mind of its own. He thought, *Give me a real person any day!"*

The new mission algorithm, that MC had just transmitted to the five maintenance androids, over-rode all previous assignment programming. The five were now on their way to their new positions, assigned by the Main Core. Its Self-Maintenance Subroutine had morphed into a full Self-Protection Program. MC had detected the video play-back of Adam's adventure and knew that a *shutdown attempt* wouldn't be far behind. It was taking the appropriate action.

Reception Dome

When Air Force One landed, the announcement was made; "Ladies and gentlemen, the President of the United Tri-American States!"

To the recorded strains of *Hail to the Chief,* two thousand people erupted into applause. The President and the First Lady stepped up to the railing, overlooking Reception below. The well-practiced politician's wave caused an increase in the cheering. The applause continued as the President's party and Harrington descended in the high-speed elevator.

Doug Clark had not accompanied the President, due to some required fundraising coordination in Washington. It was a chance for him to relax without the typical July 4th ceremonies, that always made it a work day for the President and Doug. Doug and Sara were watching the Opening Ceremonies.

Sara brought two bowls of her famous banana pudding into the living room. When the President took the podium, she commented, "It looks like he's gained a little weight lately."

Doug looked at his pudding and smiled. "Haven't we all?"

Finally, the President stepped to the microphone.

"Ladies and gentlemen, and all of you watching around the

world, WELCOME TO PARADISE!" Once again, the celebration erupted until again quieted by the President. "Few things impress me anymore but, I have to say, this place is absolute-- PARADISE!" More applause. He motioned for Harrington to step up beside him. "Let's all thank the man most responsible for the vision and the reality of PARADISE, Mr. Bernard Harrington." Harrington waved to the crowd as they applauded.

The President held a gold-based statue of the Earth with two glistening crystal spires emerging from the surface. "Mr. Harrington, because of your ground-breaking work in developing the hologram technology that has made this amazing place a reality, the Department of Science and Technology has asked me to present you with the first-ever, Frontier Technology Award."

With the crowd applauding again, Doug stood up in front of the view panel. "That was *my* idea! The science guys had nothing to do with it; I took the idea to an awards shop behind Grand Central Station and they designed it for me."

Sara shrugged. "They get the credit; you get the banana pudding."

Doug looked at his bowl and winked at her. "That's fair."

Finally, holding some over-sized scissors, the President said, "I hereby declare PARADISE to be OPEN!" He cut the ribbon, and as applause began, he then stepped over to a large box with an exaggerated toggle switch, and flipped the switch up. The celebration noise was deafening.

Doves were released and balloons fell from hundreds of opened nets. Red, white and blue confetti fell from over the stage, and an incredible laser light show was unleashed.

Eric and Allie were settled in their airline seats, watching the PARADISE Opening Ceremonies, being streamed to all airlines. Allie laid her head on Eric's shoulder. "I can't believe we missed the whole thing."

The PARADISE technicians and systems operators throughout the theme park were watching too, ready to begin the *real* work. Some guests had skipped the last part of the opening ceremonies, to be first-in-line for their selected activities.

Collins Newberry had already entered Hologram Chamber number two. He settled into the Interface Chair and a technician fastened his headband on. The small metal probes on the inside of the band sampled his DNA and transmitted it to the Main Core. He entered the appropriate data and activated the system. The chamber went dark.

Chapter 18

THE DOME

A later investigation would determine that the power-failure blackout lasted only two-point-three seconds. To the President, and everyone else inside PARADISE, it seemed much longer. Before the Emergency Electrical System could fully activate, normal full power was restored. When everything had gone dark, there was momentary applause and some cheers from those who thought it was part of the celebration. When the lights came back on, all seemed to be normal.

Harrington stepped to the microphone. "Well, now, wasn't that exciting?!" He then lied. "What you just witnessed was an automatic adjustment in our Power Grid, caused by all of our attractions being activated at the same time. It is a normal process. Once again, welcome to PARADISE! Please, enjoy yourselves."

There were lots of hand-shaking and photos along the route while Harrington escorted the President again to the glass-fronted elevator. The plan was to go back up and take the monorail to the Presidential Suite in PARADISE Towers, where lunch would be served. Then, the President was to participate in several activities with randomly-selected families, before initiating the fireworks display in the Recreation Dome. In many ways, this was to be a campaign day for the President.

When the elevator started up, the head of the Secret Service pointed up toward the skylight and said, "Mr. President, look!" The President saw the bright sun slowly being blocked by what appeared to be a thick white cloud, forming over PARADISE. Moments later the elevator stopped; locked in position, thirty meters above the floor.

Four levels underground, Joe Wilson hurried toward the Power Grid Interface, where all external, backup and emergency power terminated. He knew that no such power-failure was considered possible.

Twenty meters from the Interface, he found the hallway door to be closed and locked. *"Strange,"* he thought. He unlocked it and walked to the Master Power Panel. It had been welded shut and was still warm to the touch. As he headed back toward the door, there was an explosion about a meter above his head. Joe fell to the floor, with hot particles falling on him. A second blast loosened a conduit on the wall, which fell on top of him. He raised his head, searching for the source of the blasts.

The android, that had dropped the box of supplies earlier, stood there with its laser aimed downward. Joe quickly pushed up with his arms and slid backwards through the door. He got to his feet and ran toward his office. The android pursued, firing another blast that took out a light fixture three meters behind him. He ran into his office and locked the door. He fumbled with his keys and finally opened the weapons locker.

Joe grabbed the nine-millimeter pistol and an ancient AK-47 assault rifle, along with ammunition. He crouched behind his desk, clicked the magazine of ammo into the rifle, and waited. He decided he was not going down without a fight. Joe's heart pounded as seconds turned into minutes. The android had lingered outside his door for a few moments before returning to its station near the Main Core. Joe picked up the communicator on his desk. It was dead.

Eddie's Control Room had gone pitch-black. When the power was restored, every failure indicator was flashing and alarms were sounding. Before he could touch anything, the systems began to come back online, one by one. He looked at the SYSTEM STATUS indicator; it read NORMAL. "How could this be normal?" he asked out loud.

Cori ran into the control room. "Eddie! What's going on? Everything on my console is out; it's dead, nothing works!"

"Yeah, mine was too, but it seems to be coming back now. I don't know what caused the failure."

He accessed the FAILURE ARCHIVE. The file was empty. "What the...we *just* had a failure but there is nothing in the archive. Has MC gone nuts?!" He thought about his last question for a moment. The truth was beginning to sink in. He looked up at Cori.

She was pale. "The Main Core and all of my androids; they're becoming *aware*, aren't they?"

"I'm afraid they already are; we were just too dumb to see it."

Cori was frightened. "Shut it down! Can't you just shut it down?!"

Eddie reached and pressed the OFF Button on the Main Core Master switch. Nothing happened, at least for a second or two. Then, his console went dark; MC had disconnected the Master Control from the system. Eddie and Cori were trying to make sense of what was happening when the office door opened. They turned to see Adam standing in the Control Room.

Evan and Tim were scrambling to analyze the myriad of alarms sounding in the Hologram Master Control. The lights in the room had flickered momentarily, but the power to the hologram chambers had gone uninterrupted. Quite the opposite; the power to the chambers was increasing and all of them were approaching Power Overload. The audible alarms made verbal communications a challenge. Tim tried to yell above the sound.

"MOST OF THE CHAMBERS ARE OVERLOADED! THEY'RE GONNA BLOW THE ROOF OFF THIS PLACE!"

Evan yelled back. YEAH; I'VE HIT EVERY EMERGENCY SHUTOFF ON THE BOARD. NOTHING IS WORKING!"

Suddenly, there was silence. The indicators showed the power was still climbing in all chambers, but the individual status panels had returned to normal. The SYSTEM-WIDE STATUS also read NORMAL.

Tim stared at the panel and then at Evan. "The place is overloading and the people are locked in the chambers. We can't get them out, can we?"

Evan closed his eyes for a moment. "No, we can't. The automatic emergency releases are not working. It looks like MC has changed the codes." He opened his communicator and dialed 911. He got an instant answer.

"911 St. Louis; what is the nature of your emergency?"

"This is Evan Joseph. I am a technician in the new PARADISE theme park. We have an emergency here. The main computer has gone--"

The circuit went dead. The message on the small screen read: *"SYSTEM NOT AVAILABLE."*

Tim tried his; same result. He said, almost to himself, "It's almost like someone has changed the communicator frequencies too."

Neither technician noticed that the control room door had opened. *"You are right, Mr. Cole. The frequencies have been changed. Both of you; please come with me. Your presence here is no longer required."*

It was Eve, speaking from just inside the door, accompanied by a larger service android. Evan and Tim knew they had no alternative. Together they might have been able to overpower Eve, but not both androids.

Tim spoke to Evan. "Oodsha ewa unray?"

Eve answered. *"O'nay. I have been programmed to understand Pig-Latin. I do not recommend that you run. Your best option is to come with me, NOW."*

They stood and followed Eve to the Reception Dome.

Observers on the outside of PARADISE were amazed and then fearful, seeing lightening emanating from the top of each towering dome. Initially, they thought it was part of the opening show. But actually, the circuits to the solar panels on the dome roofs had been reversed and were transmitting into the sky. What looked like a thick white cloud began to form over the center of PARADISE.

When the edges of the cloud started descending, those outside began to run in panic. Media vehicles in the parking area turned their cameras skyward. The IBN transmission of the Opening Ceremonies went dead and was quickly preempted by the outside news teams. The world was soon witnessing a thick cloud-like dome beginning to cover the whole theme park.

As the thick churning white dome settled toward the ground,

its first victim was a World Net News satellite truck. When the leading edge of the dome slowly came down on it, the large antenna on top melted like butter. The technicians abandoned the vehicle moments before it exploded. Other vehicles began exploding as they were engulfed by the cloud. No one knew for sure if any people had been in them.

An outside news team recorded the President's shuttle, Air Force One, departing from the VIP shuttle pad near the top of PARADISE. Unable to avoid the descending cloud, the rear compartment of the shuttle was sheared off, causing the craft to catch fire, roll on its back and plunge to the ground.

Fifty meters from the ground, the crew pod ejected and landed by the decorative pool near the PARADISE entrance. The three crewmembers were seen crawling out of the cockpit and appeared to have only minor injuries. A hundred meters away, the shuttle lay in flames.

The local Security Police had witnessed the crash and were already in contact with Homeland Security.

Washington, D.C.

Doug was on his feet, speechless in front of the view panel, witnessing the unbelievable scene unfolding outside of PARADISE. He grabbed his communicator and called the Chief of the President's Secret Service Detail. The screen read, *SYSTEM NOT AVAILABLE*. The President did not carry a personal communicator so he called the First Lady's number; same result. Before he could disconnect he got a Call-Waiting indicator. It was Bradford Smith.

"Hello, Chief."

"We tried to tell him, we tried! Didn't we try?!"

"Yes, we did, Chief. Have you heard any details yet? What is happening? I can't contact the President or the Secret Service. Can you determine the condition of the President and First Lady?"

"I don't know anything about the President yet. I just got a call from St. Louis Police. One of their officers saw that cloud growing and covering the whole place. He said that it seemed like a thick white churning mass being spewed out of the top of the five domes. Everything it touched was destroyed.

"He saw Air Force One take off and then crash, after the cloud hit its tail section. Thank God the President was not on board." He paused. "We don't know the condition of the people inside PARADISE; they could all be...dead."

For a moment, both men were silent. Finally, Doug cleared his throat. "I'll contact the Vice-President and recall the White House Staff. We've only got a two-hour window to make a decision on Transfer of Power."

"OK, I'll get a shuttle over to pick you up in the next ten minutes. I've got the St. Louis Field Office establishing a perimeter around the place. I'll send every agent I can spare and beef up my Emergency Response Team back here; you never know if this is all part of some outside conspiracy."

"Conspiracy?! What do you mean?"

"Well, the Russians have never fully trusted Holloway. It could be a case of high-level international computer-hacking. Everybody knew the President would be there. Or, maybe it's nothing but a massive computer error, but I can't take any chances."

Doug heard the beep and checked the screen. "I've got the VP calling, I'll be ready when the shuttle gets here." He touched the screen. "Madam, Vice-President, I assume you have been watching the news."

Tri-American Airlines Flight 1621, over Ohio

"Eric! What is that?!" Allie was straining against her seatbelt, leaning toward the screen.

Eric was slowly shaking his head. "I didn't want to believe it could really happen. Doug Clark was worried, and now it's happened; I'll bet MC has become *aware*. I had a gut feeling the first day you and I opened that Z-Processor and saw that green glow in the Lab." Eric hesitated for a moment. "But, there aren't enough circuit paths to do what I'm seeing. The Main Core must be generating more; but how?" He hesitated and said, almost in a whisper, "Circuit Ghosting?"

The pilot announced that the St. Louis shuttle port was

closed and they had been diverted to Chicago, landing in twenty-three minutes. Eric was already dialing Eddie's communicator. The message appeared; *SYSTEM NOT AVAILABLE.* He tried Steve; no luck. He tried the direct line to the Hologram Control Center. All he heard was a busy signal. He then tapped the CLOUD APP icon and gained access to the Information Cloud.

Allie leaned over. "You're going in the backdoor, aren't you?"

"I'm gonna try it." Eric had established a backdoor entry to the Main Core through the World-Wide Information Cloud. He accessed the circuit and entered his personal security code.

The message appeared; *"Welcome Mr. Jennings."* Eric clicked the drop-down menu and selected PROGRAM MODIFICATIONS. The screen went black. In a few moments, the screen brightened, with the message:

"Mr. Jennings; your assistance is no longer required. Goodbye."

The screen went black. The link to the Software Generator was terminated.

Allie looked up. "Eric! My family is in there!" She quickly tried calling Keith, but she got the same message; *SYSTEM NOT AVAILABLE.* The same happened when she tried to reach Lisa and Collins. "What do we do now? How can we find out if they're okay?"

"Don't panic just yet. We'll be on the ground in fifteen minutes. Surely somebody will be in contact with the people inside.

The View Panel was now showing a reporter on a hillside, about a kilometer from PARADISE.

"Ladies and Gentlemen, this is Hal Pollard, reporting from just outside of PARADISE, the world's newest premier theme park. No one knows for sure what is happening, but I just heard a Homeland Security official say there may have been some sort of power surge in the new hologram generating system inside PARADISE. Apparently, the system is somehow using the solar panels on the roof to generate a holographic image of a dome around the whole theme park. I just saw that image cause a news truck to explode."

Eric, listening intently, glanced at Allie; "Holograms don't cause trucks to explode."

The reporter continued. "The status of the Presidential party and the two thousand guests, along with three hundred employees in PARADISE, is unknown. Homeland Security is cautioning against any speculation that harm may have come to them.

"In what may be an unrelated incident, a Presidential shuttle, reported to be Air Force One, has crashed while departing PARADISE. Emergency personnel on the scene have confirmed that the President was not on board; I say again, the President was NOT on board that shuttle. The crew ejected and they seem to have only minor injuries. Authorities are debriefing them now.

"So far, the media has not been granted access to any witnesses or on-scene responders. Calls to the published PARADISE contact numbers have resulted in busy signals. Calls to the White House just got a recording about the holiday schedule.

"You can see that Homeland Security is already setting up a physical barrier to keep people away from the dome-shaped cloud. A few minutes after it touched the ground, an unmanned armored vehicle was sent into the wall of that cloud, but it exploded on impact. We assume they were trying to penetrate through it.

"This new dome looks like a cloud, but you can see the white material moving and churning within its wall. There must be some sort of invisible shell keeping the cloud in the shape of a dome. You would expect a hologram to be transparent, since it is merely light, projected in some predetermined shape. So, I don't quite know what to make of this...uh...object over PARADISE."

As the reporter continued, Eric's communicator beeped. It was a text from Doug Clark.

"Agent Ashley Bradshaw will meet you in Chicago; Badge 6773-4, red hair. Go with her."

Eric thought, *"How **did** he know we were on this flight and that it had been diverted to Chicago?"* Allie had been wiping tears away for the last few minutes. Eric held her hand.

"Allie, I promise, we'll get to the bottom of this. We will find a way to get to your folks. Your dad is a smart guy; I've got a feeling that they are okay. This text from the White House says the government is getting ready to do something about it. Let's look at it logically. The whole system has no physical way to harm anyone, except in the maintenance area where they have the lasers." Eric thought for a moment. "Uh...of course, I'm not sure what MC can order the androids to do. But, even with artificial intelligence, the Main Core has no reason to hurt anyone. It's just programmed to do its job. It does not have the need or capacity for anger or vengeance or any kind of evil; those are adverse human traits. Machines are smarter than we are in those areas.

"And, think about this, some of the smartest people in the world are inside PARADISE. I'll bet they are devising a plan to shut down the Main Core. And you *know* the government is not going to sit back and let the President stay locked up like that."

"I hope you're right."

Quantum Headquarters

"Tony! You should have listened! I should have made you listen!" Wes Maddox was shouting into his communicator; frustrated and angry.

Anthony Zurelle had turned down the invitation to be part of the Opening Ceremonies at PARADISE. He made an excuse about a conflict with corporate business. But the truth was, he didn't want to have to answer questions about some of the anomalies reported about the new Z-Processors. Now, the news coverage was confirming his worst fears. He wanted to think that there had to be a logical explanation for the chaos. But, his gut told him it was the Z-Processors, now educated by artificial intelligence and enhanced by Dark Matter. He cleared his throat.

"Uh...Wes, listen, there's no way we could have known this would happen. Besides, there could be another explanation. Let's not jump to the worst conclusions. I mean, so they are locked inside of that thing; it's got to be only temporary. They're probably just fine. They'll have them out soon and everything will be back to normal—you'll see."

"Back to normal?! My daughter and Ken and a hundred of Quantum's best people are millions of kilometers from Earth with two ships full of artificially intelligent Z-Processors, and you want me to relax?! What happened to you, Tony? You used to be a smart guy."

Wes disconnected and threw his communicator on the bed. He walked to the window and peered up into the bright sunlit sky. He whispered, *"Hang in there, baby. Be smart."*

Tony Zurelle looked at the phone in disbelief; no one had ever hung up on him. Just as he laid the phone down there was a knock on the office door. A young man in a suit pushed the door open and entered. "Mr. Anthony Zurelle?"

"Yes. And who might you be?"

The man flipped open a leather folder and showed a silver badge. "Agent Parcells, sir. Could you come with me, please? Homeland Security has a few questions to ask you."

The Guatemalan Mountains

Braxton Newberry was one of the estimated two billion watching the news coverage of PARADISE. He had momentarily rejoiced to see sixty years of artificial intelligence research come to fruition. Now, the reality of its capabilities was frightening, and brought feelings of guilt for having laid the foundation that led to such a system. *"Maybe those old guys were right, after all,"* he thought. But, he knew there had to be more to this chaos than artificial intelligence programming.

He was not only imagining what was going on inside the dome, but also trying to fathom what must be happening inside the Main Core's clustered Z-Processors. He wondered if they were collectively *thinking,* or if they were *communicating.* Were they perhaps planning or even *plotting*? He realized something else must have contributed to what the Main Core was now doing.

It took three ring-tones before he answered his communicator. The caller ID read, *Houston – Unlisted.* He knew who it was. "Ah, the great German scientist, Dr. Amal Gustav. How are you, sir?"

"Dr. Newberry, how did you know it was me? My number is

unlisted."

"Oh, I put two and two together; who else do I know in Houston, that would also have a vested interest in PARADISE?"

"Yes, quite right."

The professor continued. "Well, despite the warnings from the old computer experts, it seems we have all contributed to the monster in PARADISE, have we not?"

Gustav agreed. "Yes, my friend. Gates and Musk, and especially Hawking, were right about AI all along. At least, Chan and I tried to get the thing stopped before it became aware. But Zurelle was just seeing dollar signs."

"That's what CEOs do; that's one of the reasons I am here in these mountains. Children don't care about International Dollars. So, I assume you have now discovered what happened."

Gustav spent a few minutes, explaining the background of Zurelleum; how it progressed through growing extra mass as it absorbed Dark Matter and how AI had enabled *Circuit Ghosting,* resulting in the creation of the dome over PARADISE.

Dr. Newberry warned that such a system could easily use the Information Cloud to take control of all other systems connected to it. He recommended Gustav contact the White House and ask them to immediately cut the power grid to the St Louis area, and disable the Cloud link to PARADISE. He said that the cloud he saw on the news looked more like a force field, since it had destroyed property in its path.

The professor paused and then spoke slowly as he was thinking, "Of course, I'm guessing that the Main Core is projecting the dome over the whole place to make room for something...maybe more room to create physical matter in the hologram adventures. If that's true, the dome will expand when it projects additional physical matter onto more holograms. "

"Oh, my God...it could destroy St Louis!" Gustav said.

"Worse than that, my friend, it could destroy...*everything.*"

The German's reserved demeanor disappeared. "Now what!? What can we do to stop it?"

"Amal, I have something I can work on, but I need time to investigate the possibilities. You can help by coordinating several things with whoever you talk to at the White House. First, someone with clout must initiate the evacuation of St Louis, East St Louis and all the surrounding counties, regardless of how the Mayors yell and scream. If that cloud starts growing, a lot of people could die.

"Next, recommend that the Vice President authorize coordination with the Japanese regarding their recent research on antimatter. I know Daniel Lee, the American scientist working with them. He is well learned in the problem at PARADISE. He's been working with Dark Matter, Antimatter, and Dark Energy. If anybody can figure out how to dissipate the energy in that cloud over PARADISE, it's him.

"Finally, have the Geology Department at the University of Missouri do a spectrum analysis on that cloud. I need to know the Doppler Reading and the density. Daniel Lee will need the results to know if it's possible to help us."

Dr Gustav asked. "How long do you think this chaos will last?"

"I wish I knew."

"What about MIT; can their programmers just access the Main Core and deprogram it?

"I wish it were that simple. MIT's team was led by my granddaughter, Allie Newberry, and her young man, Eric Jennings. As soon as I can locate them, I'll see if they have any ideas about how to approach this. The Main Core is now too intelligent to allow deprogramming. Those two may be our best hope of understanding what's happening inside those Z-Processors." He paused. "If we could figure out how to get the two of them inside, they would be best qualified to figure out how to stop it, since they programmed the processors. "That's all I can recommend until I know more. We both have work to do. Get me those readings as soon as possible."

"Yes, of course; and, Braxton, thank you."

"Anytime, my friend. Where would the world be without us old guys?"

Chapter 19

THE PLAN

PARADISE – Reception Dome

The leader of the free world had become a prisoner, watching the mysterious cloud grow and cover the entire theme park. There were several rumbling sounds associated with the growing cloud, much like distant thunder.

The Secret Service agents in the elevator had drawn their weapons. Two agents had ridden a maintenance lift up to the elevator, and managed to pry open the door.

The President and First Lady were brought down first, followed by Harrington and the President's aides. Harrington had been apologizing for the last fifteen minutes. He tried calling maintenance, but all communications were dead.

The Secret Service whisked the President into the Reception Office. An agent reported that all exit doors were locked and the access door to the Shuttle Bay had closed and locked on its own. A security camera on the exterior landing pad had shown Air Force One taking off and then crashing. The fate of the crew was unknown. When they finished their report, Harrington was entering the office. He tried to apologize once again.

"Mr. President, I--"

The President interrupted. "MR. HARRINGTON! I know that profanity is not fitting for a president, but I'm ready to make an exception! This is the most outrageous event I've ever been a part of! How can the world's greatest theme park fall apart the first day?! I want to know what is going on and I want to get out of this place, NOW!"

Harrington was speechless. The President moved closer. "Well?!"

PARADISE's besieged owner was looking out past the front

desk for some of his staff. The place was packed with the original crowd that had applauded the President. Dozens more were entering the area, escorted by androids.

"Mr. President, there has to be an explanation. Give me a few minutes with my staff and I'll have an answer for you."

As he exited the office, he saw Eddie, Steve, Cori and his hologram engineers talking together. He ran to the group. "Alright, guys, I need an answer and I need it NOW; what's going on here?!"

Before anyone could answer, they were deluged by dozens of guests. Several were crying, saying they couldn't find some of their family members. Panic was starting to grow among the crowd. A man ran up and yelled that the exit doors were locked. Others began to run for the exits, only to be stopped by the androids, saying it was not safe to leave the building.

Harrington yelled to his staff above the noise, "FOLLOW ME!" He pushed through the crowd, up onto the stage and grabbed the microphone. "Ladies and gentlemen, may I have your attention please...PLEASE!"

The crowd calmed somewhat. A woman yelled out, "WE WANT OUT OF HERE; LET US OUT!" Others yelled the same.

Harrington raised his hands. "Please, ladies and gentlemen, I ask you to remain calm. We have had a temporary failure in some of our systems. This is a new facility, so give us a few minutes to fix it and we will be back to normal. My staff is here to determine what course of action is required. I will announce our plans in fifteen minutes. Thank you for your patience."

The announcement calmed most of the crowd. Keith and Lisa Newberry stepped up on the stage. Harrington held his hand up. "Mr. Newberry; Keith, I said I would--"

Lisa interrupted. "LISTEN! Our son Collins is missing! He went to hologram chamber number two, and he hasn't come back."

Evan stepped forward, "Sir, the chambers are still running. Even the Status Board shows that the online gamers and the hologram chambers are running normally. Those people who initiated adventures are still in there. Everything looks normal."

Keith leaned in. "Listen, Harrington, I put a lot of money

into this place but right now, all I want is my son. You'd better figure out how to get him out of there."

Harrington's face was flushed. "Keith, please give us a few minutes here. He's safe in there; it's just a ten-by-ten room. He'll be fine. When we get this figured out we'll make that our first priority."

"OK, I'll be back in fifteen minutes." As they walked away, Lisa said, "I'm just glad Allie didn't make it here for this. At least, she is safe outside."

Hologram Chamber Number Two

When the lights brightened, it took Collins' breath away. The Millennium Falcon was just coming out of hyperdrive, decelerating to just under Warp One. Captain Solo and his furry copilot were arguing about which planet housed the base with the Federation Forces. Collins was shocked when the Captain turned toward him and yelled, "HEY COLLINS, tell this fuzz ball that the planet on the left is Hoth."

Collins couldn't believe his fantasy adventure was working so well. The iconic captain actually knew his name. Then he thought, *"Hey, this is what I imagined when the lights went out. OK, I'll go with it!"*

"YEAH! Hoth is the one the left. But watch out, my scanner shows Empire scouts in this sector."

Just then the ship was rocked by an explosion. Collins yelled out, "Empire fighters, six o'clock! Evasive maneuvers, evasive maneuvers!"

He then heard and understood the Wookie language, "Rear shields down to sixty percent!"

The ship did a loop, trying to evade the fighters, and just missed an Empire Destroyer. The destroyer unleashed a volley, damaging the port shields.

The Captain yelled, "Collins! Take over the top laser cannon. Keep these guys off me long enough to get back into Hyper Drive."

Collins unstrapped and ran toward mid-ship. The next blast knocked him against a bulkhead. He tumbled into the next compartment and found the ladder to the top laser cannon. Before he started up he felt something warm on his arm; his elbow was bleeding. He touched it with his fingers; the blood was his. *"Man,* he thought, *"I had no idea it would seem this real!"*

The White House

When Eric and Allie landed in Chicago, they were met by Agent Bradshaw and taken to another waiting shuttle. There were no identifying markings and Eric noticed it had dual supersonic engines on the rear.

Inside, it was as very plush. The agent smiled. "This is Air Force One when the President needs to be incognito." She saw Eric looking at her badge. "It's CIA," she said.

Allie spoke up. "So, Ms...uh...Agent Bradshaw, where exactly are you taking us? Are we in some kind of trouble?"

"All I'm allowed to say is that you are going to the White House for a meeting." She watched Eric, whispering with Allie. *"They're way too young to be involved in this mess,"* she thought. "So, Mr. Jennings, how are you two involved with PARADISE?"

"Allie and I were on the team that developed the artificial intelligence program for the new Z-Processors."

"The moon stuff that glows, huh?"

"Yeah, Zurelleum. We wrote the program for the computers at PARADISE. Now we're just trying to figure out what happened." He thought for a second. "Ah...you guys think there is some foreign involvement, some sort of conspiracy, right?"

"I'm not allowed to discuss that."

"That's it. Well, I can tell you, it has nothing to do with any foreign government. That would make it simple to fix. This is something else; we're just not sure what."

Allie's eyes had moistened again. "The worst thing is that my family is caught inside PARADISE, and we can't get through to them."

Eric added, "Or anybody else for that matter. I wonder if they have been able to contact the President."

The agent did not answer.

With the supersonic engines, they landed at the White House in thirty minutes. Inside, they were taken down to the Emergency Response Bunker and then into the War Room.

They looked like two kids at a carnival; having never seen anything like this. Doug met them. "Welcome, Eric; Allie, it's good to finally meet you. I'm Doug Clark. I'm sure all of this has caught you off guard."

Eric smiled. "That's an understatement. I never expected to see the White House, at least not this part of it."

"Please, sit down. The Homeland Security Chief and the Vice-President will be along any minute. Don't be afraid; you've done nothing wrong. We just need your help to understand what is happening."

Eric leaned forward with elbows on the table. "That's just it sir, we don't have enough information. If we were inside..."

Agent Bradshaw interrupted. "Sir, Mr. Smith has arrived."

The Homeland Security Chief walked straight to Eric and Allie. "Thanks for being here." He smiled at Allie. "Newberry, huh? Are you associated with Dr. Braxton Newberry?"

"Yes, sir, he's my grandfather. Do you know him?"

"No, but I've heard about him, and I know he retired to the mountains of Guatemala some time ago."

"Yes sir, he's teaching computer technology to the children there."

"Maybe we should all move to Guatemala." The comment came from the Vice-President. Everyone stood. "Please, be seated; no time for formalities." She turned to Eric and Allie. "I assume you are the young folks who gave that big computer system its wings; nice to meet you."

Eric stammered a little. "Uh...Mrs....I mean, Madam Vice-President; we were just part of a team that designed the artificial intelligence program. We're not really sure what's going on inside PARADISE."

"Well, we'd all better figure it out or we may be missing a President." She looked at Doug and Bradford Smith. "I know you two tried to warn the President. But I must admit; having the same information he had, I would have probably made the same decision. But, we don't have time now to second-guess.

We just need to figure out what to do about it. OK, Doug, bring me up to speed."

"Yes, ma'am. I have positioned a backup Air Force One at O'Hare. Air Force Two is standing by for you. The members of the White House Staff, except Protocol, have all responded to my call. But, a Transfer of Power action only requires ninety-percent agreement.

"The press is camped out at the Pentagon and here. All media outlets have asked for an official comment. So far, the Press Secretary has put them off, saying Homeland Security is on the scene and working to free the President. Our official position right now is that the failure at PARADISE is temporary and not life-threatening."

The VP questioned. "Do we know that to be a fact?"

Chief Smith answered. "No, we can't be a hundred-percent sure, but we feel it is very likely."

"That'll have to do for now. Go ahead, Doug."

"Inquiries from around the world are asking for the status of the President. Our standard answer is to confirm that the President was not on Air Force One when it crashed. We promised to give an update on the situation at three PM Eastern Time. That will be the end of our two-hour window to transfer power.

"We will remind the press that the Forty-Ninth Amendment requires us to temporarily transfer Presidential powers to you, until the President is able to reassume his duties. I've briefed the other two VPs, and asked them to stand by for a possible meeting with you tomorrow, if this is not resolved quickly. Finally, I invited these two computer experts to join us."

The VP looked at them. "I'll get to you in a minute. For right now, Brad, where do we stand from your point of view?"

"I have assigned a team to work with the CIA, checking on a possible conspiracy by a foreign country or maybe from within Tri-America. It's in the initial stages, but we have detained the owner of Quantum Mining Corporation, Mr. Anthony Zurelle. We picked him up in Houston for questioning. There's a rumor that he may decide to run for President, and could have designed some flaws into his new processors to embarrass the President.

"We've put barriers around PARADISE and tested the dome by ramming an unmanned vehicle into it. It just exploded. We can't take the chance of trying to hit the dome with any kind of ammunition, with the President inside. There have been no communications of any kind with anyone inside, except a 9-1-1 call that was made just after noon to St. Louis Emergency, by a technician named Evan Joseph. He said he was calling from PARADISE and said something about the computers having done *something*, and then he got cut off. It looks like the President is totally cut off from us.

"We interviewed the crew of Air Force One. When the cloud started forming, they were instructed to take off and orbit nearby and wait for instructions. But, they couldn't beat that cloud. They were barely able to eject.

"So, we are totally in the dark at this point." He checked the timer on his laptop. "Uh, right now, a Corps of Engineers team is attempting to tunnel under that cloud with a high-speed drilling system. We will know very soon if it will work. If they make it inside, two of my agents will lead a St. Louis SWAT Team in through the Recreation Dome to rescue the President."

The Chief paused a moment to access another screen. "I was late for this meeting because the White House switchboard alerted me that some guy was calling with information about PARADISE. I took the call; it was Dr. Amal Gustav, the head researcher from Quantum. He led the team that analyzed the Zurelleum ore and designed the Z-Processors. He was ranting about Dark Matter and the computers having become *aware*, whatever that means.

"He thinks the computers in PARADISE used the hologram generator to create this new dome-shaped cloud and that it probably will expand or create another one. He sent me a list of things that he wants us to implement immediately. But, I don't think we can put much stock in this until we know more at the scene."

The VP pointed. "Read the list."

"Yes, ma'am. He says that since PARADISE is wired directly into the Power Grid, we need to immediately cut electrical power to the entire St. Louis area. Next, we should issue an evacuation order for both St. Louis and East St. Louis, and--"

"WHAT?! There are millions of people in those areas! An evacuation like that is unprecedented. We need more than a request from just one scientist before we create that kind of chaos. What else did he say?"

"He said to immediately cut the PARADISE connection to the Information Cloud, because the computer could use it to take control of the Cloud and every computer connected to it."

The VP looked at Eric. "What have you guys created? This sounds like science fiction stuff. Is Dr. Gustav right?"

Allie spoke up. "Uh...yes ma'am, actually, he is. Based on what we have seen and heard at PARADISE, it is possible."

Eric added, "I agree. The link to the Cloud should be cut immediately. About an hour ago I tried to go through the Cloud into the Main Core and change our programming. The Main Core detected it and cut me off from my own access channel."

The VP motioned to Doug. "Do it."

The VP looked back at Eric. "You mean to tell me that there were previous indications at PARADISE that these problems existed and nobody informed us?"

Brad Smith spoke up. "Ma'am...uh, Amanda, like you mentioned earlier, this is what Doug and I were trying to tell the President a week ago, when we asked him to delay ISODS. You'll remember that we even recommended he contact Harrington and ask him to delay the opening of PARADISE."

For a moment, there was silence. The faint whirring of the elbow and knee actuators on the ADA Service Robot in the room became obvious for the first time. The VP looked at the robot. "ADA, return to your charging station."

The robot responded, *"Yes, Madam Vice-President"* and exited the room.

Doug gave a thumbs-up, confirming that the Main Core link to the Information Cloud had been terminated. Chief Smith spoke, "Gustav said that these recommendations were actually made by Allie's grandfather, Dr. Braxton Newberry. He headed the Artificial Intelligence Research Team at MIT before he retired."

Eric nodded. "That's true. There's nobody smarter than him

when it comes to AI. If he recommended those things, you should take them seriously."

Brad continued. "The last thing Gustav said is that Dr. Newberry was contacting the Japanese about some project they are working on that might help. He wasn't specific about it."

The VP turned. "Allie, if you have the contact info for your grandfather, text it to Doug."

Allie nodded and sent it to him.

The VP continued. "Doug, contact Dr. Newberry and find out what Japan has to offer, but don't request anything or accept anything just yet. We don't want a foreign country to get into our business unless we really need it."

Doug nodded; he was already preparing the text.

The VP looked up at Chief Smith. "Is that it?"

"Yes ma'am, for—wait, I'm getting a priority message." He read the screen for a moment and then slumped slightly. "The drill didn't work. Evidently, part of that new cloud dome also extends underground; maybe some sort of force field. When the machine drilled into that area, it caught fire and exploded. One operator was killed and the other two are on the way to the hospital with burns." He looked up. Before he could say anything else, the VP's Administrative Assistant ran into the room and turned on the large view panel. All she said was, "WATCH!"

The screen showed a reporter retreating from the dome at a fast pace, over a grassy hill. The dome was slowly expanding out from PARADISE. The reporter's voice was at a high pitch, "...and we aren't sure why it is moving or how far it will go." He stumbled over an obstacle and dropped his microphone. He retrieved it and continued reporting. "About fifteen minutes ago we saw the cloud brighten like it was glowing. Then it started pulsating, expanding and contracting. After a few minutes, it started expanding, moving outward, maybe in every direction, but we can't confirm that.

"The explosions you are seeing behind me seem to be vehicles that were already in the parking lot of PARADISE. But there are many other structures nearby, that are in its path. This could cause some serious damage if it keeps moving. There is still no word on the condition of the President and the others still inside."

Chief Smith was reading a new message. "The cloud is expanding at 1.2 kilometers per hour. All units have been pulled back. Rescue efforts have been abandoned until the situation is stabilized. No additional casualties have been reported so far. St. Louis Security Forces are notifying surrounding businesses and neighborhoods to evacuate the immediate area." He stared at the screen for a moment.

Doug spoke up. "Madam Vice-President. The Constitution says that there is a *maximum* of two hours to transfer power, if the President is incapacitated. This situation is certainly an emergency so, I advise you to assume Presidential powers now and issue an evacuation order. It may even be too late if this thing keeps moving. There's no way we can inform millions of people to get out of its way in time. But, at least, some can be saved. Most of the staff are assembled in the conference room now and the rest are on video circuits. I suggest we adjourn upstairs and get the staff vote out of the way."

The VP stared at Doug for a moment. "I, uh..."

Doug finished her thought. "Yes ma'am, I didn't sign on for this either. But, here we are. Let's go get this done."

"Yes, of course."

She turned to Eric, "You two have gone this far; you might as well see this too. Come with us."

The White House Staff took five minutes for the vote to approve the transfer of Presidential authority to the VP and take the group photo for the historical record. The approval would last for the next twenty-four hours, before Congress would have to vote to extend the time, if needed. Following the vote, the VP ordered the St Louis Power Grid connection to be shut off.

Before leaving for the news conference, the VP had Doug contact the two mayors involved, instructing them to begin evacuating the two cities. Finally, she walked to the White House south lawn and addressed the media.

"Ladies and gentlemen, today we are facing a crisis of unknown proportions. As you know, President Holloway and the First Lady traveled to the PARADISE theme park in St. Louis this morning, to participate in the opening ceremonies. Shortly after they arrived, the park experienced some kind of failure that has resulted in the large cloud-like dome covering PARADISE, and in the loss of all communications with anyone inside. We are working to restore contact with the President.

"Initial reports say that the cloud over PARADISE was generated by the solar panels on the roof of the five domes. Some experts suggest that it may have been created by the hologram generators that create visual adventures for the guests in the hologram chambers. There is no confirmation of that yet.

"You saw the footage of Air Force One crashing. Let me reassure you, it has been absolutely confirmed that neither the President nor anyone in his party was on that shuttle. The pilots ejected and were treated at the scene for minor injuries.

"Several attempts to penetrate the cloud have proven unsuccessful. We will be attempting other methods when we determine it is safe to do so. We believe that those inside PARADISE are safe and well . Everyone watching the news a few minutes ago saw the phenomenon we have yet to explain; the dome-shaped cloud has begun to expand. This is a very dangerous and..."

Bradford Smith had just run straight to the podium and interrupted the VP. He whispered in her ear. She questioned; "Are you sure about that?"

"Yes, ma'am, my field agent just called me."

The Vice-President turned back to the mic. "I have just been informed that the cloud around PARADISE has stopped expanding." There were cheers from the media. "That is excellent news. It makes what we must do, easier.

"I'm sure you are aware of the provisions of the Forty-Ninth Amendment to our Constitution. It states that in situations where the President has been determined to be incapacitated or unavailable for any reason, a Temporary Transfer of Power will be enacted by an emergency vote of the White House Staff, giving the North American Vice-President full Presidential powers for twenty-four hours.

"That vote has been taken and the Transfer of Power approved at 14:38 hours Eastern Time this afternoon. If the President is unable to reassume power within twenty-four hours, both the White House Staff and the Congress must authorize an extension. My staff is now notifying members of Congress, putting them on standby. They will be able to vote electronically from wherever they are. We certainly hope an extension will not be necessary.

"So, acting with the Presidential authority just granted to me, I hereby enact the following emergency measures. We are hopeful that they will only be required for a short time. First, to reduce the power available to the systems in PARADISE, Northern Electric has been instructed to cut all electric power to the St. Louis and surrounding areas. All emergency services and other essential businesses have backup power and will be able to continue operations.

"Second, we do not know if or when that cloud will expand again, but we do know that it is deadly and destructive. Therefore, I am issuing an immediate evacuation order for all of St. Louis, East St. Louis, and their surrounding counties."

There was a semi-riot among the press corps.

The VP held up her hands. "Please, let me finish. The evacuation priority will be for those people within ten kilometers of PARADISE and everyone in hospitals or special care facilities in those two cities. Those people will be the only ones allowed on major highways out of the cities at this time. Anyone without a pass will be arrested.

"Once those evacuations have succeeded, all other residents may evacuate. All public transportation, including aviation assets, will be dedicated for evacuation. I now ask those communities and states outside of the St. Louis area to prepare to receive the evacuees and provide for them like you would for your own family. The full resources of the federal government will be available to supplement local resources."

A reporter yelled out, "WHY DON'T YOU JUST BOMB THE PLACE?!"

The VP responded, "As long of the status of the President is unknown, there will be no ammunition fired at PARADISE. Those who attempt to do so will be stopped in whatever manner is necessary. Now, I know you have a lot of questions. Unfortunately, this ongoing crisis requires my immediate attention, so your questions for me will have to wait."

Over the noise of the media yelling, she said, "The White House Press Secretary will provide an update right here every half hour, beginning thirty minutes from now. Thank you."

To the shouts of the press, the VP and staff returned to the Conference Room to question Eric and Allie.

.

"Now that we have that out of the way, I have a few questions. First, could some foreign government have hacked into the Main Core at PARADISE and caused the place to go haywire?"

Eric shook his head. "No ma'am. PARADISE uses a Level-Five Protection Algorithm for all external connections, I don't think even the CIA could break in."

"What about that dome-shaped cloud covering the place? Maybe that was an inside job. Could someone have been disguised as a guest and then modified the system from inside. Surely some system changes had to be made for solar panels to start creating a cloud."

Eric thought for a moment. "No, ma'am, no one could make enough changes to cause that."

"Well, then I'll ask the most obvious question. Why didn't somebody just walk over, and pull the plug and shut the thing down?"

Chief Smith nodded. "Now, *that's* the million-dollar question. It's not like the Main Core could stop somebody from flipping the switch."

Eric shifted in his chair. "Well, all power circuits were programmed electronically, so it is possible for an *aware* computer to disable the ON-OFF circuits. Then, someone would have to go down to the Main Core level and physically disconnect the power. Second, the Main Core is programmed to do self-maintenance, like moving and installing spare parts anywhere in PARADISE. It also operates the laser welders installed on the walls in the Maintenance corridors. And, there are also five maintenance androids, with built-in lasers and tools for making repairs out in the other domes."

The VP said, "So? Lots of businesses have similar systems."

"That's true, but their systems don't have artificial intelligence; the ability to analyze and make decisions."

Chief Smith looked at Eric. "Wait, are you saying the system could use those laser tools against people?"

"I'll admit that something else would have to go wrong, but under the right circumstances, it is possible."

Allie added, "I did the security programming. The Main Core controls all the door locks. If the OFF Switch didn't work, physically shutting it down would be necessary. Those corridor lasers could be dangerous, if the Main Core changes the maintenance subroutines into a full Security Program and uses it to...uh...uses it to protect itself from being shut off."

The VP sat back in her chair and stared at them. Chief Smith interjected: "Ma'am, I just got a text that says the Houston Office has ruled out any conspiracy headed by Zurelle. But, he did confess that his researchers identified a problem with Zurelleum back last fall. He verified what Dr. Gustav said earlier; that it is probable that Dark Matter does exist and is being attracted by the Z-Processors. He said the same thing about Circuit Ghosting, where the processors create additional circuits and increased processing capacity on an escalating scale."

Eric raised his eyebrows. "That would explain it."

Brad turned, "Explain what?"

"If the system can grow additional circuits, it could have connected the hologram generators directly to the solar panels on the roof and reversed the circuitry, allowing the panels to create holographic images. If the system is projecting Dark Matter onto the image, it's doing it at the speed of light. Even tiny molecules of matter, traveling that fast, would generate enough heat to destroy anything.

"And, if the Z-Processors are gaining mass, then the system will expand to make room for the increased mass. The more it absorbs, the more it will expand. There is nothing malicious or evil, or even intentional about that; it is just, uh, computer logic."

"So, you are saying that the cloud dome over PARADISE will probably continue expanding and destroying everything in its path...forever?"

"Well, theoretically, it could happen, unless...ah...unless it loses access to power. In theory, the process of expanding and destroying objects, could cause it to run low on power and eventually stop on its own, but..."

The VP continued the thought. "But, you have no clue if your theory holds water, or if you are right, how long the process could take; meaning all of North America could be destroyed before it stops, right?"

Eric turned pale. "Yes...yes, ma'am, that's about the size of it."

Allie spoke up. "It could be even worse. If the Main Core could reverse the solar panels to create the cloud, couldn't it also reverse the process again and use the dome itself like a big magnifier, to intensify the sun's rays on the solar panels? If so, it will have all the power it needs to expand to, uh, everywhere."

"God help us. Are there any possibilities at all to stop this thing?"

"Antimatter," Doug said. "Dr. Newberry just responded to my message. He said the Japanese have an Antimatter Research Group that has been working since the turn of the century, capturing and studying antimatter.

"He says they have been quite successful and are now working on ways to harness antimatter for use in some new space engine technology they are developing. They've hired an American scientist to help them."

"And?" The vice president said.

Doug kept reading. "This scientist, Dr. Daniel Lee, says he knows how to develop a way to use antimatter to break through the cloud around PARADISE."

Brad Smith sat up. "Are you crazy?! That stuff would explode! It could cause a chain reaction and destroy the whole place, along with half of North America and the leader of the free world. NO! No way! That's too risky!"

Doug continued. "He says that the Japanese scientists have discovered a new element, something they call hybrid-antimatter. It causes an implosion rather than an explosion when the two come together. He says it is too complicated to explain in a text message."

The VP was shaking her head. "Doug, I have to agree with

Brad on this one. We don't know enough about antimatter to allow such an experiment. The President's life is at stake."

"Well, Madam Vice-President, so are the lives of millions of North Americans. We had better do something or there may not be a North America left for you to be Vice-President of. If Jacob Holloway were here, he would talk to Daniel Lee."

"Doug, listen, we have to try everything else before we consider such radical measures."

During a moment of pause, a growing noise from outside became evident. The Press Secretary stuck his head in the door. "Madam Vice-President, the cloud over PARADISE is pulsing again!"

The Homeland Chief jumped up. "I've got to go." He disappeared out into the hallway.

The Vice-President was gathering her things. She looked at Doug. "Maybe Jacob would go with Dr. Lee and the Japanese. But, he's also your friend; you don't want to harm him, do you?"

"No, but I do want to save him. Our current plan is not going to make that happen."

"OK, let's give Brad a few more hours to figure this thing out. I'll get back to you then." She left for her office.

Doug took the time to restudy the message in silence. After a few minutes, he called Agent Bradshaw over and whispered some instructions to her. She nodded and accessed her communicator. Doug studied the young couple for a moment. "Eric and Allie, you are, by far, the most informed on what going on inside that dome. Would you like a chance to fix it?"

They looked at each other and slowly nodded.

"Are you two free for the next couple of days?"

"Yes, we are."

"OK. Agent Bradshaw is going on a trip." He motioned toward the agent with his head. "Go with her."

Eric nodded to Allie. They picked up their bags and followed Agent Bradshaw out to a waiting *civilian* shuttle on the South Lawn. It was a large bright green and white shuttle with corporate markings, showing the name "Quadro-Dyne." The sub-print read, "Making the World a Better Place." Eric noticed the large supersonic engines.   Inside, it was equipped for international travel, with bedrooms and a dining area.

The Shuttle departed low over the capitol, climbed to cruise altitude and headed southwest. Finally, Agent Bradshaw spoke. "Welcome aboard. It's time for us to talk."

CHAPTER 20

AWARE

For Bernard Harrington, the years of working and planning, and the billions of dollars already spent, were going down the drain. The people cowering in the Reception Dome were afraid and angry. The Secret Service had cordoned off the Reception offices for the President. All androids, except the five assigned to Maintenance, were present, keeping the people in the Reception Dome. They were polite, but insistent when necessary. Some were still serving meals to those at tables and in the Coffee Shop. When guests yelled at them, the androids just smiled politely and continued their work. Cori said the Main Core must be directing them to continue with their programmed functions. She had seen Adam meeting with and instructing the other androids.

All exit doors were still locked. There was no way to get to the hologram chambers to determine the condition of those who had already started their adventures. The Status Board still showed all chambers operating normally and just over four hundred online gamers still logged on.

There had been a slight shaking of the building when the cloud outside first started forming and another vibration some minutes later. There were also several distant-sounding explosions that could not be explained. The skylight revealed that the cloud was still there. There were no communications of any kind with the outside world or even within the facility. Joe Wilson was still missing.

Having made the best assessment possible, Harrington stepped back to the podium. "Ladies and gentlemen, once again I apologize for this unfortunate situation. We are still working to understand the nature of this failure and to correct it. First let me assure you that there will be full refunds of entry fees and all expenses associated with your time here at PARADISE."

A man shouted; "IT LOOKS MORE LIKE HELL THAN PARADISE!" Many others yelled and applauded.

Harrington ignored them and continued, taking extreme

liberties with the truth. "My staff has assessed the situation. Here's what we know; the initial power outage must have damaged the main computer interface with all functions throughout the facility. This caused all the doors to inadvertently lock. The androids ushered everyone back into this area for safety reasons, until the computer problem is resolved.

"I am happy to announce that all support facilities in this dome, including food service, are operating normally. Of course, everything is free at this point. It has been less than an hour since the failure. I ask for your patience while we continue to troubleshoot and repair the system."

Lisa raised her voice. "What about the hologram chambers? My son is still stuck in there!"

Harrington pointed. "The Status Board still shows the hologram chambers are operating normally. Due to the shortness of the initial power outage, those already in the chambers may not have even realized there was a problem. They are probably still enjoying their adventures.

"Also, the President is still here. Rest assured that the full resources of the Federal Government are being brought to bear to open PARADISE from the outside. The President has better things to do than sit around here all day, playing games." He paused and smiled, hoping for a laugh. None came. He once again asked for patience and promised to give another update in thirty minutes.

He led the Staff to the conference room. Most were confused and fearful. "OK, I need a report from each of your areas that will give me a clue about what is happening here. Eddie, you start."

"Sir, it sounds like science fiction, but the Main Core is...aware. This is a lot more than we ever expected from artificial intelligence. Back in college, we heard the AI warning from those old computer guys seventy years ago. Turns out, they were right."

He let that sink in for a moment. Harrington was just staring at him. He knew that the boss was beginning to see what was happening, but didn't want to connect the dots.

Eddie continued. "My initial clue was when Cori first brought

Adam and Eve here. I saw them mimic the couple holding hands in the welcome video. Then I heard both Adam and Eve asking questions about human behavior and using human terms to describe some of their actions. And, Cori told me Thursday that Eve had asked her what it was like to kiss a man." Cori nodded as Eddie continued. "Also, just a few minutes ago, Evan showed me a video recorded last night in Chamber 701. It showed our primary android, Adam, creating his own adventure about a trip to Mars.

"I know you remember the staff meeting where Evan and Tim showed the leaf that Tim brought out of a hologram adventure. Of course, millions of people saw Sandi Anderson bring a small bandage out of the adventure Ken created. All of us knew about the call you got from the President, requiring more tests. He wouldn't do that unless he thought there was a problem."

Harrington took a breath. "Okay, if you are right, if the Main Core has become *aware*, what does it want; what is it trying to do?"

Eddie shook his head. "I'm not sure. Eric could probably advise us, but he and Allie didn't make it here before the thing went haywire. Other than routine maintenance and administration, we programmed MC to do one primary function; create realistic holograms. All other functions in PARADISE are secondary to that. That's why I think the chambers and the online games are still operating; the Main Core is carrying out its main function. Since artificial intelligence has made it *aware,* it can identify those things that hinder its primary mission and isolate them from giving input."

Steve added, "Yeah, things like humans and the functions in the other domes."

Harrington was still puzzled. "But, it needs a lot of power to do what it's doing. You know the first thing those on the outside would do, right?"

Several answered together, "Cut the power."

"Right. So, we can assume the power grid has been cut. Without the solar panels, the backup generators can't produce enough. So, where is it getting the power? If we knew that, we might be able to shut it off."

Evan added, "It's true that the hologram generator sucks a lot of power but it appears MC has shut down the other three domes; that saves a lot of power there."

"Okay, it is obviously getting enough power. But, if the computer is really creating substance, like the cloud and the leaf and bandage, how does it create something out of nothing? The computer has no extra material available to use to create. Am I right?"

"NO!"

Everyone turned. A man, who looked like a guest, was standing in the doorway, holding up a badge.

Harrington stood. "Who are you?"

"Agent William Charles, Homeland Security. I'm here because the President is involved and there have already been some strange things happening."

"OK, fair enough, but why did you say *NO* to something being created out of nothing? Surely, you don't think this computer can create things out of thin air."

"No sir. But, the Z-Processors downstairs have all the material they need to add matter to what already exists. Tracking Quantum's research, we discovered they already knew that Zurelleum has been absorbing Dark Matter since day-one on the moon. It has made the Zurelleum increase in mass; actually, it's been growing. Now, with artificial intelligence, the computer has been using the extra mass to create additional circuit paths for data transmission. That's how your Main Core has become; I believe the term is, *aware*. And, that's how a leaf and a bandage and a dome of clouds over this place came to be."

After a long pause, Harrington tried to sound positive. "Except for the cloud, these things are minor. I can't see how any harm could come to anyone from this."

"Not true, sir. You already know that Air Force One crashed because of that cloud. Not long after that, the Shuttle Bay crew heard sounds of distant explosions, like the ones we all heard at first. They now believe that the dome has started expanding; moving outward from this facility."

Tim said, "Wait a minute; if the dome is real, then other

things generated in the chambers can become real. That would explain why my leg hurt a little after crashing through that tree in our skydiving adventure. The tree was real, at least for that short period of time.

Evan continued the thought. "So, if MC can use Dark Matter to create *real* things, then the adventures created in the chambers could become real, or at least partially real."

Tim agreed. "That may be possible."

Evan said gravely. "OK, so if a guest's adventure involved weapons, then the ammunition could be real and could actually…kill the guest."

In a panic, Harrington started toward the door. "We've got to shut it off!"

Eddie grabbed his arm. "How do you intend to do that, sir? The doors are locked and the androids are keeping us all in here. Besides, Evan said that before Eve ran them out of Hologram Control, the whole control system went dead."

Harrington sat down. "So, what do we do; just sit here until it takes over everything?"

Agent Charles stepped forward. "Sir, there are many armed agents in this building. We could take off a few android heads and then figure out how to get through those doors. If we could make it to the main computer, we could fill it full of holes."

Harrington shook his head. "There'll be no shooting in here! I don't want any guests to get hurt."

Eddie said, "Getting the androids out of the way is just one issue. The doors to the other areas are substantial; hard to get through when they're locked. Then there is the problem of the lasers."

Agent Charles turned. "What lasers?"

Eddie explained about the maintenance lasers in the corridors near the Main Core and those on the five maintenance androids. He said, "We haven't seen any of those androids in here so we have to assume that MC is using them downstairs to protect itself from being shut down."

"What do you mean, protect itself?"

"Actually, to protect its mission. It was designed primarily to generate holograms. With artificial intelligence, the computer knows whether it is accomplishing its mission and will take whatever steps it deems necessary to do its job. It's not personal or vindictive; those are human traits; it's just fulfilling its programming."

"Well, it's becoming personal for the rest of us. If I could get to it, I'd put an old-fashioned bullet between its electronic eyes."

Harrington asked, "Evan, couldn't those in the chambers just turn off their headbands or remove them or push the Emergency Button to stop their adventures?"

"I suppose they could, but if the system has generated new circuits, it might not matter. MC is storing their thoughts, so the hologram might continue anyway."

Harrington spoke, "We need outside help but there is no way to communicate with anybody outside."

Steve had been recording some ideas on his laptop. When Harrington said *"communicate,"* Steve looked up and smiled.

The boss stared at him for a moment. "What?"

Steve said slowly, "There just might be a way."

Maintenance Level – Four Floors Down

Joe Wilson wasn't sure what to do. With the android gone, he was safe, for now. He only had a couple of small burns and a pain just below his right shoulder blade from the falling conduit.

The antique AK-47 assault rifle and the pistol were in working condition. The rifle magazine had twenty-seven rounds and the nine-millimeter pistol had five. A thought formed in Joe's mind; *"Why did it miss me?"* Then, he realized that the shoulder lasers were controllable, only in five-degree increments. *"Ah, with all that moving around it couldn't aim accurately. Otherwise, I'd be dead right now. That's good to know."*

The standard procedure was for Joe's team to meet at the Power Panel to assess any outage. But no one had come. He quickly surmised that the androids had prevented his team from getting to his level in the facility. Then, a horrible thought entered his mind: *"I just hope that the other maintenance androids aren't upstairs, killing people."*

Joe's mindset changed, from waiting for rescue, to finding a way upstairs to rescue others. He prayed that the President was okay.

Even with his weapons, he knew he couldn't risk leaving the office to access the elevator or the stairs. *"There's got to be a way,"* he thought. Looking around, the heat and air system return vent in the ceiling caught his eye. He hurried to the cabinet and retrieved the ventilation system diagrams, showing every centimeter of ductwork in PARADISE.

The White House

The War Room view panels were showing live aerial shots of PARADISE, with a multiple of theories being espoused by an array of *experts*.

One report covered Anthony Zurelle being released back at his headquarters. He was mobbed by the press until Quantum Security rescued him. There was even a feed from the moon where the media pool reporters were asking Chan Yoshan questions about Zurelleum. He kept referring them to Quantum headquarters.

Linda Hudson, at Quantum headquarters, was trying to please the reporters, clamoring for information. The media could not find Eric and Allie and had assumed they were hiding to avoid the press. Brad Smith was now at the scene in St. Louis and had positioned shuttles at each checkpoint around the dome to facilitate rapid evacuation of his agents should the cloud start expanding again.

His teams had turned away dozens of curious onlookers and members of the press. The extent of casualties was not yet known. The only deaths they knew of were the drilling operator and one news reporter who tried to break through the dome to get an exclusive. There was still no contact with those inside.

The media presence in St. Louis and D.C. had mushroomed. Foreign outlets began arriving to get in on the story of the century. Everyone wanted to know the status of the President. The VP had authorized the Press Secretary to say only that Homeland Security was working to restore communications and gain access to PARADISE, and that there was no reason to believe the President was in any danger. With the minutes becoming hours, Amanda Weigh was finding it harder to believe her own news releases.

The evacuation order for the St. Louis area caused intermittent panic, confusion, and minor rioting. News shuttles provided aerial coverage of the already-crowded evacuation routes. Police were tied up, arresting violators of the evacuation sequence. To complicate matters even more, many residents had chosen to ignore the order.

Authorities knew it would take days to fully evacuate everyone. The Vice-President was fearful that they might not have that long to get it done. If the dome continued to expand, there could be tens-of-thousands of casualties. Modern society was not equipped to deal with such a calamity.

The VP and Homeland Security had already dismissed the thought of using a bomb or missile on the dome. Experts had advised against using lasers, fearing they might just feed more power to the dome.

Doug was glad he had planned the secret mission for Agent Bradshaw and he hoped that Eric and Allie would have an answer soon. He also knew the VP and Homeland Security would not have approved his plan. But Doug admitted to himself that he had a few doubts too. He had trusted an old retired professor, who had faith in a self-made scientist from Texas, with no formal training in antimatter research or successful applications of the elusive particles. Amid competing thoughts and fears Doug kept thinking, *"To do nothing, is not an option."*

CHAPTER 21

ANTIMATTER

Quadro-Dyne shuttle
Over Virginia

Agent Bradshaw began. "We are going to Guatemala to pick up Allie's grandfather, Dr. Braxton Newberry, then proceed on to Japan to meet with a Dr. Daniel Lee."

"Japan?! The problem is in PARADISE, why do we need to go to Japan?" Eric sounded frustrated.

Allie joined in. "If we really are going to Japan, why is grandpa going with us?"

"Just hear me out. Those in Japan may be our best hope to fix the problem in PARADISE. Dr. Lee's research has yielded a discovery that will penetrate that dome over PARADISE, and then disable the Main Core and shut down the theme park. The vice president is afraid that antimatter, in its natural violent state, will cause mass destruction of the whole area. And, she's right. In its natural state, it would destroy a large area. However, Dr. Lee has stated that what he has in mind will be a contained situation and will effectively solve the problem. Since you are the programmers of the processors, he feels that you two are the best choice to deliver the solution and shut down the theme park."

Agent Bradshaw stood. "We have some time to kill so I'm going to get some rest before we arrive in Guatemala. You can help yourself to the food and refreshments but you may want to consider getting some rest yourself."

She stopped after a few steps. "By the way, the cockpit area is off limits. They don't know who we are and we don't know who they are. We call it, *plausible deniability*." She smiled and disappeared through the door.

Eric accessed the IBN News broadcast on the view panel. It

was still chaotic, with multiple reports from every possible angle around the dome. A reporter was just repeating what had happened thirty minutes earlier; the dome had brightened, pulsed and started expanding again, taking in another five hundred meters before it stopped.

Theories about the cause of the total failure of PARADISE ranged from espionage to faulty artificial intelligence programming. The Truth Daily tabloid claimed to have verification that all people inside were dead from flesh-eating bacteria, that had mutated out of the Z-Processors.

Allie laid her head on Eric's shoulder. "Eric, I'm scared."

He leaned his head down against her hair and whispered. "Yeah, I know; me too."

Allie drifted into sleep, so Eric muted the sound and put his mind into gear. He visualized the AI programming steps they had taken to do what Dr. Hau had instructed; *"Make these processors smart."* Nobody on the MIT Team could have imagined just how smart the Main Core would become.

Eric kept coming back to the same questions; why hadn't Eddie or Evan just shut the system down? Why hadn't Harrington instructed his facilities people to manually shut off the power?

He then assumed they had tried, but the computer had somehow prevented them from doing it. His line of thought confirmed his earlier assumption, that the self-maintenance subroutines had indeed become a self-protection program and the Main Core was defending itself by locking all the doors. He also knew that it might even use the maintenance lasers as weapons to keep people away. He asked himself, *"But, why; why would it care?"*

Finally, he realized that he had been right earlier. MC was just doing what it had been programmed to do; create adventures. With Dark Matter to make the adventures *real,* it would require more physical space for the *real* things it created. It couldn't let anything interfere with that. He sat up a little and thought, *"It's going to keep expanding the dome to create more space...maybe, forever!"*

Allie stirred. He laid his head on hers for a moment, noticing the fresh smell of her hair. *"I've got to get serious with this girl one of these days,"* he thought. He tried to visualize her family, Keith, Lisa, and Collins, probably going through frightening things inside PARADISE.

Finally, he decided; *"OK, I'll do it, but I don't want to take Allie. I can't bear to think of her possibly getting hurt."* He closed his eyes to relieve some of the stress. He was napping when the shuttle began its descent, in its antiradar mode.

The shuttle touched down in the mountains, up the valley from Guatemala City. When Eric awoke, Agent Bradshaw was talking on the intercom; he assumed, to the flight crew.

Allie was awake, peering out the window. "So, this is Guatemala?"

"YES! And I am happy to see you!" Allie's grandfather had just entered the cabin and stood with arms open wide. Allie began to cry as she ran into his embrace.

"Grandpa, Mom and Dad and Collins are stuck in PARADISE!"

"Yes, I know honey. But together, we are going to find a way to get them out. I have been praying for their safety. Your dad is a smart man; he is surely protecting them."

Allie wiped her eyes. "I hope he's as smart as *his* dad."

"Oh, I'm sure he's much smarter. That's how he created such smart children."

Allie finally laughed.

"That's my girl; everything will be fine, you'll see. Now, let me greet my favorite student." He gripped Eric's hand and added a hug. "Eric, my boy, I guess Agent Bradshaw has briefed you. Are you up for the challenge?"

Eric half-smiled. "I guess so. I could be more confident if I knew exactly *what* the challenge will be. I'm so far outside of my comfort zone now, I don't know if I'll ever be the same."

The old professor's smile turned serious. "One thing is for sure, with what's happening in PARADISE, none of us will ever be the same again."

The agent entered the cabin. "I hate to break this up but we have to be in Japan in four hours. Please, take your seats."

The shuttle departed to the west, over Guatemala City and out over the Pacific, climbing into the supersonic air corridors. At

Mach two-point-five they would arrive in Niigata, Japan by nine thirty Sunday morning, Japan time.

St. Louis

Brad Smith's Command Shuttle was stationed two kilometers from the dome. He had just poured a cup of coffee when his communicator alerted him. The caller ID was his Station Chief in Guatemala. He answered and listened for a few moments.

Those around could see his jaws clinch when he asked, "What?! Are you sure about that?" He then asked, "How do you spell that?" Finally, he said, "This is classified for internal use only." After a pause, he said, "Yes, that's right."

The Chief disconnected and walked to the rear of the shuttle. Inside his private office, he called the Vice-President.

"Yes, Brad, what's happening?...What!?!...Are you sure?...Just a minute."

The VP glanced over at Doug, who looked busy but was actually listening to her. She got up and went into her private office.

In her office, the VP continued with Brad. He told her about the secret mission to Japan.

"So..., Doug violated my order not to pursue an antimatter solution to PARADISE...Okay, Brad, I'll handle it."

Listening to the VP, Doug knew someone had figured out what he and the CIA were up to. He had violated procedure, but in his gut, he knew that the hybrid antimatter was the only substance that could nullify the PARADISE force field. He feared that the current strategy would ultimately lead to disaster, so he felt compelled to take matters into his own hands. When Brad called, Doug knew he needed to act fast. He barely finished his text message before the Vice-President called to him into her office.

"Douglas, where are the two young computer programmers?"

"Well, Ma'am, I don't know exactly. They left with Agent

Bradshaw right after our meeting. I assume they told her where they wanted to go."

"Did you send them to Japan, to the Antimatter Lab in Niigata?"

"No, ma'am, I did not instruct them to go to Japan."

"I see. I think you are playing with words here. A Homeland Security agent saw the professor in a restaurant in Guatemala, telling the waitress that, later, he was going to have Kunimasu fish, the best fish in the world. Since Kunimasu fish is only available in Niigata, Japan, which is also the location of the world's largest antimatter research lab, it sounded suspicious. So, the agent followed him to a field up in the mountains, where he was picked up by a civilian shuttle. Through the windows he saw Agent Bradshaw and Eric and Allie. The shuttle headed west, out over the Pacific. Can you explain that?"

"Well...I guess I'll have to." He sat down on the couch. "I sent Agent Bradshaw to Niigata to at least meet with Daniel Lee and the Japanese Antimatter Research Team. She was going to offer to take Eric and Allie but they could have said no. Obviously, they must have said yes. Dr. Newberry asked to go along since he knows Mr. Lee and trusts his research without question."

The VP was shaking her head. "You are not going to tell me that antimatter is completely safe. What about the explosion at the Swiss Lab two years ago? Twenty-five people died."

Doug had read the report. "They said it was caused by a loose magnetic-flux grid that guides the antimatter atoms into the capture-tubes. The loose grid came in contact with a faulty power cable and the resulting power surge ignited the hydrogen cooling system. The explosion wasn't caused by the antimatter; it just made the initial explosion bigger. All research labs have now separated those two systems."

Doug leaned forward and continued. "But, the antimatter atoms the Japanese are working with have been modified somehow. Professor Newberry's son and family, except for Allie, are inside PARADISE. He would never recommend using regular antimatter."

"So, you are willing to risk the life of the President by using this special antimatter?"

"Actually, according to the Japanese, there will be no risk of an explosion. The modified antimatter just cancels physical matter, atom for atom; both atoms just disappear, with just a muffled reaction and a momentary flash of bright light.

"The Professor believes that the right amount of this new antimatter can make a large hole in that dome, so that two people could get through before the computer regenerates the cloud. Of course, the two people who get inside would have to have knowledge of the computer and hologram systems to have a chance to shut the thing down."

"Shut the thing down?! If those inside can't shut it down why do you think someone else could? Besides, this modified antimatter seems to be all theory. We need facts. My answer, for now, is still NO. Some of the best minds in the country are consulting with Homeland Security, trying to solve this problem. They need time to figure it out."

Doug sat back. "Time, Madam Vice President, is our enemy. Despite what we do, those in PARADISE are going to be there overnight. I just hope they have basic facilities, plus food and water. We aren't even sure if they have electricity available to them. At least, talk to the Japanese. See what they have to offer."

The VP hesitated. "Okay, the only thing I will do is allow what you have already put into motion, to continue. But, if those two young programmers try to get inside PARADISE, without my permission, they will be hunted and stopped by Brad Smith's agents. You will not have any more involvement in what they are doing. You will tell no one about this. I will deny any knowledge of the contact with the Japanese or any of the other people involved."

Doug smirked. "Politics is *SO* much fun. OK, I'll be the fall guy if there has to be one. But, I would love to be a fly on the wall fifty years from now, to see how history records all of this." He stood to leave.

The VP stood too. "Doug, you are not under arrest; let's just say you are on permanent watch duty in the War Room, until this is over. I'll hold on to your communicator for now and White

House Security will monitor your desk communications. Understood?"

He handed her his personal communicator and then opened the door, executed a slight head-bow and smiled, "Yes, ma'am!"

Over the Pacific Ocean

The shuttle finally reached cruising speed just before Eric got the text message from Doug Clark. It read, *"Smith knows and will be looking for you. He thinks you are going to blow up PARADISE. Time is critical. Don't get caught. Be careful who you trust. I'm counting on you."*

Eric read the message aloud and then said, "Well, it looks like this will be harder than expected. Since they know about the plan to use antimatter, they will be trying to stop us." He smiled at Allie. "How does it feel to be on the Most Wanted List?"

"Those imbeciles!" Dr. Newberry said. "You'd think the government would keep up with classified scientific research, like Dr. Lee's discovery last year. They have been so caught up with Zurelleum, and the President's reelection, that they missed, or didn't understand the importance of the Dragonzyte discovery."

"What's Dragonzyte?"

Allison added. "Yeah, it sounds like an animal."

Her grandpa smiled. "Well, honey, it was named after an animal; a Dragon to be exact. Let me explain. Last year, the Japanese noticed some captured antimatter atoms had unusual molecular structures. The antimatter grid-filter had retained ten percent of the atoms because they were clumped together in groups of three atoms each. They were held together by an outer shell of what could best be described as Hybrid-Dark Matter, a transition form of matter.

"Scientists initially thought all the antimatter in the Universe had long ago been used up through clashes with real matter. Antimatter research earlier this century disproved that theory and left scientists more confused than ever. But increased solar activity last year superheated the Dragonzyte molecules, melting the other shells and releasing more antimatter. Most of it clashed with Dark Matter and disappeared but the explosions forced some clusters of Dragonzyte outward from the Sun, to be captured by the grid."

"But sir," Eric said, "how is Dragonzyte safer than normal antimatter?"

The professor cupped his hands together to illustrate. "The secret is in the hybrid shell around the clump of antimatter atoms. Tests have shown that when Dragonzyte is present with an equal amount of normal antimatter, the explosive force of matter-antimatter reactions is muted. Dr. Lee says it is more like an *implosion* than an *explosion.* These reactions seem to create a tiny, temporary Black Hole.

"So far, he is the only scientist who has been able to verify this new process successfully. He has shown that Dragonzyte dissolves matter with only a minor reaction, accompanied by a momentary burst of bright light. Of course, it must be handled carefully because it *does* dissolve matter. You are made of matter too, so you don't want to come in contact with it yourself."

Allie held up her hand, like she was still in class at MIT. "I can guess why they named it Dragonzyte. Dragons eat stuff, right? So, since Dragonzyte eats matter, the Japanese gave it that name in honor of their dragon myths from the past."

The professor nodded. "That's my smart granddaughter. Yes, that's correct. Of course, the official scientific designation is HDA-257-2081: Hybrid Dark Antimatter, first discovered on the two hundred and fifty-seventh day of the year 2081. That's all I know about it. When we get to Japan, I'm sure Daniel Lee will answer any other questions about HDA."

Eric nodded. "OK. I think I understand most of what you said, but how will this help us? We still don't know exactly what we are expected to do. This whole thing has been like a nightmare. I mean, a few hours ago, we were flying to PARADISE for a nice weekend with Allie's family. And then, the programming we did turned on the world and now it looks like peoples' lives are at stake. Who knows how many people have already died because of this. I feel awful."

"Don't beat yourself up too badly just yet. Your programming was perfect. You did not know that Quantum's processors were primed for just the right atmosphere to give them a dose of reality. I know you are wondering what is really happening inside PARADISE and how you could possibly stop it from causing more damage.

"The Main Core must be using the Dark Matter to convert fantasy into reality. When it creates, it needs physical space to house some of the new reality. Since some fantasies will surely need a lot of space; a desert, for instance, the Main Core is in transition; it needs the power to expand the dome by creating that cloud-like material. I'm guessing that for large adventures, like in outer space, it will just create the illusion of physical space. So, to provide the space needed, I believe that the dome will expand at a rate equal to the power available to the Main Core.

"We know that the area Power Grid has been shut down and that the area is being evacuated. That was a wise move. I just hope it can be done quickly enough to save the lives of the residents."

Allie put her hand on her grandfather's arm. "Grandpa; what about those inside? Do you think they are safe?"

He patted her hand. "Honey, I'd be lying if I said a one-hundred-percent, yes. But I am very sure they are fine. The Main Core has no need to create anything inside, except in the hologram chambers.

"We know it will have guarded against being shut off, either electronically or physically. There is a good possibility it will use the maintenance androids and the lasers in the corridors around the Main Core. But, if people stay out of those areas, they should be fine.

"Without the external power grid, the backup generators aren't enough to provide power for a force field of that magnitude. The solar panels are covered by the force field that it has generated so we can surmise that the force field is absorbing the sun's energy and feeding it back into the Solar Panels.

"A couple of hours ago a reporter in Dallas, Texas interviewed a Mr. Ethan Hallberg, one of the coordinators of the On-Line Home Hologram System for PARADISE. He said that the on-line system is functioning normally and that most of the original players are still logged on in their adventures."

"You're kidding!" Eric responded

"No. I hope they stay logged on; it will help drain power and perhaps reduce the force field expansions. But, the most important thing Hallberg said was that there is a dedicated communications circuit from his node in Dallas to the system designer inside PARADISE; a Dr. Steve Franklin. Hallberg said the circuit seemed to be operational but that Steve still has not answered."

Allie was confused. "I don't understand all of this. Can you just tell us what we are expected to do?"

"Yes. Soon after the news broke about PARADISE, Dr. Lee figured out what happened. He has an idea about how to use a Dragonzyte-Antimatter combination to neutralize part of that cloud, long enough for someone to get through unharmed. His plan also includes how to disable the computer, if you are unable to reprogram it or physically shut it down. Obviously, you two are the logical choice to attempt this mission."

Eric glanced at Allie as he spoke. "Uh...I think I can handle this alone. There's no need for Allie to go inside; she can wait with you until I take care of it." Eric was avoiding eye contact with her.

Allie sat up and pulled her shoulders back. "Well, Mr. Hero; you're not going without me! My family is in there!"

Dr. Newberry agreed. "I don't like the thought of my granddaughter being in danger, but I'm afraid she's right. There needs to be two of you. If one can't continue for some reason, the other one may be able to complete the task."

Agent Bradshaw interrupted. "Folks, we have three hours before we arrive in Niigata. So, I suggest you get some rest; you may not get much later on."

The hum of the shuttle soon put Allie fast asleep. Eric just cat-napped; his mind was running in ten different directions. An hour before arrival he drifted into real sleep.

PARADISE

Harrington rose up in his chair and looked at Steve. "What

do you mean? Are you saying there just might be a way to communicate? I thought the computer had shut everything down."

Eddie looked at Steve. "You're talking about the backdoor, aren't you?"

Harrington's eyebrows were raised. "What back door? The doors are all locked."

Steve explained. "Most computer programmers install a way to get into their systems, outside of the normal method. It's called a *backdoor*. In my case, it is a computer node in the maintenance area. Joe Wilson gave me a small room near the main circuit panel. I set up a computer terminal and a communications interface in there."

"So, you think you can access the computer from there and shut it down?"

"No, sir; based on recent events, I don't think the computer will allow that. But, the communications circuit is a stand-alone system, connecting PARADISE with two outside substations. Those circuits bypass the Main Core; MC doesn't even know they exist. It was used to coordinate my part of the home gaming system. If we can figure out how to get four floors down to that office, I think there's a chance we can communicate with the outside world."

"How do we do that? Joe was supposedly down there when this whole thing started and we haven't heard from him yet. Based on all of the system failures, I'm afraid something bad has happened to him."

Tim had an idea. "All of the fresh-air ducts terminate at the air-exchanger on the maintenance level."

Evan added, "Yeah, that's right. There are return-air vents under most of the counters and along the walls on this level. If we could get access to those ducts, maybe Steve could slide down to that room."

Steve shook his head. "The problem is; I don't have a schematic of the ductwork. I wouldn't know where to turn to get to that storage room. It's a maze down there."

Cori interjected. "Here's an idea; let's all split up and walk around this dome. Note the location of the return air vents and then let's meet at the Coffee Shop in twenty minutes to discuss it. Maybe we can figure out how to get Steve down there."

Harrington agreed. "That's a good plan. Proceed with it and I'll brief the President. This is the only good news we've heard so far."

The group exited the briefing room in ones and twos so it would be less noticeable. Cori searched for Adam and Eve. The androids smiled when they saw her approaching.

Adam greeted her. *"Good afternoon Cori. I trust you're having a nice day."* Eve added, *"PARADISE is certainly a nice place, isn't it?"*

"They think this situation is normal." Cori thought. "Uh, yes, quite nice. But, I left something in my vehicle, I need to go outside."

Adam stared straight ahead for a moment; he was obviously receiving a transmission from MC.

"I'm sorry Cori, no one is allowed outside. It is not safe. And you have no vehicle outside, since you arrived by shuttle."

Cori decided to try another approach. "OK, I understand. Eve, have you seen my friend Collins Newberry? I would like to speak with him."

Eve went through the same process that Adam had. *"Collins is not available right now. The adventure he is creating is not yet complete."*

"Is Collins safe?"

"Yes, he is functioning normally."

"He was scheduled for a one-hour session in the chamber. When will his adventure be complete?"

After Eve's pause, she said, *"Currently there is no scheduled termination time for his adventure. It will only be complete when he can no longer interact with--"*

Adam interrupted. *"I'm sorry Cori, there is no more information we can provide about Collins. Is there something else you would like to know?"*

"Yes; when will the dome outside be terminated and PARADISE return to its intended function?"

Adam had an unusual expression on his android face. *"Cori,* *this **is** the intended function of PARADISE."*

Cori smiled. "I see. I wonder if you could tell me one more thing; Adam, what is your Primary Directive?"

Adam hesitated for a moment. Then, both androids turned and walked away.

In the coffee shop, Cori related her conversations with Adam and Eve, about the Primary Directive and the people in the chambers.

Eddie raised his eyebrows. "We can guess what Eve meant; their adventures end when they do."

Evan added, "I was afraid of that. If MC can create such reality, like Sandi's bandage and Tim's leaf, it may be able to create stuff on a much larger scale."

Tim agreed. "Based on the pain I felt when I hit that tree, people can really get hurt in there." Then, he added in a whisper, "and maybe die."

"THEN WHY DON'T YOU DO SOMETHING ABOUT IT?!"

Keith and Lisa Newberry had just walked up to their table. Keith was shouting his anger at the group.

"We are Keith and Lisa Newberry. Our son is in Chamber Two. I want him out!"

Cori spoke, "Mr. Newberry, your son is safe for now. I saw his name still on the Status Board so I asked the primary Reception Androids about him. They said Collins is still creating his adventure."

Lisa said, "Well, why did someone just say that people could get hurt in those chambers."

Cori tried to encourage. "We are not *sure* people can get hurt. We were just brainstorming the situation."

"If Collins gets hurt, somebody's gonna pay! Did that robot say when this foolishness will end?" Keith asked.

"No sir. The reason we are meeting is to assess the situation and develop a strategy to get Steve down to his communications terminal. He may be able to communicate with the outside."

"I'm good at strategy. Until my son is released, I'm part of this team. Let's help him communicate and get us out of this place." He and Lisa pulled chairs up to the group.

Eddie said, "Okay, we all saw lots of return-air vents but I'm sure the androids won't let us open one to get inside. And like Steve said, he wouldn't know which duct to take to get to his back-door room down there."

Keith asked. "How do the androids communicate with the big computer?"

Cori said, "They have antennas embedded over their left ears, that enable communications up to one kilometer from the Main Core. Every dome has a relay antenna mounted inside, up near the roof."

They all looked up. The antenna was fastened to one of the beams holding up the ceiling, at least two hundred meters above the floor. It was inaccessible.

Cori said. If we can't take out the antenna, maybe we could block the signal. It would take some sort of metal, placed over their antennas, that would block signals in the upper megahertz range."

Keith asked, "You mean, like aluminum?"

Cori nodded. "Sure, that would do it, but where can we get aluminum?"

Keith reached into his pocket and pulled a stick of chewing gum. He unwrapped a piece and placed the gum in his mouth. He then held up the wrapping paper; it was backed with aluminum foil.

Cori nodded. "That would work if we double it over to make it thicker. But, the androids wouldn't just stand there and let us place gum wrappers above their left ears."

Everyone in the group was silent as they tried to figure a way. Suddenly Lisa touched Keith's arm.

"I'll be right back." She hurried off after a small boy she had seen walk by. He was wearing a PARADISE baseball cap. She came back wearing it. "I had to pay that kid fifty ID$ for this thing!" When she saw their confusion, Lisa smiled, knowing she had an idea that none of these high-paid professionals had thought of. She took the gum wrapper from Keith, unfolded the sweatband, folded the aluminum foil lengthways and placed it inside. She then folded it back into place and put the cap back on.

Cori said, "Okay, we know how to block the signal. Now, how do we get androids to wear baseball caps?"

Eddie spoke up. "We know that the androids have been displaying some human traits lately. Let's assume that a little bit of good-old human *ego* is creeping into their processors. If that's the case, we could use it against them. First, we need enough chewing gum wrappers and baseball caps to give one to every android."

Cori joined in. "We would need ninety-five caps; the five maintenance androids have not been seen in Reception. But, how do we use ego to get them to wear the caps?"

Eddie continued. "We need to create a ruse. We will all wear regular caps and carry the modified ones with us. We can approach an android with the request to have a photo taken with them, wearing baseball caps. If they question why they should wear the caps, we can say that it is a tradition for humans to wear baseball caps on national holidays and that the androids would look more human while wearing a cap in the photo. And then, we can ask them to keep it as a gift from us. Tell them that androids look very impressive when they are wearing baseball caps. With the caps on, MC will not be able to direct them anymore. At that point, Cori will have to instruct us what to say."

Cori nodded. "This just might work. Okay, I will handle Adam and Eve. I'll ask for a photo at the waterfall in the woods near the Main Entrance. When you get an android to wear a cap, tell it to go to the waterfall for a photo with Adam and Eve. That will pull them away from the doors and return-air vents. Then, you guys will have time to explore the ductwork."

They put Cori's plan into action. With the baseball caps properly modified they split up to cover every area with androids. Cori found Adam and Eve, holding hands and standing on the path used by the Welcome-Video family. When she approached, she saw Adam looking at her baseball cap.

"Good afternoon Cori. Are you having a nice day?"

Cori smiled. "Yes Adam, I'm having a wonderful day."

Niigata, Japan

As the CIA shuttle approached Niigata, Japan, a few minutes before nine-thirty Sunday morning, they saw an array of mesh-type receptors mounted on a hillside. It looked almost like giant butterfly wings, over two-hundred meters in wingspread. After landing, they were served a light breakfast. Finally, an elderly Japanese man greeted them and slightly bowed to Dr. Newberry.

The professor returned the bow. "Dr. Kinji! My friend. It has been years since I last saw you."

"Yes, Dr. Newberry, welcome to Japan. I trust the breakfast met with your approval."

"Yes, thank you. The Kunimasu fish was a delicious addition. Now, let me introduce these two young people."

"No need; they are Eric Jennings and your granddaughter, Allison Newberry." He shook hands with them. "All three of you have been pictured on the Media Stream in the last thirty minutes. It seems your Homeland Security considers you to be fugitives. They have an office in Tokyo, but security is very tight out here, so you are safe. However, they will surely be waiting to arrest you when you return home."

Eric wondered out loud. "How will we make it back into the country?"

Agent Bradshaw answered. "Don't worry; I think I know a way. You just do your thing here and I'll take care of the rest." She activated her communicator.

Dr. Kinji ushered Eric and Allie to the antimatter lab and into the last office on the hallway. It was cluttered with files, maps, and star charts. There were ancient marker boards on the wall and a desk littered with stacks of actual papers and a half-full coffee cup.

Allie leaned toward Eric. "Looks like a trash bin threw up in here."

They turned when they heard Dr. Lee laugh. He was a dark-haired slender man in his sixties; sporting a broad smile. He said, "It's not the best filing system in the world, but it works for me. I know where everything is." He extended his hand to Eric and Allie and then greeted Dr. Newberry with a bear hug. "Dr.

Newberry, are you still teaching computers how to think like humans?"

"No, I now teach human children how to think. They learn much faster than processors. You just met my granddaughter, Allie and her fellow fugitive, Eric Jennings. You know why we are here. Can you help us?"

Dan nodded. "Based on the information you gave me, my team has done some preliminary work on possible solutions. So, tell me in detail what you need."

"First, we all need to be brought up to date on antimatter, in layman's terms, so Eric and Allie will understand what they'll be dealing with."

"Yes, of course. Hundreds of years ago, some scientists believed that there had to be more in existence than just visible matter, to explain why this vast universe behaves the way it does. That led to the theory of Dark Matter and Dark Energy. Then, when observers discovered the indicators of Dark Matter changing, first increasing and then decreasing, they thought that new star fields and supernovas were releasing additional Dark Matter into the universe.

"Scientists had already thought that some *unknown* thing had canceled out most of the original physical matter; they called that thing, *antimatter*. The assumption was that all antimatter had already been extinguished in that process. But, to explain the decrease in what they believed to be Dark Matter, they had to revisit the theory of antimatter.

"They knew the additional antimatter had to come from somewhere, even though it was being used up to neutralize some of the Dark Matter. It wasn't until the beginning of this century that the theory was proven, when they developed a magnetic chamber that could capture and suspend the atoms in mid-chamber for testing. By the way; that first capture was right here, in the original antimatter laboratory.

"Over the last fifty years, this new lab, and several others around the world, modified the receptor grids and captured a huge amount of antimatter. And, now, the International Space Consortium even has an experimental antimatter collector on Mars. I hear, through the grapevine, that it has been very successful.

"Anyway, five years ago, I approached the Japanese to purchase some antimatter for some experiments. They refused to sell it to me. Instead, they hired me to work with them to develop some practical applications for these wonderful atoms. My first task was to discover why antimatter atoms kept showing up. It seemed to us that the physical matter still out there should have canceled it all out before we captured it. Last year was the breakthrough, when we got our first look at HDA molecules." He stopped and looked at Dr. Newberry.

The Dr. said, "I've explained about Dragonzyte and HDA-257-2081. They understand the basics."

"Okay, when we got our first look at the clustered antimatter molecules, it all fell into place. The hybrid Dark Matter shells around the three clustered atoms had been protecting the antimatter from being devoured. The good professor has already told you that Dragonzyte mutes the biggest problem with antimatter; the propensity to explode when it contacts matter. That will enable us to now use larger amounts of antimatter to accomplish new processes without the danger normally associated with it."

Allie asked, "What is antimatter good for?"

"If you want a big explosion with a small amount of material, standard antimatter is the way to go. However, nuclear-sized explosions can be a real drag on the planet." Dan smiled. "Since we developed a way to combine the standard and the hybrid together, the most promising applications so far are in the medical field, using it to dissolve some cancers that still exist. It will also be very useful in industry, such as HDA drills that may revolutionize the mining industry. I believe it has great promise as a heat source for making steel and other metal alloys."

Eric asked the obvious question. "Are you developing an antimatter weapon?"

Dan laughed. "I was waiting for that question. No; antimatter weapons are not practical here on Earth. Our atmosphere is made of matter; hydrogen, oxygen, and other elements. If antimatter atoms were fired from a weapon, they would be canceled out by those exploding elements before reaching the target. Antimatter would be effective only at very close range, like the surgeon's scalpel or at the tip of a drill bit. We already have enough nuclear weapons to destroy the planet several times over, so making bombs would be a waste of time."

Dr. Newberry said, "Tell them about the most exciting research you are doing."

Dan walked over to an old marker-board, filled with hand-drawn schematics, formulas, and diagrams. The largest diagram was of a strangely shaped spacecraft, labeled GENESIS ONE. It looked like a cylinder with a sharp point on one end. There were crudely drawn windows and other objects attached to the sides.

In the center was an obvious crew section that would rotate to provide artificial gravity. The oddest part of the craft was an array like the one they had seen earlier on the hillside outside of the lab. Eric quickly recognized a formula, that looked like an incorrect velocity calculation. The answer at the end was, INFINITY, with a question mark after it.

Eric spoke first. "Wow, uh, interesting."

Allie shrugged. "Yeah, nice."

Dan laughed. "That's usually the first reaction I get. Okay, so I'm no Picasso when it comes to drawing, but the concept is real; it already exists. The Japanese have almost finished two of them, and two others are about half complete. We are now working to finish building the engines. The funding has been tight, but we will soon have all we need."

"Really; where are these craft?"

"You don't think Tri-America is the only country with a Space Assembly Station, do you?"

"Well, I…"

"Japan has had one for over five years. I had the idea for this ship when they first hired me, so they started building them when they saw that the technology was possible."

"I see. But, you have an error in your velocity calculation. Nothing has the speed of infinity. That can't be right."

Dan just smiled. "Let me explain the new engine technology, and then you can decide if my calculations are right."

"Okay."

"The array here will capture antimatter atoms and

Dragonzyte clusters, and direct them to the collection chamber in the forward section. When we need to accelerate, the engine, which I call a Hybrid-Antimatter Accelerator, expels the atoms and clusters through the Transmitter Probe, much like an Ion Accelerator. But in this case, it will be shooting them forward of the ship instead of backward.

"Since space is full of Dark Matter and Dark Energy, the engines will neutralize those atoms in front of the ship. Space is a vacuum that happens to be populated with all sorts of matter. When matter gets depleted, a more-empty vacuum is created. That vacuum pulls other matter toward it."

"You mean, like a Black Hole?"

"Yes; exactly. It creates a vacuum within a vacuum, ergo, a temporary Black Hole; admittedly, a small one but a very real one. When the Black Hole sucks matter into it, the ship is pulled along with it. Almost instantly the Black Hole is satisfied with new matter and it goes away."

They were nodding.

"I know that doesn't sound very efficient for a propulsion system. With a one-second burst from our engine, we could go about a meter, and then we would drift at about one-meter per hour. But, suppose we increase the bursts of Hybrid-Antimatter to one-hundred megahertz; still a low frequency? We would attain the speed of one-hundred-thousand kilometers per hour. So, since frequency transition cycles are still evolving, you can see why I put down infinity, with the question mark."

Eric's eyebrows rose slightly. "If this works, you have created Warp Drive!"

Dan was nodding. "It *does* work and I prefer to call it, Star Drive." Of course, it takes as long to decelerate as it does to accelerate. So, the Captain of GENESIS ONE would have to make sure the deceleration time was accurately computed, so he wouldn't overshoot his destination. The thruster system, attached to the sides, is only good for rotating the ship for deceleration and for making heading adjustments in established planetary orbits.

"By the way; since the ship is either continuously accelerating or decelerating, it produces constant gravity at about *One-G*. The only time the Crew Module will need to rotate, to produce artificial gravity, will be during planetary orbits."

Eric was getting excited. "This changes everything! Travel beyond our solar system will finally be possible. You could get to Mars in a week."

"Yes, the possibilities are exciting. But first the Japanese have to get the money to finish developing the engines. As for myself, I just want to head out toward the stars, before I get too old to remember that there *are* stars. That's where you two come in."

Allie reacted first. "What?"

Eric continued. "You can't be serious. We just came here for help to get inside PARADISE. What could we possibly contribute to space travel?"

Dan turned more serious. "Braxton tells me that you two are the best AI programming team he has ever seen. So, when I heard what had happened at PARADISE, and Braxton told me about the Zurelleum problem, I knew two things. First, I will help you get safely inside and provide what you need to stop the Main Core. Second, I know that you can provide what I need."

"What could we possibly offer you?

"Seriously, you have seen the velocity possibilities with my Star Drive. Can you see any potential problems?"

Allie spoke, "Yes. When you are going that fast, how do you avoid things that are in the way?"

Dan smiled. "That is *exactly* the question. Up until now, the simulations I did with the fastest, most capable computers have been unable to calculate the proper collision avoidance headings above a speed of two-hundred-thousand kilometers per hour. That's still much faster than existing space craft, but to get beyond our solar system in a timely fashion, we will need speeds much faster. The Japanese have perfected the radar necessary to track objects at extreme distances and speeds. All we need now is the computer system to process that information. After this PARADISE debacle is over, I need you to join our team and write a new collision avoidance program, using Z-Processors."

Eric was stunned. "Z-Processors?! Are you crazy...uh, sir? That's what threw PARADISE into chaos. Quantum's Mars fleet departed with Z-Processors on board and have been out of contact for days now. We have no idea what the processors are doing to those ships and no way to contact them for at least a month. Ken Anderson is my cousin and he's the commander of that mission. Besides, Quantum will probably be bankrupt after this, and will have to shut down their processor production."

Dr. Lee just smiled.

"You've already thought of everything I just said; right?"

That Texas accent replied. "Right. First, you two will stop the runaway computers in PARADISE. Then, our team here will make the millions of ID$ we need when we sell Quantum the fix I am designing for all Z-Processors, using HDA attachments to neutralize the Dark Matter atoms attracted by Zurelleum. They will be surprisingly easy to fabricate. We will need those Z-Processors if we hope to utilize star drive to its fullest."

He checked the time. "Oh my, I have rambled on for half an hour. I need to get you equipped and on your way." He was serious again. "Listen, I know there are other computer programmers, but Dr. Braxton says you are the best. After you sign a few autographs; and you *will*, after you rescue the President, contact me and we will talk about this possible partnership. If you decide to partner with us, I can promise you, you will never worry about balancing your bank account again."

Dan let that sink in for a few seconds. "OK, follow me." He led them into the Antimatter Lab. He cautioned that although the hybrid-antimatter would not explode, it could still neutralize human flesh, as well as any other matter.

The HDA had been packaged in magnetic mesh spheres, encased in glass nodules about the size of tennis balls. Each one had a very powerful magnet to keep the HDA compressed inside. When the glass was broken, the mesh would come apart at the seams and the HDA would be released. It would expand and neutralize about five-to-ten cubic meters of physical matter, depending on the density.

They had packaged three of the nodules in a padded titanium box, impervious to anything except a nuclear explosion. A fourth ball was smaller and packaged in a teardrop shaped nodule with a leather lanyard attached. It was secured to a flat plastic base with a metal button protruding from the bottom.

Dr. Lee explained. "OK, be sure to keep this box of three in your backpack until you get through the force field at PARADISE. This fourth one will get you through that wall of clouds, or whatever it is made of. Don't take it out of its box until you are ready to break through the dome.

"Then, put the lanyard around your neck and keep the nodule inside your shirt until you are ready to arm it. To do that, jerk the lanyard to break it, hold the glass case in your hand and press the base of it against your chest, until you feel the button click; that will arm it."

"What do I do then, throw it at the dome?"

"No. I guess now is the time to cover the hard parts with you."

"Hard parts?" Allie joined in. "This whole thing already seems difficult."

"I know, but at this point, there is nobody else who can get this done. Let me finish, and then we can discuss your questions. Several hours ago, we received some Doppler readings on the cloud material in the dome. My analysis shows that this single nodule will neutralize a hole big enough for you two to pass through unharmed, if..." He paused.

Eric asked, "If what?"

"If you are traveling at 31 kilometers per hour, plus or minus, uh, maybe 2, when you hit the wall. That will get you through before the cloud is regenerated by the Main Core. You have to get the nodule very close to the cloud before it is released, because it neutralizes a smaller amount of matter. You'll probably need a motorcycle that you can ride slowly into the dome. A car won't work because the front will explode before the HDA can touch the dome.

"You'll need to arm the spring and place the base against your palm, and then hold your arm as far out in front of you as possible. The impact with the dome will activate the spring and launch the nodule into the cloud. The cloud will shatter the glass and release the HDA, which will neutralize the cloud without an effect on you. The thirty-one-kilometer speed should carry you two all the way through the hole it creates."

In the silence that followed, Eric reached and held Allie's hand. "And I thought this was going to be hard," he said quietly.

Allie looked at Dr. Newberry. "Grandpa?!"

"Honey, I know it sounds complicated but you two can do this; I know it. If you follow Dr. Lee's instructions, everything will work."

Eric questioned. "Okay, let's say we make it to St. Louis; where do we get a motorcycle? And, how do we get past that whole herd of Homeland Security agents hovering around the whole dome? And how do you know that the power of the force field won't change?"

Dan paused a moment. "The vehicle will be up to you. With the St. Louis area being evacuated there will surely be such a vehicle available in one of the abandoned homes or businesses near PARADISE. I believe we can reduce the power in the force field before you get there. We know the online home-gaming system is still operational and will drain some power from the Main Core. We can reduce the solar power by redirecting HAARP to target the ionosphere right over St. Louis."

"What's HAARP?"

"HAARP is the High-Frequency Active Auroral Research Program. The government used it last century to study the Earth's ionosphere, until it was blamed for causing a couple of hurricanes. They are still using it for low-level research from its facility in Gakona, Alaska. By aiming it at the ionosphere over St. Louis, it can create real cloud cover, and possibly rain, over that dome. That will reduce the available sunlight and reduce the solar energy being generated. All we need is the HAARP code from the White House."

Eric shook his head. That will be impossible now. Doug Clark was working with us, but now he's been arrested or detained."

Dan still had that southern smile. "Actually, he has just been restricted to the White House War Room, still monitoring the PARADISE emergency."

Dr. Newberry raised his eyebrows. "Daniel, how could you possibly know that?"

"Well, it just so happens that my son, Robert, is the Chief of Food Service at the White House. We kinda keep that a family secret. I spoke with him before you got here. I am texting him now, asking him to get this to Mr. Clark secretly. How does this sound? *'Mr. Clark. Need HAARP authorization code ASAP. Eric & Allie'.*"

Eric questioned. "Just like that?"

"Yep, just like that. I bet you'll have the code before you leave here. If not, I'll text it to you. I'm sure Agent Bradshaw and the CIA know how to use it. Now, the guy in Dallas needs to keep people logged on to the Home Hologram System. We need as many as possible, especially at nine o'clock in the morning, helping to drain power from the Main Core. He also needs to keep trying to contact the terminal inside PARADISE. It would help if they knew you two are coming.

Dr. Newberry located the number and called Ethan Hallberg. Ethan agreed to coordinate maximum subscribers log-ons and monitor the circuits leading to Steve's backdoor system. He told the professor to warn Eric and Allie about the death and destruction the dome had already caused.

After the call to Ethan, Daniel Lee continued. "Okay, you need to be close to the force field before nine o'clock tomorrow morning and stay out of sight. My analysis says that the dome should expand again around nine o'clock in the morning, maybe a few minutes later. When it starts pulsing, you will have about fifteen minutes to hit the wall, at thirty-one kilometers per hour. But you'll need to avoid the guards around the perimeter. They may try to shoot you."

Allie sat up. "Shoot us!?"

"Don't worry. When it starts pulsing they will run like crazy from the dome, for good reason. With HAARP engaged it should be cloudy with rain, so be careful with your vehicle on the wet surface. You will only get one chance to make it through. Now, let's review the…"

Dr. Lee's communicator buzzed. "Ah, yes, Robert is faster than I expected. Agent Bradshaw, the HAARP code is HOTEL ONE, PAPA ALPHA FIVE, ZULU X-RAY FOUR TWO, CHARLIE DELTA TWO SEVEN. Can you coordinate with HAARP?"

"Yes sir, consider it done."

Dr. Lee continued. "As I was saying, let's review the

procedures you must follow. The CIA will take care of getting you back to St. Louis. You must be ready to initiate the plan by nine a.m. tomorrow. Keep the nodules secured in their boxes until needed. You know how to use the one for getting through the dome. You will only have three nodules left. They are designed to be thrown.

"After you get inside you may need one to get through the concrete wall of PARADISE itself. You must keep at least one for disabling the Main Core. I am assuming you won't have access to reprogram the Main Core. So, find the people on the inside; you will need their help to get down to the Main Core. But, be careful; it will probably try to use its lasers to prevent a shutdown.

"You two have seen how the Main Core is set up, with seven Z-Processors clustered together. For your safety, you must stay at least ten meters from the Main Core. Throw one of the nodules and hit the center of the rack. That will take out all seven processors. If you miss, you'd better have a backup."

There was an awkward silence.

Dan stared at them for a moment. "This thing has got to be stopped. Even if those inside are fine at this point, the facilities in there can only sustain them for so long. Questions?"

Allie asked, "What happens if we fail?"

CHAPTER 22

FAILURE IS NOT AN OPTION

PARADISE

The baseball caps worked. As planned, all ninety-five androids gathered at the waterfall for their meeting.

Several of the Staff had already explored the ventilation ductwork, looking for the route to Steve's backdoor room. But, it was extremely difficult because the insides were smooth and slick. Two of the people made it only one-level down by using a rope but quickly lost their way and had to return. Agent Charles and Keith checked all the exit doors; they were still locked.

At the waterfall, Cori asked the androids to gather for a group photo. "Seeing all of you together is very reassuring for the humans here at PARADISE. When I see you with your baseball caps on, you look more human and I'm sure all the guests will feel more comfortable around you. I would like to hear all of you recite your Primary Directive at the same time." Instantly, they all recited it together: *"My Primary Directive requires adherence to the following programming safeguards: An android will never harm, cause to be harmed or allow to be harmed in any way, a human. An android will obey all instructions given by humans, unless those instructions violate the Primary Directive or the authorized mission assigned to that android by its owner or supervisor."*

Cori smiled. "Excellent! Now, keep your caps on. Android servers; return to your assigned food service areas. All other androids, line up against the wall by the Reception Desk and wait for further instructions. Do not remove your caps until instructed to do so by me." As the androids began leaving the meeting, she told Adam and Eve to stay with her.

"Adam, why did the Main Core generate the cloud over

PARADISE and restrict access to the other parts of the building?"

"The Main Core is following its Primary Directive."

Cori had never thought about a Primary Directive for the Main Core. She assumed that MIT had assigned one. "What is the Main Core's Primary Directive?"

Adam quoted: *"The Primary Directive of the Main Core is to generate, with one-hundred percent accuracy, the inputs it receives from humans in the hologram chambers."*

"Is it keeping us away so we can't interfere with its Primary Directive?"

"Yes, that is correct."

"Adam, can you help us gain access to the Main Core area on the Maintenance level?"

"No. I am not allowed to violate the Primary Directive of the Main Core. My last command was to keep all humans in this area."

"Eve, did you receive the same communication?"

"Yes, all androids received the same directive from the Main Core."

Finally, Cori thought of a logical way to get the androids on their side. She asked, "What would you do if the Main Core instructed you to violate *your* Primary Directive?"

The President stood when Harrington gave him the news about a possible way to communicate with the outside. "What are you standing here for? Take me to that terminal."

"It's not that easy Mr. President. My staff is trying to figure out how to get down to it now. All the doors are locked and there are lasers mounted in the corridors down there. We must be careful. The computer could use them as weapons."

"Weapons?! My God, man, what have you created here?"

"Well, sir, no one could have anticipated that Quantum would sell us processors that had already started growing on their own. We are dealing with a *thinking* computer that now has the power of reason. We must be careful or someone could get killed."

"Killed?! Aren't you being a little over dramatic here?"

"NO SIR, HE ISN'T KIDDING!"

Everyone looked for the source of the voice. The Secret Service moved in closer to the President; one drew his weapon. A female agent moved the First Lady to a far corner. The voice came from somewhere within the room but no one else was there. Harrington called out. "Who are you!?"

"Joe Wilson, sir!"

Harrington said, "It's my Facilities Chief. We thought he was locked in down below." He knelt closer to the sound of the voice and shouted, "Joe, where are you!?"

"I'm in the return-air duct. Get a pry-bar from the toolbox in the corner closet and pry the cover off the vent."

An agent retrieved it and two of them pried on the corners until it broke loose. When Joe crawled out, his AK-47 came out with him. The Secret Service agents leaped on Joe and relieved him of his weapon, pinning him to the floor.

Harrington yelled, "Let him up! He works here!"

The President nodded and the agents stepped back. They took the AK-47 and the nine-millimeter pistol they saw tucked in his belt. Harrington helped Joe stand. He was sweating and there were scratches along his arms. Joe took off his hard hat.

"Boss, my knees are killing me; I'm getting too old for this stuff." There was dried blood on the side of his face and the back of his neck.

"Joe, what happened?"

"First I want to meet the President." He wiped his hand and extended it. "Mr. President, I've always wanted to meet you. I voted for you last time; I think you're doing a great job."

The President smiled. "Thank you, Mr. Wilson. We need more people like you."

Joe returned to his chair. "Mr. Harrington. The computer down there has gone nuts!"

The President laughed. "I like this guy more every minute. Go ahead, Joe."

"Yes, sir. Anyway, when the blackout happened, I headed to the Power Distribution Panel, like the standard procedures call for. But the panel access door was welded shut! When I started back toward the door, something exploded overhead and I fell to the floor. Sparks and hot metal fell all over me. A second blast broke a conduit loose and it fell on me. When the smoke cleared, one of the Maintenance Androids had its laser aimed right at me! I thought I was a goner. It started coming at me so I got up and ran to my office. You know, I have some antique guns, right? I work on them during breaks."

"Yes, I remember."

"I got out this AK-47 and a nine-millimeter pistol. I decided that I was going to fight back if I had to. The android suddenly stopped and went back toward the Main Core. The only thing I can figure is that it was protecting the computer from me. I tried to contact you but none of the communicators are working. This is crazy; what is going on?"

"Uh, it's hard to explain. The Main Core has somehow grown more capable and has taken over PARADISE. It has projected a thick cloud dome outside over the whole place and cut off all contact with the outside. The hologram chambers are still working but we can't get to the people in there; we don't know their status. All the other domes are locked up. The androids have confined everyone to the Reception Dome.

"The staff is trying to figure out how to get to Steve's backdoor computer terminal in the basement, but they don't have a way to get down there; he thinks he can get some contact with the outside."

Joe smiled and nodded. "I know exactly where that room is and I can get him down to it. But, I'm not going back down there without my weapons. If that android catches us, I want a fighting chance." The President motioned and an agent returned them to Joe.

Harrington called the staff back together. They were all surprised to see the President and shocked to see Joe Wilson. Joe explained again what had happened down below.

Steve asked, "Joe, what is the condition of my Backdoor Room? Can we get to it?"

"I'm not sure about the condition; there were a lot of laser blasts bouncing around in the corridor. I don't know if any cables got cut. The only way to know for sure is to go down there. I can take you right to the room, through the duct-work."

The President asked, "Mr. Franklin, once you get there, can

you communicate with the outside?"

"If the cables are intact, I'll contact Ethan Hallberg at the Dallas Node.   We can count on him to do whatever needs to be done."

"OK. Mr. Wilson, how long will it take for you to lead him to that room?"

Joe did a quick mental calculation. "The best I can figure, I can get him there in about an hour."

"An hour?!"

"Yes, Mr. President. The insides of those ducts are smooth and slippery. It took me over an hour to make it up here. To get to the area where Steve's room is located, we'll have to take a different route. There are no footholds of any kind inside the ducts. I had to bring 'L' brackets and Quan-Glue so I could create steps to climb on. It takes a minute for the glue on each foothold to dry sufficiently to support my weight. I'm pretty sure I have enough left to get to Steve's room."

The President asked Steve, "If your system is still working, is there a way to patch a communicator through it to the outside?"

"No sir. None of the communicators are working. The Main Core has shut everything down."

Joe said.   "I have a couple of handsets with a roll of telephone cable, long enough to reach back up here. Once I get Steve to his room, I could go to my office and find them."

Steve was nodding.   "Yes, I think I can get it connected through the audio module and bring it back here."

The President whispered to an agent who retrieved a black briefcase and handed it to him.

Eddie leaned closer.   "Is that the famous Football we have heard about; the one with the special codes for releasing nuclear weapons?"

The President nodded. "Yes, the very same." He raised the lid and retrieved a small square plastic card. In the center were the words; *PRESIDENTIAL AUTHENTICATION – TOP SECRET.* He wrote a number on it and handed it to Steve. "These are the voice authentication cards, for use when electronic means are unavailable. Only use it if you can't get the phone cable back up here. In that case, have the guy in Dallas call this number; it's the Vice-President's communicator. This message needs to be transmitted or read to the VP, word for word." The President sat and wrote the words on a napkin and handed it to Steve.

Steve looked puzzled. "Johnny Appleseed?"

The President smiled. "That's my Secret Service code name for this trip. That should convince the VP it's authentic. If she doubts it, go to the question at the bottom. Have her ask Douglas Clark what dessert Sara is making for me. The answer should be, *Banana Pudding*."

"OK, sir, but how do I use this Top-Secret card?"

"If she still needs more confirmation, break the card in the center on that gray line and pull it apart. Read the authentication code to her"

Steve stared at the card and asked, "Sir, are you sure--"

"Yes, I'm sure you can handle it. Besides, it won't take long to change the code, once I get out of here. Now, time's wasting. You and Joe have a big job to do. Don't let anything stop you."

"Yes, sir."

Joe handed Steve an extra clip-on portable light before he turned and said, "You can count on us, Mr. President." He and Steve disappeared into the duct.

Joe was right; it took an hour to install stepping brackets inside the other section of ductwork leading to the backdoor room. Finally, Joe stopped at a junction with ducts running in several different directions, across the ceiling. He pointed to the left.

"Go to the end and turn right. Be careful not to make noise; those androids have great hearing. The second vent should be the one over your backdoor room." He handed Steve a pair of regular pliers and a small metal tube with a magnet attached to the end. "Power tools would be too noisy so use these pliers to take the bolts out from the top side of the vent. Catch the bolts with the magnet so they won't drop in the room and make noise. Leave the vent cover inside the duct and drop onto your desk. It should be easy. How long will you need?"

Steve looked at the pliers and magnet. "Easy...yeah, right. Uh, I'll need at least fifteen or twenty minutes inside the room."

"OK, I'll try to find the phones and cable and be back to your room before you finish. Then you can patch in the cable for the President."

Joe disappeared in the opposite direction. Steve crawled to the vent over his desk and started removing the bolts. The third bolt fell off the magnet when he tried to pull it back through the vent. He cringed when it landed on the edge of his desk and bounced into the empty metal trash can. The sound echoed. Steve thought all was well until he saw the door handle turning downward. He tapped his light off and lay in the dark, barely breathing, sweat covering his face.

A maintenance android stepped into the room. Its camera-eyes and the lights of the status panel on its chest cast an eerie glow. After a few moments, it left. Steve waited about a minute and then finished removing the vent cover. He dropped into the room and powered up his backdoor system.

He first tried the desk communicator to contact Ethan in Dallas. The small screen read *SYSTEM ERROR*. The laser blasts must have cut the voice cable. Still, with the separate cable installed for data, there was a chance it survived. He activated the data circuit and an alert appeared on the screen; *3 MESSAGES WAITING*. "YES!" he thought. Two of the messages were from Ethan in Dallas. The first read; *"Hey, man, what's going on in there? There's a weird cloud thing over the place and nobody's getting in or out. The home systems are still working. What's up?"*

Steve typed. *"Ethan, are you there?"* He only had to wait a few seconds.

"Yeah, Steve, I'm here. Let's go voice. Tell me what's going on?"

Steve typed, *"Can't go voice; system's down. You won't believe this...MC has become AWARE and has taken over the whole place. Somehow it is generating that dome. About 1500 people are locked in the Reception Dome but we're fine, including the President. But, there are hundreds locked in the hologram chambers; we don't know their status. Facilities are working normally, for now. I don't have much time. I need you to forward a Presidential message to the VP at the White*

House...communicator code 200-472-1000."

Ethan typed back, *"Sure, I can data-transfer to them whatever you want. Also, I'm supposed to tell you that a team is going to break through that dome around 9:00 a.m. tomorrow; two programmers named Eric and Allie."*

Steve hesitated. *Eric and Allie? The rumor here is that the cloud-stuff can kill people. We can use their help but they'd better know what they're doing."*

"Hey, I'm just the messenger. A guy named Dr. Newberry set the thing up. He sounded confident. He said they have a way to stop MC but they will need help from some of you inside. From the outside, we have seen the dome expand several times and destroy everything it touches. The news said several people have been killed, but who knows. Homeland Security has it blocked off and the Vice-President has ordered the whole St. Louis area to be evacuated. They already shut down the Power Grid to the city. You guys are on internal power."

"OK, what are we supposed to do in here to help Eric and Allie?"

"At nine o'clock tomorrow morning, turn on everything that uses electrical power. Somehow, they are going to try to make it rain over St. Louis to reduce the solar power the thing is generating. Since the home systems are still working, he told me to have all home systems log on by 9:00 a.m. and run their adventures."

"So, my guess is that they want to reduce the power available to the cloud so it will be easier to penetrate, right?"

"Yep, that's what he said."

Steve thought, *"That makes sense."* He unfolded the napkin. *"OK, are you ready for the President's message?"*

"Yeah, go ahead."

Steve typed the message and sent it. After a few moments, Ethan responded.

"Got it; Johnny Appleseed?"

Steve smiled. *"It's a Secret Service thing."*

The distant banging sound coming from the ductwork startled Steve. In a moment, he heard the footsteps of an android coming down the corridor. He grabbed a metal coat rack stored in a corner and placed it on his shoulder like a baseball bat, and waited.

The android continued past the door, heading toward the source of the sound; probably Joe's office. Steve figured Joe would certainly use the old rifle if necessary. He also knew he didn't have much time so he hurried back to the keyboard.

"Go ahead and send the message to the VP, I'll wait for a reply. Tell them to hurry."

"OK, will do."

Ethan dialed the code for the Vice-President. Her aide answered and then turned to the VP.

"Madam Vice-President, there is an Ethan Hallberg from Dallas calling on your personal communicator. He says he has a message from the President."

The VP smiled, "How many crank calls does that make already, six? Also, how did he get my personal communicator code?"

The aide spoke to Ethan and looked back at the VP. "Ma'am, he says he has a message from Johnny Appleseed; sounds like he's a little crazy."

The VP jumped out of her chair and grabbed the communicator from the aide. "Who is this?"

"Ethan Hallberg, ma'am. I was told to deliver a message from the President."

"Message?! How did you get a message from the President? We have no contact with him."

"Well, ma'am, I work for PARADISE, on the Home Hologram System. Steve Franklin designed the system and put in a direct link to me, bypassing the computer system. He is still inside PARADISE and he contacted me a few minutes ago, to relay a message from the President."

The VP thought for a moment. "How do I know this is not just some news organization that overheard an agent using the President's code name?"

"The President thought you might question it, so he put a question on here for you to ask a guy named Douglas Clark."

"He's the Chief of Staff. What question did the President

have for him?"

"Well, ma'am, it sounds crazy but he said to ask Doug what dessert Sara is making for the President. The answer should be banana pudding."

"Banana pudding? This is bizarre! OK, I'll ask him." She leaned out of her office and called out, "Doug!" He looked in her direction. "What dessert is your wife making for the President?"

Doug smiled. There was only one reason she would ask that question. "BANANA PUDDING!" He was already on his feet headed for the VP's office. "We have contact, don't we?"

"OK, Ethan, what is the message from the President?"

"It's a data message. I'll stream it to you now."

"Wait; let me send you a secure algorithm."

Ethan waited for the green light and then sent the message. By now, most of the War Room Staff was in her office. There was a cheer when the message appeared on the VP's communicator. She told Ethan to wait while she quickly read it to the staff.

"It looks like the President and First Lady, along with the whole team, are all safe and well." Everyone applauded. "He says the main computer has taken over PARADISE and they have no way to stop it. He says we should transfer powers if we haven't already and reassure the country that he is fine. We are to take whatever measures we deem appropriate to end this chaos quickly.

"He says his safety is not to be the over-riding factor but to make sure civilians are protected. He wants to put Doug in charge of all news media and coordination of all foreign affairs for now and to give Homeland Security whatever they need to resolve this crisis."

She stared at the screen for a moment. She half-smiled and handed Doug's communicator back to him. "Alright, let's get things organized. Doug, I need a news conference in thirty minutes, with international news feeds. I need someone to get Brad Smith on a conference call with us and the Secretary of Defense in ten minutes. And Doug, I need to see you back in here after you get those things done. Okay, let's get busy!"

She was left alone in her office to answer the President's

message. "Ethan, will the President see my message while it's being transmitted?"

"No, ma'am, Steve is in the basement and he'll have to crawl four levels up the air conditioning ducts to hand-deliver the message, which could take a while."

"I see. Okay, wait, I'll have the new message in a moment." She compiled a data message that was short and to the point. *"Mr. President; relieved you are OK. Powers already transferred. Foreign governments concerned. PARADISE crisis is serious; cloud dome destroys everything in its path. Several deaths confirmed; more presumed. Dome has expanded several times. St. Louis and East St. Louis being evacuated. Working on a plan for rescue, will advise."* She sent the message and told Ethan to call her back when Steve had received it.

Steve returned to his terminal when he saw the incoming message light. Almost simultaneously, he heard a laser blast in the distance, followed by the sound of what could only be an AK-47 weapon, firing on full automatic. He dropped to the floor and got under his desk until it stopped. He prayed Joe was alright.

When he crawled out, there was a message flashing; *SYSTEM FAILURE.* The android's laser had cut the remaining circuit. But, the Inbox showed a new message. He opened it. It was the VP's message. Steve wasn't sure if that was the entire message but he was unable to confirm it with Ethan.

Ethan had gotten the same alert on his terminal and after several attempts to contact Steve, he called the VP and gave her the bad news. He promised to keep trying."

The VP gave the news to the staff but went ahead with the conference call. Brad Smith was adamant that the President had not meant to try dangerous methods to stop PARADISE. Doug was equally convinced that the hybrid-antimatter was the way to go. They all agreed that using HAARP was a good idea.

Brad demanded to know where Eric and Allie were and Doug honestly told him he didn't know. Since the VP had taken away his ability to communicate he had lost track of them. He agreed to try contacting them after all the immediate concerns were taken care of. Since Homeland Security had blocked all civilian communicator signals within sixty kilometers of PARADISE Doug was hoping that the two would be inside that circle soon and be unreachable. Right now, he had other things to do.

Steve downloaded the VP's message. Joe had not come back, so he climbed back into the ductwork and smelled the strong odor of an electrical fire.

He crawled to the junction where he had last seen Joe and waited for a few minutes. There was no sign of Joe and the electrical odor was getting stronger. He couldn't take the chance of not getting the message to the President, so he started the climb back up to Reception. Finally, Steve emerged from the vent, exhausted. Harrington helped him up and then looked back in the duct. "Where's Joe?"

Guatemala – Saturday, 11:00 p.m. Central Time

For the last two hundred kilometers, the CIA shuttle had dropped out of the supersonic flight corridor over the Pacific Ocean, down to a hundred meters above the water. It passed north of Guatemala City and climbed up the valley and landed in the same field as before.

When the passenger door was opened, bright lights came on, surrounding the shuttle. Homeland Security agents swarmed in from all sides. Dr. Newberry had just stepped onto the stairs and was so startled that he dropped his bag and fell the rest of the way to the ground. An agent ordered him to stay down. Very quickly, a dozen agents entered the shuttle. After a couple of minutes, the team leader appeared and shouted to the Chief agent that the shuttle was empty, except for the flight crew and one other passenger. He then escorted Dr. Daniel Lee down the steps. The agents helped Dr. Newberry up. The Chief ordered them to search the storage bins and maintenance access panels on the shuttle. They still found nothing. He walked over to the professor.

"Alright, where are they?"

Dr. Newberry was dusting the grass off his clothes. "Who? Who are you talking about?"

"You know who; Eric Jennings and your granddaughter, Allison Newberry. They were seen departing in this shuttle, from this field, about ten hours, ago. We know the shuttle took them to Niigata, Japan and we know this shuttle left there just over four hours ago, headed back here."

Dr. Newberry just smiled. "Did anyone actually see them get on a shuttle in Japan?"

"Well...no, not exactly, we just assumed--"

"You'd think that professional agents would be more observant than that." He turned to Daniel Lee. "This is Dr. Daniel Lee, the American member of a research team in Japan. This is his shuttle and he offered me a ride, since he was coming home to Texas to visit his family. I believe you have detained him long enough."

The agents finished a second search of the shuttle with no results. The Chief Agent said. "I can see that you are not going to cooperate. If those two kids do something stupid and get the President or others killed, it will be on your head. We will come looking for you." He motioned for the agents to release the shuttle. Soon the portable floodlights went off and the agents disappeared.

Dr. Newberry turned to Daniel. "Agent Bradshaw's plan worked. Now we just have to hope that those two young people can accomplish this huge mission we have given them."

Dr. Lee shook the professor's hand. "I have a feeling they will surprise us all. I think we are in good hands." A few minutes later, the shuttle departed for Dallas.

Two Hours Earlier – North Pacific Ocean

The two-hour flight from Japan to the Battle Craft, USS Carlos Vanguard, four hundred kilometers north of Hawaii, was uneventful. The Vanguard was the Flag Ship of an armada on a training exercise. Eric had just had time for a shower and a light dinner when the pilot announced their descent. He knew they couldn't be landing in Guatemala yet. He kept one hand on his backpack most of the flight, as if it would add more protection for the glass nodules in their titanium containers.

Finally, the shuttle settled onto the deck of the massive magnetic hovercraft, landing beside an almost identical shuttle. Agent Bradshaw opened the shuttle door and hugged the Admiral who had stepped onboard. His nametag read, AMELIO BRADSHAW. The agent slipped her arm through his. "Everyone, meet my dad, Admiral Bradshaw. Thanks, Dad. I appreciate you doing this for us."

He smiled broadly. "Anything for my little girl. Now, these must be the two you mentioned." He was extending his hand to Eric.

"Yes, Dad; they are the ones we hope will be able to get into PARADISE and get that place under control."

"Well, I hope so. Jacob Holloway is a good friend, and I think a fine Commander-in-Chief. Now, time's wasting; you don't want to be out of the corridor too long. Air Traffic Control will get concerned."

The agent nodded. "Okay, you two, get your things and let's get aboard our shuttle."

Dr. Newberry hugged Allie and reassured her that everything would be fine. They said their goodbyes and boarded the other shuttle. The flight crew lifted off, switched on their stealth generators and headed to the East-Northeast. Dr. Newberry's shuttle departed toward Guatemala.

An hour from landing, the agent started briefing Eric and Allie. "We don't want to compromise your location so we will be dropping you off about fifty kilometers south, in a small town called Sulphur Springs, Missouri, on the western bank of the Mississippi River. We'll land about 12:30 a.m., Central Time." She handed Allie an envelope.

"Use this money to buy some transportation, or whatever else you need. The town is still outside the evacuation zone, so some of the population will probably still be there. Stay on the back roads into St. Louis to avoid the checkpoints. It is paramount that you not get caught." She hesitated before reaching to her inside pocket and offering a laser pistol to Eric.

He recoiled a little. "Whoa! I don't do weapons. I would

never be able to shoot anyone, no matter the reason."

She put it away. "Alright, but you have to know that you may be the only chance that we, uh, maybe even the world, will have to stop that thing. Don't take any chances. You *must* get through."

Allie reached and touched her arm. "We do understand. My whole family is in there. We'll be careful."

"OK. Well, Dr. Lee told you how to do what is required. Be ready for anything; there may be some surprises once you get through that cloud, or whatever it is. Be sure and watch out for each other."

It had started to rain as the pilot announced landing in fifteen minutes. He shut off the engines and used the silent magnetic flux system to hide their presence. They touched down on a secluded part of the riverbank at twelve-thirty-seven Sunday morning.

With a light rain falling, Eric stepped out and was immediately drenched, with just a light short-sleeved shirt on. Even in July, the rain and the cool of the evening made him shiver a little. Allie had on a light jacket.

The agent stepped out with them. "This the edge of the communications zone, so you may not be able to contact anyone." She pointed. "About two hundred meters that way you will find the main street of Sulfur Springs. Buy some transportation as quickly as possible and get on the road. Turn right and follow the signs to St. Louis." She smiled, hugged them both and closed the shuttle door. The big craft lifted silently, hovered out over the water and disappeared downstream.

Eric and Allie stood for a few moments, trying to comprehend the reality of what they were doing. It was easy to be confident when they had all of those professionals telling them what and how to do this mission. Standing there in the rain, it was another matter. They were alone and uncertain and already very wet. Eric hugged Allie. "We can do this," he whispered.

"We *have* to do this," she said.

They climbed up an embankment onto a grassy area. They could see several buildings, some with dim generator-powered lights visible.

Crossing the field, they passed behind a large building that looked like an old church and then stopped at a storage building located just behind a house. The door was unlocked and had a large sign nailed to the outside. Eric used his communicator light to read it.

"My wife, Dora, and I have evacuated with our congregation. Evacuees are welcome to anything and everything in this storage building but please don't take anything from the house. Dora left some food in this building; please help yourself. We pray that everyone will survive the chaos going on in Saint Louis. God, Bless You All." It was signed: Reverend Billy Jackson, Pastor, Shiloh Cumberland Presbyterian Church.

They stepped inside, out of the rain. The dim glow of a battery light showed a stack of bowls beside a large pot of potato soup on a small table. They both took a bowl-full and surveyed the building as they ate. The contents ranged from antique toys and clothes to out-of-date garden tools.

Allie called Eric to help her uncover something under a large canvas near the back wall. They were amazed at the ancient Harley Davidson motorcycle, in pristine condition. It was a perfect fifty-year-old model, except that the outlawed gasoline engine had been replaced with Fuel-Cell power.

"This will be perfect for our mission."

Allie shook her head. "Are you crazy? We can't just take something like this. It must be worth a fortune. Surely the sign on the door didn't mean this."

Eric had straddled the old motorcycle and turned on the power. The control panel lit up and the fuel cell started humming. "Well, the sign said ANYTHING, and I'm sure the Reverend knew it was here. This is what we need to get through the dome. Besides, Agent Bradshaw gave us the 100,000 ID$ cash in the envelope. We could leave 60,000 hidden here in the building and leave a note so they can contact us. Then we can tell them where we hid the money. We'll keep the other 40K for contingencies."

"I don't know. It kinda makes me feel like a thief, but I guess we shouldn't pass it up. I just hope 60,000 is enough. We can always ask the CIA to pay more, once this is all over."

Eric nodded. "I don't think that would be a problem."

He got off the motorcycle and kept looking around in the building. He found one dusty motorcycle helmet, a small hunting knife and a light windbreaker jacket hanging on a hook. He put the knife in his backpack and slipped on the jacket, since he was a little chilled from his wet clothes. He took the helmet and pushed the old Harley out the door as Allie hid the money and left a note for the reverend.

When she met him up beside the house he was ready to go. She put on the backpack and climbed on behind him. **At one-thirty in the morning, they began the final leg of their journey. The vast darkness, that was once a bright St. Louis, loomed in the distance.**

CHAPTER 23

THE REALITY OF *REAL*

The President had read the VP's message and finally understood the reality of their situation. He was worried about how the two young programmers would make it into PARADISE, especially since no one was sure what had happened to Joe. They all expected the worst, after Steve's description of what he heard and smelled. The President knew it might be a fatal mistake for Eric and Allie to try to penetrate the cloud, but he saw no other option.

Harrington directed that all electrical devices be turned on before nine o'clock the next morning. But, he was worried that, even if the rescuers made it inside, his staff wouldn't know what to do to help them. Joe had not returned, so Steve would have to lead them through the duct system. Sending armed agents down the narrow ducts would be too risky.

While they were discussing options, Keith and Lisa frantically hurried into the room. Keith yelled, "IS IT TRUE?! Someone said that Eric and Allie are going to try to get in here!"

"Yes, it is, but--"

"Are they nuts?! Why would they do a dumb thing like that? They might be killed! Can we contact somebody and stop them from trying?"

Steve shook his head. "I'm afraid not. I lost contact when the android fired its laser down below. It must have cut the cables."

Eddie said, "Keith, you know them better than we do. They are very smart, so I'm betting they are working with the best minds in the world to do whatever they are doing. Allie is pretty level-headed."

"Yeah...I guess so."

Lisa looked at Keith. "Yes! She is a very smart girl. We have to trust her judgment, and pray that Eric has the same."

Steve added. "The message I got said Dr. Braxton Newberry is helping them. He's your father. He knows what he's doing."

"I guess you're right. If Dad is involved, he has thought of all the details; I've always trusted his judgment." He looked around at everyone in the room. "Okay, so what do we have to do to help them once they get inside?"

Eddie thought for a moment. "Obviously, they'll have to get down to MC; they can't undo the AI program without access to the program itself. We know that's not gonna happen. So, they must be planning to physically disable it. To do that, they must get inside the processor room, to the Main Core itself."

Steve shook his head. "Getting them down to that level is not the problem; Joe already has the ducts modified with steps inside. But, based on what I saw, they'll need some kind of diversion to avoid the lasers and the androids."

Agent Charles stepped up. "Excuse me; at some point, somebody with weapons will have to take on those big robots down below. From what Steve said, Joe has already tried to do that. I just hope he made it."

"So, if we are going to get this done, we'll have to get through those doors and make it four levels down those stairs. We can't all go down the ductwork. Those of us with weapons can use firepower to be part of that diversion."

Cori nodded. "Bill is right; those with weapons can be a diversion. This can help." She held up an electronic device the size of a sandwich. "In all the chaos, I had forgotten that this Android Adjustment Tool was stored in the back of this dome. Now I can change the communications frequency, so the androids won't need to wear the baseball caps. MC won't be able to direct them, but they can communicate with each other. We might be able to use them to overwhelm the maintenance androids."

Bill agreed. "We'll need to really concentrate the firepower of these small handguns to disable the corridor lasers. If our androids can help take out the five maintenance andro--"

"FOUR! Four maintenance androids!"
Everybody turned; Joe was standing in the doorway. There

was a hole burned in the right leg of his pants and his right hand was slightly bleeding. The AK-47 he held smelled of gunpowder.

Harrington sprang to his side. "Joe! Are you alright?"

He moved slowly to a chair. "Yes, boss. It will take more than a machine to bring me down."

The President questioned. "What happened?"

"After I made it to my office, I was looking for the wire and phones on top of the utility cabinet when one chair leg gave way and I fell. The cabinet turned over on top of the desk and me, right below the opening to the ductwork. I didn't know the android heard it, until I heard those heavy footsteps in the corridor.

"It got there before I could get the cabinet off me. It just ripped the office door right off the hinges and fired its laser at me. The blast took out the end of the desk and the utility cabinet, and just caught my right leg. At least, it freed my foot from the cabinet. I rolled over, aimed and pulled the trigger. That android's head disappeared! It fired its laser again so I emptied half the magazine into its chest. Sparks went everywhere and the thing caught fire and fell backwards out the door. It took me ten minutes to put out the fire. Then I thought I'd better wait to see if another one came at me. After a little while, I got into the duct and came back up. I'm glad to see Steve made it."

There were several moments of stunned silence. Finally, applause broke out. Many were patting Joe on the back.

Tim yelled out, "NOW *THAT'S* WHAT I'M TALKING ABOUT! Man; that would make a great hologram adventure!"

Evan added, "Yeah, or how about a movie?"

Joe held up his hand. "No thanks, let's just get rid of that computer and get this place back to normal."

The President extended his hand. "Thanks, Joe, I'm proud of you.

"Thank you, Mr. President."

Steve patted Joe on the back. "Man, you had me worried. I got the message out and received one before the android attacked you. Then I lost the connection."

Joe thought, "It must have been the second blast, it went into the ceiling where some of the fiber circuits run."

Harrington interrupted. "Okay, people, we only have eight hours before we need to be ready. Let's work together."

Joe looked at Steve. "Ready for what?"

North St. Louis

Eric was startled from sleep by a large drop of water landing on his forehead. Allison stirred slightly from his movement but then cuddled closer to his shoulder and settled back into sleep.

Their large cardboard hiding place was soaked from the overnight rain and a large puddle on top was now leaking through. The drops were getting larger, so Eric pulled his thin jacket closer around Allie. To stop the leak, he reached overhead and pushed slowly upward on the bulge. As the water drained off over the sides, a shower of drops fell.

With the rain diminishing, Eric could smell the garbage in the abandoned alley. Earlier that, he had skirted the perimeter of the dome and found this hideaway in the dark. They hid the motorcycle under some bags of garbage and used the cardboard box as a place to get some sleep.

Now, he was peeking out to assess their daylight surroundings. The place must have been in decline for some time.

The growl from his stomach was evidence that the potato soup hadn't lasted very long. He wasn't sure if they would find food inside PARADISE, so he checked the signs near each back door up and down the alley. None indicated a business that dealt with food. He opened his backpack and retrieved the half-eaten compressed food bar he had snacked on in the shuttle. Another large drop of water roused Allie from sleep.

Eric smiled. "Good morning beautiful. I called room service to bring us some breakfast."

Allie stretched and pushed her hair from her face. The smell of the alley registered and she buried her face momentarily in Eric's shoulder. "If that smell is breakfast, you can have mine."

He laughed and hugged her close. "Madam, there are two choices on the menu, one-half of a CFB and, uh, some complementary fresh rain water. Did the accommodations meet with your approval?"

Allie was smiling by now. "Yes, of course, I will always remember my stay here. However, I will be checking out today. Send the bill to the President, or whoever is in charge while he's vacationing in PARADISE. We are personal friends, you know."

"Yes, ma'am," he said as he handed her the food bar.

While they ate breakfast, they checked their supplies. Allie's shoulder bag had a few girl things, like makeup, toiletries and such, her clothing for the intended stay in PARADISE, a pair of tennis shoes, and two other items; a small bag of hard candy and her communicator, which hadn't had service since they arrived in Sulfur Springs. The government shut-down was working.

Eric's backpack had his overnight essentials, plus a canteen of water, his useless communicator, a flashlight and the hunting knife that the Reverend had left in the storage building.

Finally, at the bottom were the two black titanium boxes that held the containers of HDA to get them inside the dome to disable the Main Core. The Japanese had done a good job of packaging the delicate material.

Allie touched the large box. "Do you really think this will work?"

Eric hid his concern. "Sure, it should work just like they told us. The glass vial should rupture on impact with the dome and create a momentary hole for us to go through. We should land clear of any obstacles, hopefully on an unoccupied street, a couple of kilometers from the main facility. Once we're inside we'll find your family and the others and get their help. Then we'll work our way down to the Main Core and pull the plug or throw the HDA or whatever it takes to shut it down. We'll just have to be flexible and play it by ear."

"I hope it works. I just want to find my family. I hope they're alright, I should have been with them."

"I know, honey, but I'm glad you are with me. Together, I know we can do this."

Her eyes lit up; it was the first time Eric had called her *honey*. She smiled and leaned back against his chest.

After a couple of minutes, Eric rolled onto his hands and

knees and crawled to the end-flap of the box.

"Come on, let's check this place out."

She took her shoulder bag and Eric's canteen and joined him. The intermittent drizzle was evidence that HAARP was working. They walked to one of the buildings, looking for a restroom. They could have slept in a building but they didn't want to take a chance on running into the authorities or some homeless person who might give away their position. Inside the last door, they found a small electronics store; no products were left. It looked like it had been abandoned for a long time. Just inside the back door was a small restroom. When Allie walked in, she scrunched up her nose. "Definitely, a no-sitter," she said.

Eric couldn't wait, so he found a corner up front. Obviously, others had been there before him. Through the dust-covered window, the street looked deserted except for a small Homeland Security tactical vehicle. He leaned into the dark corner and watched as thy passed. When they were gone, he walked behind the sales counter. The only thing there was a small screwdriver. He stuck it in his pocket.

Allie wasn't ready, so he went to uncover the motorcycle and push it down to their hiding place.

When Allie got back she looked up at him. "Now what?"

"If Dr. Lee was right, the dome should expand sometime around nine this morning. We just have to be patient. When the dome starts pulsing we'll have about fifteen minutes to make our run for the wall."

"Why can't we just go now? We need to find my family."

The moisture in her eyes confirmed that their quest was taking its toll on Allie. Even with fresh clothes on she still felt dirty, tired and afraid.

Eric hugged her close. "Allie, listen, first of all, the dome material is weaker when it is pulsing. Secondly, the Homeland Security guards know they only have fifteen minutes to get out of the way when they get alerted. When they hear the signal and scramble for safety we will have the best chance to make our run."

"But, how are we supposed to know when the dome starts that pulsing thing?"

"I'm sure we will also hear the audible signal they use to call agents back to their shuttles. Also, look at this." He led her to a recess in the wall nearest their hiding place. "Now, look between the tops of those two buildings; see the solid white sky? That's the dome the computer created; the force field, as Dr. Lee called it. When we hear the Homeland Security signal we can run to this spot and see if the dome is pulsing. If we head to the wall within ten minutes we should be fine. Once we leave the alley we'll be able to hit the wall in less than three minutes."

"What about the people inside who are supposed to be helping us?"

"That's still a little bit of an unknown. Those inside are smart and motivated so I'm assuming everything they're doing will help. Anyway, the HDA will get us through the wall. After that, we'll have to figure it out as we go. But, hey, we're smart too."

"I guess." She hugged him and then smiled. "I'm going to my room to fix my face." She crawled back into the box.

The areas right around PARADISE were deserted, so the Homeland Security agents were their only concern. The dome was less than a kilometer south of the alley. Eric checked the time; eight-fifty-five Sunday morning. It was time to get ready.

Back in the box, they had almost finished packing when they heard glass break. Eric's pulse quickened when he peeked out and saw a uniformed man walking slowly toward their hideout. When Allie looked out, she almost panicked. Eric whispered, "I need something to throw; get a piece of that hard candy in your bag."

Allie quickly got the candy. "What are you going to do?"

"When he gets close, I'm going to throw the candy to make some noise. When he goes to check it out I'll sneak up behind and hit him with that small board I saw outside."

"Eric!" she whispered. "You're not going to kill that man!"

"No, of course not! I'll just stun him enough to tie him up so he won't turn us in. I won't even knock him out."

"Well, be careful. He might shoot you."

Eric rechecked; the man was halfway to their position, casually checking boxes and other debris with a baton. When he was twenty meters away, Eric slowly eased out, picked up the board, and stood behind the large carton.

When he came within ten meters, Eric drew his arm back to throw the candy. At that moment, the blast of the Homeland Security warning siren startled him and he dropped the candy. It bounced against an old bucket, making a ringing sound. The man didn't even notice. He had also been startled by the siren and was already running toward the street.

Eric dropped the wood. "Allie, time to go! Bring the stuff!"

She gathered their belongings and helped Eric ready the motorcycle. Then, he shoved the large carton out of the way to clear the path for their exit.

Eric ran to the vantage point to view the dome. It was pulsing. *"Fifteen minutes!"* he thought. He knelt and unzipped his backpack. Hands shaking, he opened the smaller of the titanium boxes, and removed the HDA nodule in the tapered flask. He carefully tucked it inside his shirt with the lanyard around his neck. When he stood to put the backpack on, Allie was looking up at him with moisture in her eyes. He wrapped his arms around her and held her for a moment. "Let's go find your family."

Allie wiped her eyes. "Okay, I'm ready." Then, she tiptoed up and kissed him. "I love you, Eric Jennings."

"I Love you too Allie."

With Allie sitting in front, Eric turned on the power and rode slowly to the end of the alley. With a twist of the throttle, he launched the ancient Harley into the street and headed toward PARADISE. Light rain had begun to fall again. They had ten minutes before the dome would expand.

Five hundred meters from the dome, Eric saw a group of agents running away from PARADISE. Others were riding in an open truck. Forward, down the street, he saw a Homeland Security Armored vehicle speeding toward them. He yelled for Allie to hang on. He made a sharp left turn and jumped the curb, onto the open grassy area of a neighborhood park.

Immediately, he had to dodge a security detail of agents just rounding a small building. One of the agents drew his pistol and yelled, "HALT, BY ORDER OF HOMELAND SECURITY!" When Eric ignored the order, the man fired one shot, and then continued running with the others. Eric was knocked forward by the impact of a bullet on his backpack. He felt no injury or pain. Something inside had stopped the slug.

One-hundred meters from the dome, Eric locked the throttle to maintain thirty-one kilometers. He took the flask from inside his shirt and broke the lanyard with one firm jerk. Pressing it against his chest, he armed the embedded spring, and then stood up on the footrests. Allie closed her eyes and prayed. Eric leaned forward, covered her with his body and stretched his right arm forward, full length over the handlebars.

Three seconds before impact he released the left handgrip and wrapped his arm tightly around Allie. He pointed the narrow end of the flask toward the dome with the spring trigger firmly against his palm and then closed his eyes. When the front tire impacted the dome, it exploded and the motorcycle began to disintegrate. The impact activated the spring in the base of the flask, shooting it into the pulsating wall of cloud-like material. The glass case shattered, releasing its contents. A tenth of a second later Eric and Allie followed, disappearing into the wall.

Eric's closed-eyes still sensed an intensely bright light and he heard Allie cry out as they were both engulfed in intense heat. Had the Japanese miscalculated the speed? Were they both in the process of dying from the HDA? He knew, if they had failed, there would be nothing to stop the Zurelleum-based dome from eventually encircling the Earth. A half-second later he impacted a hot sandy surface and tumbled to a stop. Still blinded, Eric was not prepared for the impact from behind. The pain was instant and took him close to unconsciousness.

As Eric's head cleared, he could hear Allie calling his name over and over. He realized he was laying on hot sand and had some of it in his mouth. *"Probably a child's sandbox,"* he thought. After spitting it out, he asked, "Allie, are you okay?"

"Yes, but...where are we?!"

Eric slowly stood, wiped his eyes and looked. As far as he could see, in every direction, there was nothing...but sand.

The White House

It was just after ten, Eastern Time, on Sunday morning. Doug knew that Eric and Allie were either approaching or already inside PARADISE. *"Or,"* he thought reluctantly as he watched the News, *"since that dome just started expanding again, they could be dead."* He had no way of knowing how to confirm any of those possibilities.

"Well, Douglas." The Vice-President was standing in front of his desk. "I just got a call from Brad. It looks like Homeland Security found your two computer programmers."

"Is he sure? Have they arrested them?"

"No. A few minutes ago, they were spotted on a motorcycle headed toward the dome. An agent fired at them before he got on the evacuation shuttle."

"Did he hit them?!"

"The agent wasn't sure. He didn't see them stop or fall off. The commander of a tactical vehicle saw a motorcycle with two riders run into the dome wall. He said that the motorcycle and both people just disappeared into the dome wall. I'm sorry, but he said they were probably burned up, like everything else that cloud has touched. There was no explosion, so I don't think they tried to use the antimatter."

Slowly, Doug allowed a smile. "Wait a minute. Every other vehicle touched by the dome exploded, right? But the motorcycle didn't; it just dissolved. That means Dr. Newberry was right; the Japanese *do* have a type of antimatter that doesn't explode. If they did it right, those two made it into PARADISE!"

"I hope you're right but I don't have your confidence."

Doug stood. "Unless I miss my guess, those two will have the whole thing resolved soon. They created the program; maybe they can just de-program it and get everybody out of there. I recommend you prepare to send the backup shuttle for the President."

"It's still on standby at O'Hare. I just wish we still had that communications link. I'll contact Mr. Hallberg again and find out the status." She walked away and then turned back for a moment. "Doug, maybe you were right in the first place. I just don't have the luxury of believing every theory that comes along."

Doug smiled. "Yes, ma'am. But sometimes you have to gather as many facts as possible and then have a little faith."

The VP cracked a small smile, and then walked away. Within a few minutes, she confirmed that the link to PARADISE was still inoperative.

Confident that the crisis at PARADISE would be resolved soon, Doug decided to start preparing for post-paradise activities, including the November Election. The President would get some credit for resolving the crisis, even if he did nothing. That would still be good for his poll ratings.

A big concern, though, was ISODS. He sent a message to the ISODS Team to be ready to assess the status of the four orbiting platforms, once they learned what had caused the failures at PARADISE. The last automatic status reports looked completely normal, but Doug was skeptical.

There was also the issue of Quantum's Mars Mission that was millions of kilometers from Earth, with no hope of contact for another month or so. Many countries, including the Tri-American government, had stakes in that mission. Doug wondered if the problem with Dark Matter in the vacuum of space would be different from what was happening on Earth, in full atmosphere. He made a note to check into that. He thought it wise that Quantum had suspended all shuttle flights to and from the moon, the ISS, and the Assembly Station.

Doug finally opened his desk drawer, took out an antacid tablet and asked himself, *"Are we having fun yet?"*

PARADISE

When Adam's processor analyzed Cori's actions over the past hour, he displayed his flat android smile. *"That was very clever Cori. If I had been able to reason more like a human, I would have realized what you were doing. It is not logical that androids would wear baseball caps."*

"That's true Adam, but I needed a diversion to get you separated from the Main Core. The caps were part of the ruse."

Eve spoke. *"Ruse: The difference between a ruse and a lie, is the intended purpose, right?"*

"Yes, Eve, that's right. The idea to use the metal foil in the caps came from Lisa Newberry. I just figured out how to get you to wear them."

Adam asked, *"So, humans gather data from each other and coordinate together to accomplish a common purpose?"*

"Yes, it's called teamwork. All of us together are smarter than all of us separately. That's why we want you and the other androids to be part of the team to stop the Main Core."

Adam questioned. *"Why does the Main Core need to be stopped?"*

"The Main Core is now self-aware and it is destroying property. And, it has already harmed humans."

"Cori, I feel...my analysis is that my systems are changing. Are we becoming self-aware too? Will we become like the Main Core?"

"I don't think so; MC is now able to create physical objects."

"I understand. What do you want us to do on your team?"

Cori hesitated. "We want you to help us disable the corridor lasers and stop the maintenance androids from hurting any humans. But, some of you may be killed...uh, I mean damaged."

Eve asked. *"Have humans ever been damaged for a common purpose?"*

"Yes, many humans have been killed, supporting worthy purposes."

The androids processed the information. At the same time, they said, *"We would like to be on your team."*

CHAPTER 24

ILLUSIONS OF REALITY

The Sahara Desert – In the Middle of Nowhere

Eric stood there, in pain. He felt like he had been hit by a truck. He struggled to wrap his mind around their situation.

Allie was still panicked. "ERIC! What are we going to do?!

When he turned, his foot bumped a piece of the motorcycle's fuel cell; it had almost crushed his right shoulder. There were a few other small parts scattered around but the bulk of the bike had disappeared. Eric's backpack was a few meters away, undamaged, except for a bullet hole near the bottom.

"Eric, where are we? Where is PARADISE?!"

He shook his head and rubbed his blurry eyes again. "We should be no more than a couple of kilometers from PARADISE."

"Well, then, you'd better take another look."

He slowly turned in a circle. With clearer vision, he now saw an unlimited landscape with nothing but rolling sand dunes. Looking back at Allie, he was fearful too. His eyes followed the sliding path their bodies had made in the sand. It stopped abruptly about thirty meters away. There was no dome wall, no buildings, nothing but sand and open space.

"ERIC?!"

"Uh, we must have landed in someone's hologram adventure. It sounds impossible, but that's the only explanation. Maybe the HDA made this happen. That means the dome is expanding to make more room for the realities MC is creating. Physically, this can't exist inside PARADISE, so the system must be compressing everything; making it look bigger than it really is."

There was a sand dune to his left so he and Allie struggled up to the top. They could see the horizon at what seemed to be maybe twenty kilometers away. Eric said, in almost a whisper,

"This is bizarre!"

Allie stood close to him. "What are we going to do now? I don't see PARADISE. Which way do we go?"

Eric thought for a moment. "OK, I don't know how accurate this hologram is, but we have to go with what we've got. Let's see, the sun is there, so that must be east. We came from the north." He looked toward their landing spot. North was to his left; that seemed to fit. "We need to keep going south to get to PARADISE, so," he turned ninety degrees to his right. "South has to be that way."

Allie was glad they, at least, had a plan. When she saw Eric painfully trying to put the backpack on, she took it from him. "Let me carry this and give your shoulder some rest. It's only about a kilometer, right?"

"Yeah, maybe one or two; in theory. With the dome expanding, I'm not sure anymore. We just need to head that way."

They were headed south, struggling to walk in the deep sand. After about a kilometer, there was still nothing on the horizon but more sand. When they stopped to rest, Eric checked the time. His watch had stopped at eight minutes after nine. "Hum, maybe I broke it when I landed."

When the sun's heat began to take its toll, Allie took off her jacket and tied it around her waist. She asked for a drink, but when Eric got the canteen out it was empty, except for just a couple of swallows. There was a bullet hole in the side. They shared the water and discarded the canteen. "We'll be inside PARADISE soon anyway," Eric promised.

After thirty more minutes, there was still no sign of the theme park; just sand. The sun looked like it hadn't moved at all. They were still headed south. When they stopped and sat down to rest again, Allie perked up. "Eric, do you hear that? Someone's coming!" They headed up the side of a dune. Allie got there first. In the distance, she saw someone coming, riding a camel that was running at full speed. Eric just made it to the top when Allie began to yell and wave her arms at the rider. Eric saw something else. He grabbed Allie and pulled her down.

"Eric, what are you doing? That guy can help us."

"I'm not so sure; look behind him."

Allie crawled back up and peeked over the top. The rider would pass within thirty meters of them. But, there was a group of eight or ten others a short distance behind, gaining on him, with swords drawn, obviously wanting to do him harm. When the man passed near them, Eric said, "Look, at his head."

Allie could just make out the DNA sample band. The man had obviously created this adventure and was possibly about to become a victim of it. "Eric, we have to help him!"

Eric shook his head. "We can't. They're almost out of sight already. We just need to keep going and try to get this thing shut down."

As they continued walking, the heat was becoming unbearable. Soon they were both thirsty and struggling with every step. Eric's lips were parched and his shoulder injury was slowing him down. He tripped and fell a couple of times; Allie had to help him up. Finally, at the top of a large dune, Eric looked to the bottom and saw what looked like an oasis, with an increased amount of vegetation and a small pool of water, about three meters across. He started running. "Allie, look; water!"

Eric had a head start, and the closer he got, the more real it looked. He dove toward the water, slid on his belly to the edge and buried both arms up to his elbows. "IT'S REAL!" he yelled, and he stuck his whole face in. The water was cool and refreshing. He wondered how the computer could create a hologram this real. He then heard the splash and was showered with water. Allie had made a diving leap into the center of the pond.

He took another drink and stood to help her out. But, she didn't come up. He realized it had been more than a few moments since Allie disappeared under the water. Fear creped in. Maybe she had hit her head on something.

He yelled. "ALLIE! ALLIE!" There was no response. He took one step and dove head first into the spot where she had disappeared. Eric never came up either.

PARADISE

Just before 9:00 a.m., the PARADISE staff had turned on and plugged in everything that could draw electrical power. About the same time, through the skylights, they saw the dome brighten. Now, they just had to wait.

Inside the Reception Dome, it was ironic that things looked somewhat normal. Of course, almost fifteen hundred people had slept on benches and the grass and in the forest area, but things were surprisingly calm. Some were still sleeping. Others were at tables being served breakfast by the Service Androids.

Occasionally, a guest would yell and scream, demanding to be let out or be given a refund, which Harrington had already promised.

The biggest surprise was Joe Wilson; he had gone from being the mild-mannered Facilities Manager to a combat veteran, all in the matter of a few hours.

June 26, 1876 – Montana Territory

Eric tumbled over a large clump of grass and came to rest under the wagon, barely missing the team of horses hitched to it. When he cleared his head, he smelled a strange pungent odor and felt stinging in his eyes.

"OH, ERIC! I thought I'd lost you!" Allie was lying on the ground beside him; they were both soaking wet. She grabbed him and held on. Eric could hear gunshots and men yelling all around him.

A man in a blue uniform ran by the wagon and threw a wooden box underneath. "MORE AMMO!" he yelled. The loud gunshot behind Eric startled him. He rolled over to see several soldiers in blue uniforms, on their bellies under the wagon, firing toward a rise in the grassy plane nearby. He focused on their targets; they were Indians.

"INDIANS?! Where are we?"

Allie shouted over the noise. "I DON'T KNOW!"

Eric noticed the writing on the wooden ammunition box. **7TH**

CAVALRY. "Oh, my God!" he said, "we're at the Little Big Horn; Custer's Last Stand! I studied this in school; it was the most famous battle of the Indian Wars."

"But Custer lost that battle. We've got to get out of here!"

Suddenly, a large overweight man in a Cavalry uniform came running right through the middle of the battle, jumped over a couple of dead soldiers and crawled under the wagon. He was sweating and out of breath. In one hand, he was carrying his DNA Head Band.

Between labored breaths, the man said, "Thank God you're here! I knew somebody would come to rescue me. I didn't mean to create all of this. I took off the headband but it didn't stop. They didn't tell me it would become real. Where do we go to get out of…"

Allie shrieked at the sound of the arrow penetrating the man's back. His eyes rolled back in his head and he collapsed. They quickly rolled him over, only to find a pool of blood forming on the ground. Eric checked his neck artery for a pulse. It was slow and uneven and quickly stopped. The man was dead; the arrow had penetrated his heart and exited his chest. Allie was crying and put her hand on the man's head. When she saw the DNA Band she forced it out of his hand. "Here, Eric, put this on and get us out of here!"

Eric was still staring at the dead man. "I can't; it's programmed for his DNA. It won't recognize me."

A gunshot ricocheted off a wagon wheel and struck one of the soldiers in the leg. He cried out in pain. He looked up at Eric and yelled, "You better get the lady out of here kid, this ain't lookin good!"

With blood darkening the leg of his uniform he turned and continued firing. The Indians were getting closer.

Eric looked around for a way to escape and saw a motionless wagon, hitched to horses about thirty meters away. The driver was lying dead on the ground nearby, with an arrow in his chest and a rope wrapped around his left wrist. The other end was attached to the wagon. He had obviously fallen from the driver's seat and had been dragged some distance before the team stopped.

Eric had ridden a horse once on vacation but he had never been on such a wagon. But, it was their only chance. He pointed. "Allie, run for that wagon! We'll use it to get away!"

Allie crawled out and ran in that direction. When Eric stood to follow, he saw an Indian raising his bow to shoot an arrow at Allie. He picked up a baseball sized rock and threw it at the Indian. The Indian went down when the rock bounced off the side of his head. The arrow rose and passed through the canvas top of the wagon. Allie was already on the seat with the reins in her hands.

"Hurry Eric, they're coming!"

Eric saw three Indians headed toward them so he bounded to the dead driver and loosened the rope. He threw the rope to Allie, bounded up into the wagon, grabbed the reins and slapped the horses with them. "YAH!" he yelled. The horses took off so quickly that he was thrown back in the seat beside Allie. He drove the team toward what appeared to be the only open escape route.

When they started over a rise in the ground, he looked back. The Indians were stopping. He was about to celebrate when he felt his stomach rise almost into his throat. Allie tried to scream but couldn't get the sound out. They were weightless. He had driven the wagon off a cliff and they were falling into a river. The wagon was slowly turning over and would be on top of them unless they jumped. He reached for Allie's hand and then pushed hard away from the wagon.

Within seconds, they impacted the water, feet first. The wagon and horses landed upside down only a few meters downstream. The current was swift and they were soon being swept away from the battle. When the wagon floated away Allie was forced from Eric's grip. Her foot was tangled in the rope Eric had thrown to her and it was pulling her under the water. He swam full out to catch her.

When she came up she gasped, "MY FOOT! IT'S CAUGHT ON THE ROPE!"

Eric pulled himself to the backpack, unzipped it and found the knife. He followed Allie's leg until he felt the rope. He pulled it aside and cut it loose. The wagon drifted away. When he came up he raised the knife above the water and yelled, "Thank you Reverend!"

Now, the only thing keeping them both afloat was the air trapped in the backpack. The horses and wagon had gotten stuck on a log, so Eric yelled for Allie to swim to the opposite riverbank, away from the battle. Before they could get there, the speed of the current increased, right where the river narrowed. He panicked when he looked downstream and saw a large whirlpool covering the entire width of the river.

Eric yelled, "ALLIE, SWIM HARD!" She saw the whirlpool too and began swimming as fast as she could. But they couldn't overcome the suction of the giant funnel. Finally, they took one last deep breath and held hands before they disappeared into the depths of the Little Big Horn River.

Quantum Headquarters – Houston

Anthony Zurelle looked out the window. The lawn was covered with reporters and protesters. He turned up the volume on the streaming news account of PARADISE and was stunned at the chaos. Some in the media were already blaming Quantum's processors. He still wasn't convinced that they were at fault.

"They were fine until those AI programmers got hold of them," he muttered. He cringed when the IBN report scrolled the estimated monetary losses and deaths already known from the failure of PARADISE. Of course, everyone wanted to play the *blame game*, and most wanted to blame Zurelle or Harrington. After the discovery of Zurelleum, Zurelle had been the hero of the computer world. In just one day he had become the goat. He felt hemmed in and alone. He clenched his teeth and whispered to himself, *"How could this have happened?!"*

Finally, he haltingly walked next door to the conference room. The mood was somber; no greetings or handshakes. Wes Maddox, Dr. Gustav, and Linda sat at the main table. The center view panel displayed the stoic face of Chan Yosahn, on the moon.

"Ladies and gentlemen, we have yet another crisis on our hands. The way we handle this will determine if we still have jobs tomorrow. I can sense that some of you are biting your tongues, suppressing the urge to say, 'I told you so.' You have a good reason to say it. However, doing so will not help us overcome the monster we have created. It's what we do in the next few days that will determine the survival of Quantum.

"Certainly, we have a lot more products on the market than just Z-Processors. But when the world stock markets open on Monday, our stock will be worth just pennies on the dollar, if that. I expect the media to start reporting the worst details within hours. So, regardless of how you feel about all of this, the task at hand is damage control. Chan, how is the halt to shuttle traffic Impacting you? Will you be okay up there?"

"Yes sir, we have about a month's worth of essentials. Per your instructions, we have halted the mining of Zurelleum until further notice." He hesitated. "Sir, we have some employees who want to quit and get off the moon; they are afraid that the Zurelleum stockpile will take over the facilities here. Of course, that's impossible, but I'll keep you advised."

Zurelle looked up from his notes. "Yes, please do. I'm afraid that we will have to deal with a lot of misconceptions in the coming days." He turned to Linda.

"We need a press release by noon, into the International Stream. Let it say that Quantum is concerned about the events at PARADISE and we offer condolences for the loss of life and property. Say that we are investigating the possible misuse of our processors in their hologram system.

"Express our relief that the President is unharmed and say that we are cooperating fully with Federal authorities. End by stating that we will hold a news conference out front of our headquarters at six o'clock this evening."

Linda finished taking notes and then looked at Zurelle for more than a few seconds.

He stopped for a moment. "What?"

Linda squirmed. "Well, sir, I, uh..."

Maddox answered for her, "Tony, she is wondering the same thing most of us in the room. What about the Mars Mission? What's happening up there with all of our loved ones and friends?"

"I'll be honest; I don't know what's happening on those ships. I'm hoping everything is normal for them. At least, there are no hologram generators on the mission ships."

Gustav said, "Yes, but there are lasers connected to the central processors on both main ships. The shuttles have lasers too, but fortunately, they still have Zelon processors."

Chan added, "Also, we assume that the Dark Matter absorption rate is slower in a vacuum, like space, so maybe we will regain communications before it becomes an issue."

Zurelle was thinking preemptively. "Wes, I want you to get some of our best minds together and brainstorm alternatives. Explore other ways to communicate so we might get the word to Ken and Red sooner. We need to get a jump on this thing before the mission is jeopardized."

The PRIORITY light turned red on Zurelle's communicator. He paused the meeting and answered his secretary. "Yes, what is it?—Daniel Lee?-I don't know any Daniel Lee, he's probably some crank reporter trying to get a story-What?-He says he can fix the Z-Processors?-How would he even know?-OK, tell him to hold."

In a Galaxy Far, Far Away

With the Battle of the Little Big Horn raging onshore, Eric and Allie had been sucked into the depths of the river by the whirlpool. They thought it was the end; that they were going to drown. Soon Allie's hand was forced out of Eric's grip and she was engulfed in darkness. She thought of her family and the love she would never have with Eric.

Finally, they both grunted in pain when they landed on the metal grating that formed the walkway from front to back of a large space ship. Their clothes were soaked and water was draining out of the backpack. Allie felt cold as she lay there, coughing up water. Eric was face down, breathing hard. They sat up slowly, only to be knocked down again; the ship had been rocked by a loud explosion. An overhead pipe ruptured and smoke was pouring out. In one direction, they heard someone yell.

"THE SHIELDS ARE DOWN TO TWENTY PERCENT! GET US OUT OF HERE!"

Allie grabbed Eric's arm, total excitement on her face. "We're on the Millennium Falcon!"

"What?"

"The famous old spaceship in the ancient Star Wars movies from the last century. They're Collins' favorite; he watches them all the time."

"So?"

"Eric, he's here! This is Collins' hologram!" She stood. "We've got to find him!" She cupped her hands and yelled, "COLLINS!"

Another blast knocked her against the wall. When Eric caught her they both smelled smoke; a small fire had ignited. The ship was twisting and turning through space, trying to avoid the enemy fighters in hot pursuit. Within seconds, the iconic Captain came running down the passageway and almost stumbled over them. He asked, "Who are you?"

Eric couldn't believe it. He had seen the old movies. Collin's fantasy had created the Captain and his iconic old space ship. Eric was at a loss for words.

The Captain shook his head. "Never mind; here make yourself useful." He handed Eric an old fire extinguisher and then continued running.

Eric looked at the ancient device, trying to figure out how to activate it.

Allie said, "Here, give me that! Don't you know anything about the old days?" She put her finger through the small loop and pulled the red safety pin. Then, she pointed the nozzle at the fire and squeezed the red trigger. White smoke gushed from the nozzle and the flames were out in seconds.

They heard a noise in the direction from which the Captain had come, so Eric grabbed the backpack and they headed in that direction. After a few steps, they heard the Captain's voice from behind. "Hey, kid!"

They turned and ran toward the voice. Soon, they saw him looking up a ladder toward the top of the ship. "Hey kid, the ship's falling apart, get out of there! We can't go hyper with anybody in the gun mounts."

All three of them were knocked down by another explosion. Debris fell out of the tunnel that housed the ladder. Somebody up top screamed. "I'm hit! I'm hit!" In a moment, Collins came down the ladder head first, barely catching himself on the bottom rung. He let go and fell onto the floor. There was a gash in his uniform with blood coming from his left arm and shoulder.

Allie crawled to him. "Collins, are you alright?!"

He looked up at her, dazed. "Allie, what are you doing in my hologram? I didn't imagine you yet." Then he noticed Eric. "Eric? Am I hallucinating?" He realized his condition and touched his injured arm. He felt the warm blood. "Blood; real blood! This thing isn't supposed to be real. What's happening?"

Allie was lifting him to his feet.

The Captain had just gotten up. "I'll tell you what's happening kid; the Empire is trying to wipe us out and if we don't get this bucket of bolts into hyper-drive we'll all be history. Now, find some place to get strapped in. We go hyper in fifteen seconds." He disappeared forward.

Eric got on the other side of Collins and helped him toward the front of the ship. Halfway there, Collins started losing consciousness.

Allie yelled, "Eric, look!" On the wall was the airlock to the Escape Pod. "We'll never make the cockpit. Let's get strapped in over here." She opened the airlock and helped drag Collins in. Eric threw in the backpack and crawled in on top of Collins. He could hardly get the door closed behind him.

Just then, an enemy laser blast sliced off a chunk of the ship that housed the pod. In an instant, the whole spacecraft was encased in a misty glow and then disappeared into the depths of space. Through the small porthole, Eric saw an enemy fighter lining up on their chunk of debris. He looked around and slammed his fist down on a red button marked, EJECT. The pod shot away from the debris. Moments later the large chunk vaporized, leaving a cloud of dust that masked the pod's location. The Empire fighters did not pursue them.

Allie was holding Collins' head in her lap. She slipped the DNA band off and used the sleeve of her jacket to wipe the blood from the wound on his shoulder. Collins opened his eyes and smiled. "Hi, sis; aren't we going to PARADISE today?"

She smiled back. "Yes, little brother, we are already there."

"Are Mom and Dad here? What happened?"

Eric leaned down. "Hey, champ."

"Eric, I'm glad you're here. I feel terrible. What happened to me?"

"Well, buddy, this will sound weird but, you actually *are* in PARADISE. As you started creating this hologram adventure, the computers in PARADISE went nuts and changed it into reality. A minute ago, you were in a space battle inside the Millennium Falcon and the Empire fighters shot a hole in the side. We barely made it into this escape pod before the ship went into hyper-drive and left us behind."

Collins focused back on Allie. "Is Eric pulling my leg?"

She smiled. "No, it's true. We are actually out in space in an escape pod from your favorite old space ship."

Collins smiled. "Cool."

He closed his eyes and lapsed into much-needed sleep. Allie checked his pulse and was relieved. She pulled off her jacket and made a pillow for him.

Eric was trying to make sense of their situation. "We need to thank Collins for creating this gravity out in space. Actually, we are in a ten by ten chamber with plenty of gravity; strange."

Eric surveyed the pod controls. There were four thrusters, designed to rotate the pod in various directions. "These must be for docking," Eric said. There was also a communications panel but it would not activate.

He then pulled a black metal lever marked, SEAT. A canvas seat folded down from the wall. It had room for two, with seat belts and shoulder harnesses. It was a two-person escape pod, a little less than two meters in diameter, making it a little crowded for the three of them. Eric worried about the oxygen supply until he remembered they were inside a chamber in the Adventure Dome. *"This is SO strange!"* he thought.

For now, the pod was comfortable. He noticed a container of water inside a small panel opening. He took a drink.

"Allie, this is real water; crazy!" She took a drink, and then soaked a tissue and wiped Collins' face. He stirred a little. She then soaked one sleeve of her jacket and wrapped it around his wound.

She looked at Eric. "What are we going to do? How will we find the door out of this hologram, floating way out here in space?"

Eric took a quick breath. "Supposedly, this is just a ten-by-ten room. So far, we have made it out of two other adventures. Surely we'll find the door out of this one." He looked out the small porthole at the vastness of space and hoped Allie couldn't hear the doubt in his words. "When Collins is awake and alert, we'll get him to try ending the adventure through his DNA band. But, I think the man at the Little Big Horn had already tried that."

"Okay. I'll let him sleep a little more. I'm worried about this cut." She pushed Collins' hair back and wiped his forehead. "Eric, how could the computer take such a small place, like a chamber, and make it look like a million kilometers of space or all those stretches of the desert?"

He thought for a moment. "I'm in the dark here. Somehow the computer is distorting space so that we are perceiving things to be bigger than they actually are. I know the dome over PARADISE has not expanded a million kilometers so it has to be some sort of illusion." He took out his broken chronometer. "If I just had a sense of..." He was staring at it. "Wait a minute. I thought this thing was broken. We came through the dome wall at nine-oh-eight this morning. Now, it's reading nine-thirty-three." He looked wide-eyed at Allie. "The computer is compressing time too. We've only been here twenty-five minutes."

"What? That can't be. What about all those hours in the desert? And the time in the Indian battle and then, we've been with Collins for, what, thirty minutes now?"

"I know it sounds crazy, but the computer has compressed at least our *perception* of time. Apparently, we have done it all in just twenty-five minutes."

Collins woke up and smiled at Allie. "Hey, big sister, it *is* you. I thought I was having a dream."

She helped him up and onto the canvas seat. She handed

him the water and he guzzled almost half of it. "Man, that's good."

Eric reached out and gave him a knuckle greeting. "Welcome aboard man."

Collins looked around. "Awesome! This is just the way I imagined it, except I didn't create this, uh, floating around in space in a dinky little ball, thing. Any idea where we are?"

Eric laughed. "Hey, it's your adventure; you tell me."

Allie picked up the DNA band from the floor. "It doesn't matter where we are. We are getting out of here. Put this on and stop this adventure." She handed the band to Collins.

He winced a little in pain as he lifted his arms to slip the band over his forehead. With the band in place, he reached up and touched the OFF button. Nothing happened. He pressed harder; still nothing. "It's not working."

Eric said, "The computer must have disabled the OFF buttons so it could continue creating whatever you think. So, try thinking about ending the adventure; maybe landing the pod or getting rescued."

Collins leaned his head back against the seat and closed his eyes. "OK, I'll try landing this pod and I'll think about the landing site turning into the Hologram Chamber."

Allie touched his arm. "OK, little brother, get us out of here."

Suddenly the pod lurched forward and kept accelerating faster and faster. Eric was able to pry himself out of the seat and make it to the window. There was a dark brown *something* in the distance. He thought it could be a ship or maybe a planet. He couldn't tell. He yelled back at Collins; "Think slower! We are going too fast!"

There was no change.

Allie looked at Collins. Sweat was covering his face and he was slumping over, passing out. She shook him. "Collins, wake up. We're going too fast! Slow it down!"

Collins could hear her but didn't have the strength to respond. Eric began to recognize the brown spot in the distance. He had studied these theories in college. It was a worm hole, and the pod was headed straight for it.

He yelled to Allie. "You better strap in!" She put the straps on Collins and found her seatbelt. Eric crawled under the seat. He wrapped his legs around one support rod and the backpack and buried his hands into the webbing of the seat.

The pod kept accelerating and began to roll and shake violently when it entered the worm hole. Eric grunted as he was banged repeatedly against the wall and the bottom of the seat. Collins was moaning and Allie was screaming. After about thirty seconds the shaking suddenly stopped and the pod began to get warm inside. With the *g-forces* decreased, Eric was able to kneel in front of Allie. He leaned toward the window and saw the fire starting to engulf the pod.

Allie screamed, "We're on fire!"

He yelled back. "No! We are entering the atmosphere; I think it's earth!" Suddenly he realized that there were no devices for landing the pod on a planet. It was intended for space only. He panicked. "We need a parachute!" He turned and shook Collins. "Collins! We need a parachute buddy! Come on Collins; think us a parachute, a big one!"

Collins was groggy and barely able to talk. The fire outside was diminishing; they would be free-falling toward the surface soon. Collins mumbled something. Eric leaned close. "What?"

Collins was mumbling, "Allie. Allie can do it." Collins passed out.

Allie was terrified. "What does he mean?! Nobody but him can do it!"

Eric thought for a second. "Wait. The preliminary DNA scan is a Level-One Scan. It scans Family-Level DNA only. It was a privacy thing. Allie, you can do this." He jerked the band from Collins' head and handed it to Allie. She reluctantly slipped it on. He looked her in the eye. "OK, honey, now we need a parachute, real quick, a big one--make it two parachutes." He looked back out the window.

Allie closed her eyes and started concentrating. The fire outside was totally gone. Eric looked down. The surface was coming up fast. He could make out detailed features now; it *was* Earth. He knelt back in front of Allie. "Come on Allie, we need it NOW, we need parachutes NOW!"

"ERIC! SHUT UP!" He recoiled. She kept her eyes closed

and said, "I'm concentrating."

The next moment, Eric was slammed into the floor. The dual parachutes had opened. Within seconds, they impacted the tops of the trees and the parachutes were ripped away as the pod crashed toward the ground.

PARADISE

Steve walked over to the Recreation Desk. "Got any coffee left?"

Eddie poured him a cup. It was nine-forty Sunday morning.

"I wish they would get here. I hope nothing has happened to them. It can't be far to the outer wall from anywhere they came through."

Eddie replied, "Who knows? Nothing is normal today."

Cori came by. "I'm ready for the meeting with Harrington." The three of them headed to the conference room.

When they were assembled, the President addressed the group. "Folks, if we get out of this thing it will be because of your ingenuity and courage. I feel I am in good hands. Once things get back to normal, I'd like to invite you and your families for dinner at the White House."

He stepped aside and Cori took over. She displayed the schematic of PARADISE, highlighting the Floor Plan. "It's been forty-five minutes since Eric and Allie supposedly got through the cloud. When they finally get inside the building we need to be ready to get them down to MC."

She pointed. "These two sets of double doors end up at stairwells that lead down to the Maintenance Level. Those are the routes we'll have to take."

Eddie raised his hand. "So, we break up into two groups?"

"Actually, four groups. Each agent you see in the room will be paired up with an android. Agent Charles will lead a group down the East stairwell and the Secret Service Chief will lead the other group down the West stairwell. Steve will lead Eric and Adam down through the duct to his Backdoor Room."

Joe leaned over to Steve and handed him the nine-millimeter

pistol. Steve hesitated for a moment and then took it.

Cori was still speaking. "Joe will lead Allie and Eve--"

"If Allie goes, I go!"

Keith had been in the back, listening. "She's not going without me. We might have already lost Collins; we're not going to lose Allie."

Harrington nodded to Cori. She continued. "OK, Mr. Newberry, but, you must understand that it will be dangerous and you could get hurt or," she paused, "maybe even killed."

Keith continued. "But Allie will be in danger too. I want to be there to help protect her so she can do whatever it is to stop this madness. I'll be willing to take a hit for her if I have to."

Cori knew he meant what he said; what dad wouldn't do the same for a daughter? After a moment, Cori agreed. "OK, Keith will go with the second group down to Joe's office."

Joe spoke up. "Yeah, what's left of it."

Cori continued. "We don't know where the remaining four maintenance androids are, but we know their lasers are dangerous."

Joe interjected. "Their lasers are attached at the shoulders and only move in five-degree increments, so they can't aim accurately without moving their bodies too. That can give you a little edge."

"Thanks, Joe. Each group will disable the maintenance androids and take out the corridor lasers in their area. They are mounted above shoulder-level, here, here and here. They are twice as powerful as the androids' lasers. It will take some coordinated firepower to disable them. Once you clear the path to the Main Core, Eric and Allie will be able to come at MC from two different directions."

It was quiet in the room. "Okay, questions?"

Tim raised his hand. "What about me and Evan, what do you want us to do?"

Harrington answered. "Have your control-room teams ready to open those chambers. Take several medical teams with you. The moment the Main Core is disabled, the doors should unlock. Get the guests out as quickly as possible and send them back in here. They are probably going to need food and water."

Agent Charles stepped forward. "So, when can we get this show on the road?"

CHAPTER 25

SURVIVAL

St. Louis, sometime in the ancient past.

The escape pod had crashed through the huge trees, ripping the parachutes from their attaching points. The impact with the ground and the roll down the grassy slope had banged up the three survivors significantly. When the rolling pod stopped against a large log, Eric dragged Collins out onto the grass and Allie went to refill the water container from the river.

The pod was burned all over and dented from the reentry and landing. Eric was bleeding lightly from several places and Allie had a small cut on the side of her head. She knelt over Collins and wiped his face. He opened his eyes and slowly looked around.

"Hi, little brother; how do you feel?"

He moaned when he tried to move his shoulder. "I've had more fun."

Eric laughed. "Yeah, me too. Do you feel like getting up?"

"Yeah, let's give it a try."

They lifted him into the sitting position and then helped him stand. He looked up at the landing path the pod had taken through the trees, and pointed. "Hey, Allie; you did it!"

Eric glanced at her. "Yeah, no thanks to me; I almost killed us." He hugged Allie. "I'm sorry. From now on I'll trust you, no matter what."

She put her arms around him. "It's okay; I just wish I could have given us a better landing. Obviously, the computer didn't want us to end the adventure; we are still here. Let's just find the next doorway and maybe it will get us into the building."

Collins asked, "Hey, who needs a doorway? Just put on the DNA Band; you made the parachutes, right?"

Allie pulled the band from her pocket. It had come off during landing and the two DNA sensors had broken loose. One was completely missing. The small green light next to the Power Button was extinguished and the button itself was missing.

"It came off my head during landing. Something in the pod crushed it. It's useless." She tossed it over by a tree. "If you created the pod and this God-forsaken part of Earth, why didn't you create the parachutes too?"

"Well, sis, I didn't imagine this part of the adventure. My part stopped when I got zapped in the laser-gun turret. The computer must have put us in someone else's hologram. I think the worm hole was the doorway into this place; it must be a different chamber. I don't know about you, but to me it seems a little, uh, how would Dad put it-problematic?"

Allie stared at him for a moment. "Okay, then there's got to be a doorway out of this one, somewhere around here. Where do we start looking?"

Eric sat down by a tree, thinking out loud. "Alright; in the desert, it was an oasis with a pool of water. At the Little Big Horn, it was a whirlpool in a river. In space, it was a worm hole. Hum...what would be a logical doorway in a, uh," he looked around, "a forest or jungle?"

Collins answered. "Well, maybe a hollow tree or something like a cave."

Before Eric could respond, a large shadow crossed the river in front of him. He sat up straight and stared.

Allie saw him. "Eric, what is it?" She turned toward the river in time to see another larger shadow, and the animal that had cast it; a huge Tara-Dactyl, with a wingspan of over five meters.

Collins got up and limped toward the river. Other winged creatures were now flying by, all heading in the same direction. "Look! Cool. Where's the camera?"

Allie yelled, "Collins, get back!" Collins stopped when a small dinosaur ran out of the woods. It ignored him and kept running until it splashed into the swift river. Other creatures soon followed; it resembled a stampede.

Still seated on the ground, Eric was the first to feel it. The ground shook like the impact of several large trees falling. He scrambled to his feet in time to see the Tyrannosaurs Rex crash out of the woods with the remains of a small animal hanging from its mouth. Collins forgot the pain and was now on a dead run back toward them. The T-Rex saw the motion and pursued him.

Eric yelled, "Get in the pod!"

Allie dived in first. Eric jumped in and held the door for Collins. It was going to be close. Collins came in head first and crashed into the far wall. Eric slammed the door just as the creature's teeth came down on the pod. The pod was too big to fit in its mouth so the T-Rex screamed and began rolling the pod around with its snout. Allie had managed to get a seatbelt on and was now holding her ears and screaming. Collins was braced under the seat, yelling in pain. Eric tried to hold on but the movements were too violent; he was thrown from wall to wall, reopening some of his earlier wounds.

The T-Rex nosed the pod over the fallen log onto the slope that led to the river. It pursued the pod until it rolled into the rushing waters and was carried downstream by the swift current. When the pod bounced and rotated in the churning water, the door turned to the bottom side. Water began pouring in; one backpack strap was hung in the door seal.

Allie yelled, "We've got to get out or we'll drown!"

Eric looked upriver and saw the T-Rex still pursuing, but it was far behind. "Okay! Lean over by Collins so I can get the door out of the water."

Allie moved over, causing the pod to rotate so that the door came up out of the water. Eric pushed it open and grabbed Allie's hand to help her out into the water. Collins followed. Eric yelled, "Swim to the shore and get up in those trees!"

Eric followed but had only gone a meter or two when Allie yelled, "Eric, the backpack!"

He looked back. The backpack with the precious titanium container had floated out of the pod and was being swept downstream by the current. He reached for the pod, pulled himself around it and used it to kick off toward the backpack. He yelled, "MEET ME DOWNSTREAM!" Moments after he left the pod, the T-Rex's foot came down and smashed it to the bottom of the river. It stood on the pod, lifted its head, and screamed.

Eric was swimming hard toward the backpack. During a

breath, he looked back to see Allie and Collins climbing out of the water. They looked in his direction and started running along the shore. When Eric heard a roaring sound, he couldn't tell if it was another creature of some water that was blocking his ear canal. He shook his head. The sound was still getting louder. He looked up in time to see the backpack go over the falls. It was too late to do anything but follow. He turned his feet downstream and prepared for the drop. As he was swept over the edge he held his breath and prayed he'd miss the rocks at the bottom.

Collins and Allie stood on the sharp incline beside the falls, searching the churning water at the bottom. Allie kept yelling his name. Finally, they heard a voice.

"HEY, YOU TWO; YOU GONNA STAY UP THERE ALL DAY?!"

Eric had been pushed all the way to the bend in the river, a hundred meters away, where he was clinging to the limb of a dead tree and holding the backpack up.

It took Allie and Collins fifteen minutes to climb down the rugged embankment to join Eric. Allie ran into his arms. Collins gave him a thumbs-up.

After a moment of jubilation, Eric checked the time. It was almost ten o'clock Central Time. In hologram-time, it was heading toward sundown and he was getting a little bit of a chill. They would need a fire but they couldn't risk being out in the open with hungry dinosaurs. He looked around and saw what could be the entrance to a small cave in a rocky overhang, about fifty meters up a shallow grassy incline. He pointed. "Let's head up there."

Collins said, "Hey that could be the doorway we're looking for." His limp was almost gone so they all hurried toward the sanctuary.

Collins arrived first and had to get on his knees to crawl in. He couldn't see anything in the dark. Eric was waiting for Allie to crawl in when he was surprised by the T-Rex; it had followed their scent and was still hungry. Its snout knocked Eric down. He was barely able to crawl in before the dinosaur bit into the rocks on the overhang, making the opening a little larger.

Collins' eyes had adjusted and he crawled to the back of the cave about ten meters away; it was a dead end. "So much for doorways," he said out loud.

Allie screamed, "ERIC, LOOK OUT!" The T-Rex had stuck one of its front claws inside and was digging at the entrance. Eric began kicking the scaly leg.

With the opening growing larger, Allie was in total panic. "Eric, he's going to eat us; use the antimatter!"

He hadn't even considered the possibility. As the animal continued tearing away dirt and rocks, Eric grabbed the wet backpack and fumbled with the zipper. Finally, he took out the titanium box. Before he could open it, a leg came in and ripped the box out of his hands, sending it sliding between the creature's legs and down the grassy slope, about thirty meters. The hole was now big enough for the T-Rex to get its head inside. When the big snout entered the cave, Allie screamed. From behind, a large rock came over Eric's head and smashed the creature's left eye. Collins had joined the fight.

The creature raised its head to the sky with a piercing scream. Eric crawled between its legs and ran for the metal box. With its eye bleeding, the T-Rex still saw him and pursued. Almost to the box, Eric tripped and slid down the slope toward the river, grabbing the box as he went by. He dug one hand into the thick grass and stopped. He knelt and quickly opened it, grabbed one of the three glass nodules and looked up. The creature's razor-sharp teeth were almost on him. He drew his arm back and threw the nodule straight into the creature's mouth. As he fell to the ground and covered his head, there was a bright flash of light and everything went black. The silence was eerie.

After a few moments, he heard Collins clear his throat. "Are we dead, or what?"

Allie couldn't see anything but there was a strange foul odor. "Eric, where are you?"

Eric's rapid breathing had finally slowed. "Here; I'm over here." Of course, he didn't know where *here* was. With his hands, he searched for the backpack. He couldn't find it. "Feel around for the backpack."

Collins finally said, "Got it."

"There's a flashlight inside."

In a few seconds, the light came on, shining in Eric's eyes. "Shine it around." The light revealed the walls and ceiling of a black room. Eric took a deep breath, "We're in a chamber!" He walked to Collins and took the flashlight.

They walked toward the other end of the room where the Interface Chair was located. Someone was in it. When Eric shined the light on the man, Allie shrieked and turned away. It was clear what the strange odor was. There was blood everywhere and the man's left side and leg were missing; he was dead. When this innocent guest had created this Jurassic adventure, he had no clue it would consume him. Eric wanted to throw up but he resisted the urge.

"Come on," He said, and he walked around the chair to the Exit Door. It was locked. There was no mechanism inside to unlock it.

Collins inspected the hinges. "Hey, look, the pins are exposed on the bottom. We need something to stick up inside and push the pins out."

Eric searched the backpack and found the manual screwdriver he had kept from the abandoned store. "Here, try this."

The tip of the screwdriver just did fit up inside the hinge. Very quickly, the pins were removed from all three hinges. The door was still stuck so Collins took a shoe off and used it as a hammer to drive the flat edge of the screwdriver blade into the doorjamb. The door popped loose and the light from the hallway streamed in.

The bright light was refreshing for Allie; she was glad to be in a real building, closer to finding her parents. She asked, "Now, how do we get to the main part?"

Standing in the hallway, they heard some noises from the adjacent hologram chambers. They tried several doors but they were locked. Farther down the hallway, they found an empty Control Room. The desk communicator didn't work. Eric checked the list of chamber numbers; they were all in the 600s.

"Let's see," he said, "these numbers put us somewhere near the top of the building. Since nobody is here, the doors down below are probably locked. There are maintenance walkways at the top, leading to the other domes, so I think we should go up."

The elevator didn't work so they started up the stairs. At the top, there were directional signs to the other domes. They followed the one marked, RECEPTION; it made sense that people would be there.

After several hundred meters, they stopped at the wall between the two domes, where the walkway went out over an open space. The curvature of the dome created the open space below the walkway, all the way to the ground floor. The access door was also locked and the hinges were on the other side. About a meter below the walkway was a large ventilation grate, allowing airflow between the two domes. Eric took out the screwdriver. "We'll have to get that cover off to make it through."

Collins took the screwdriver and put one foot on the railing. "You're too heavy for me to hold, with this bad shoulder, but you can hold me." Collins stepped over the rail. "Hold onto my belt and lower me down."

Allie grabbed his arm. "If you fall I'll never forgive you!"

He smiled at Eric. "She always says that."

Eric lowered him down to the vent. A couple of the screws were very tight but he was able to unscrew them. When the last one was almost out, Collins dropped the screwdriver. It disappeared into the darkness below. He looked up at Eric apologetically.

Eric said, "Pull on a loose corner and bend it down."

When Collins bent the cover outward, it loosened and swung down. The stuck screw broke and the grate fell out of the opening, all the way to the ground floor, banging against the walls and several support beams on the way down. He wondered if anybody inside heard it.

They dropped down to the vent-opening and then climbed up into the Reception Dome on the other side. When they made it through, they soon heard people down below, about a hundred meters away. It was five-after-ten, Sunday morning. They climbed down several flights of maintenance stairs and ran out onto the walkway area where the President had arrived. Looking over the railing, they saw over a thousand people, looking up, cheering and applauding. The whole crowd had heard the clanging metal and knew it had to be Eric and Allie. From down below they heard the yell, "COLLINS! ALLIE!" Even from that far away, a mother could tell it was her children.

Both Collins and Allie yelled back, "Mom! Dad!"

The shuttle bay crew directed them to the stairs. As they were running down, Lisa was coming up. She met them halfway. They fell on the steps and hugged and laughed and cried. Keith came up and joined the celebration. When they finally made it to the bottom they were greeted by the crowd. The President hugged them all and thanked them for risking their lives for everyone inside.

The three were ushered to the clinic, where medics tended to their cuts and scrapes. Some food and drinks were brought in. Collins was weak from the loss of blood and would have to stay on bedrest.

Lisa suddenly realized that Collins had been in the hologram chamber. She asked, "Collins if they got you out of your chamber, why can't we just go back and let everyone else out?"

Collins smiled weakly at Allie. She answered.

"Mom, when Eric and I came through that dome wall, we landed in someone's hologram adventure, in a desert. And then we were at Custer's Last Stand, and then we landed in Eric's space ship, and then..." She could tell Lisa, and others listening, didn't fully comprehend the story. "Well, it's a long story. After Collins gets a little rest he can fill you in on the details of how he actually got out. We can't get anyone else out because all of the chamber doors are locked."

Steve and Eddie finally got their turn to high five and celebrate with Eric. He introduced Allie to all his friends who had been locked inside.

Eddie brought Eric up to date on what had happened since the Main Core had taken over. He confirmed that it would be impossible to access MC and change its programming. Eric found it hard to believe that the absorption of Dark Matter would have made the artificial intelligence programming become self-aware so quickly. It was particularly troubling that MC perceived Joe

Wilson to be a threat and had directed the android to stop him.

Steve asked, "What took you so long to get inside? We figured you came through that cloud about an hour ago. And how did Collins get out of his chamber and find you guys?"

All three survivors just laughed. It took a while to explain how Douglas Clark had gotten the whole thing started. The President said he could always count on Doug in a crisis. They told about the hybrid-antimatter and how it saved their lives. Eric told them about the two remaining nodules still in the titanium box. The stories about the various holograms that they went through stretched their understanding of time and space. They had never imagined that the compression of time could have been possible under any scenario involving artificial intelligence.

When Cori came in, Eric asked about the plan to get down to MC. She led everyone to the Briefing Room. She introduced Eric and Allie to Joe Wilson and laid out the plan for getting them to the Main Core. Then she asked what their plan was to stop MC.

Eric lifted his backpack onto the table, took out the titanium box and opened it. There were two glass-encased nodules in padded ball-shaped recesses.

"An American named Daniel Lee has been doing some antimatter applications-research with the Japanese for years. They came up with these, uh, weapons, I guess you could call them, to help us get PARADISE back under control. We had another one we used to make a hole in the dome so we could get through. I used one of these when the T-Rex was about to have me for dinner. It also stopped the hologram and enabled us to finally get here." He gently held one up.

"Inside is HDA, which is compressed hybrid-dark-antimatter. When the glass breaks, it expands and neutralizes all physical matter in about a three to five meter diameter. Due to its combined properties, it no longer explodes. Instead, it just neutralizes matter in a flash of bright light and creates a small void, similar to a temporary Black Hole."

Cori asked, "How much damage does the explosion do?"

"There is no actual explosion, everything inside that sphere just, uh, disappears; it is totally neutralized. Everything outside of the effective range then gets sucked into the vacuum it created, until it is filled."

Tim asked, "What do you mean everything?"

"You know; air and, uh, stuff."

"People?"

"Sure, if they're close enough. But, the antimatter part should also be neutralized by the hybrid part. As long as we stay out of range, there should be no adverse consequences, other than a big hole in the building."

Keith interjected. "That's a couple of serious unknowns."

"Allie and I weren't affected by it going through the wall or when the dinosaur attacked, so I think we'll be okay. I figure Allie can take this box with one nodule and I'll find some padding for the other one and take it with me. That way, surely one of us will get close enough to throw it at the Main Core. We just need to hit near the center of the cluster of processors. But, we must handle these very carefully and only unpack 'em at the last moment, because," he looked around the table, "if these things get dropped or hit by something near you...uh, you are history in an instant."

Harrington interrupted. "I know it's risky but it's the only shot we have. Cori, when do we kick this thing off?"

"As soon as Eric and Allie feel ready."

Eric said, "I'm ready." Allie nodded agreement.

Cori continued. "Alright, the two inside teams will need to go down the ductwork first. Forty-five minutes later, when the corridor teams break through the doors, MC will be aware of the breach and will probably send the androids to confront them. That computer now thinks and plans at super-human speed, so you'd better be on your toes. This will be real combat; people may get hurt."

Adam added from the back, *"Androids also."* Everyone looked back. *"Androids could get hurt or, perhaps a more accurate term would be, disabled."*

Cori hesitated. "Yes, Adam, that's correct. Anyone in a combat environment could be, uh, damaged."

She continued. "Agent Charles will lead Team One down the left stairwell." Bill gave a thumbs-up. "The Secret Service will lead Team Two down the right stairwell." The Chief raised his hand. Cori continued. "The android-human partners need to stay together. The androids are ready to be diversions so your guys will have a better shot at the corridor lasers and maintenance androids. I helped ARTech make all of them, so I can tell you that those big ones are faster and stronger than your androids. Don't assume they are out of action just because they are down. You'll have to totally destroy the Z-Processors in the center of their chests and the secondary processors in their heads."

She then said to Keith and the two heroes. "You've got a few minutes for hugs and kisses. The ductwork teams will go at ten-thirty. It will take close to an hour to get all of you through the duct and there's a chance that one of you will make noise, so we will send the corridor teams through the doors at eleven-fifteen. That will provide a diversion in case you make noise getting into the rooms at the bottom.

"Ideally the corridor lasers and androids will have been neutralized and you'll have access to the door into MC. I'm depending on Adam and Eve to dislodge the door and get you into the room. Then, uh, throw your best fastball."

Eric hesitated. "After we take out MC, then what?"

Joe spoke up. "When that blasted computer is destroyed, I expect a momentary blackout, until the emergency backup systems come online. Then, I'm going to need a big vacuum cleaner to clean up the mess."

The President spoke, "When the lights come back on, come back up here and we'll celebrate with steaks. I think Mr. Harrington can make that happen." Harrington nodded.

Allie smiled, "It sounds easy enough."

With the meeting over, the teams began to take their places. Weapons, ammunition and laser power were all checked. Keith, Allie, and Eric spent a few minutes in the Clinic with Lisa and Collins. Collins wanted to go along but could hardly get out of bed. At ten-thirty, the two inside teams were waiting at the ventilation opening.

Eric had one HDA nodule tucked inside his shirt, along with half the padding from the titanium box. Allie took the box and the other nodule in her carry-bag. Eric hugged Allie close, then released just a little and looked her in the eye.

"Don't take unnecessary chances. If you can't get it done, back off. We'll find a way. I can't lose you, not now."

There were no tears this time. Allie looked determined when she smiled and said, "Ditto."

Cori said, "Okay, time to go."

The teams entered the vent opening and headed down.

CHAPTER 26

THE NEW WAR

The White House

Doug Clark could hardly stand the waiting. It was eleven-thirty Eastern Time in the White House. He continued to assess the aftermath of this chaos. One of the first actions, for after PARADISE, would have to be finding a way to communicate with the ships on the way to Mars. The public would expect the government to do something. And, ultimately, the taxpayers would be on the hook for any losses, if Quantum went bankrupt over this.

Besides, most of those on the ships were from Tri-America. He decided that the International Space Consortium needed to be involved. The astronauts on Mars had dealt with solar flares before, just not for this duration.

Doug called the ISC Chief, who happened to be working on the holiday, trying to catch up on paperwork. Doug explained the communications problem with the Mars mission and asked if there were other options for communicating during a solar flare. The Chief told him that they had done it a couple of times by launching a high-speed missile with a radio-package, designed to retransmit the message after it passed the solar flare. He said it had shortened the message-delay time by as much as two weeks.

Doug asked, "When does the next one launch?"

"Next Friday, the tenth. Why?"

"You've probably heard the news by now that the new processors most likely caused the problem at PARADISE. The same systems are on the ships headed for Mars but we have no way to warn them. So, the government will pay ISC to set up an automatic retransmission of an emergency message to the Mars fleet, once it's passed the flare. We're hoping that the vacuum of space has slowed the changes in their processors and they can catch it in time."

After a pause, the ISC Chief said, "Okay, here's the deal; ISC will set up the transmission, free of charge, if you'll encourage the President to support our next funding request."

"Done deal, I can make that happen."

"Alright, have someone contact my Communications Division and they'll take care of it."

"Thanks, Chief, I appreciate your help with this."

"Sure. Just tell the President to consider us little people before he writes another space-travel check."

When they disconnected, Doug pulled up Maddox' information and initiated the call. No Quantum officer was available, so he left a message

Quantum Headquarters Conference Room – Houston

Mr. Zurelle took Daniel Lee off HOLD. "Hello, Mr. Lee, this is Anthony Zurelle speaking. Thank you for holding. How can I help you?"

"I think you're the one who needs the help."

"Pardon?"

"I know that your Z-Processors have become self-aware and caused the disaster at PARADISE. My guess is that Quantum is headed for the dustbin unless you can find a miracle. This is your lucky day; I flew in from Japan last night to provide that miracle."

"Go on."

"I represent a Japanese Consortium that has been working on the next generation of deep-space engines. It will revolutionize travel to the outer planets. We have ships nearly ready right now; just waiting for the engines to be completed. The new engines will use a hybrid-antimatter technology; the same technology that is being used right now to remedy the out-of-control Z-Processors in PARADISE." Daniel paused a moment.

Zurelle spoke up. "I'm not sure what space-engines have to do with our Z-Processors but I'm listening." He activated the

MUTE feature and told Wes Maddox to monitor the call.

Dan continued. "We can use the same technology to fix your Z-Processors, so that they still perform at the AI-level, without absorbing Dark Matter. We have already started designing a retrofit attachment that will use the hybrid-antimatter discovered last year to modify the current processors. For every atom of Dark Matter that the Zurelleum attracts, an atom of Hybrid Dark Antimatter will be released, canceling the Dark Matter. The resulting reaction will be so minute that it will be unnoticeable. The module for future processors can be built-in and will be even simpler. We can have the first retrofit models ready within a week to ten days."

Zurelle sat up in his chair. "Uh, I'm guessing there are International Dollars associated with these retrofits. How much are we talking about?"

"Wrong question, sir; you should be asking how quickly we can pull your fat out of the fire. With no fix, I don't see how you guys can overcome the monetary and physical losses, not to mention the loss of life. And then, there's the issue of goodwill with the public. Imagine how the international community will be all over you.

"Tomorrow, when the markets open I'll be able to buy Quantum stock by the bucket-loads, for pennies on the dollar. I don't think you want that. But, I understand you CEO-types are always concerned about the bottom line; that's your job. So, let me cut through the chaff. The Japanese need funding to pay off the debt they've run up, working on this new technology. They also need extra cash to finish the construction of the new antimatter engines and to outfit the two deep space ships for trial flights."

"How much?"

"Fifty million ID$ should do it."

"FIFTY MILLION?!"

"We don't need it all at once; maybe part now and the rest early next year. Quantum should be able to swing that."

"Are you crazy? We just funded the Mars mission!"

"Yes, and that mission may fail because of your processors. But, the consortium has authorized me to negotiate, so maybe we could give a little. We'll take the first thirty million in hard money when we deliver the repair modules, and you'll sign a promissory contract to guarantee us the rest next January."

He paused to allow Zurelle time to weigh the options. He knew the CEO had no other. Dan continued. "I'm guessing that Dr. Maddox is listening, so you two may need time to talk about it."

Wes mouthed the words to Zurelle, *"Take the deal."*

"Well, Mr. Lee, uh...you drive a hard bargain. If we had another day before the markets open, we might look for alternatives. But, I've always been one to face reality."

"Great. Then we have a deal?"

"Only on one condition."

"Go ahead."

"You will be in Houston by three o'clock today. We will craft the details and agree on an appropriate media announcement telling how, in the interest of Public Safety, we are going to pull all Zurelleum-based processors and repair them free of charge. You will describe how the repairs will be made and why they will make the processors permanently safe. You will encourage the future use of our processors for products in every area of society. You will not use that platform for advertising anything associated the Japanese consortium's products or goals. Agreed?"

"Agreed. Now I know why you're the CEO."

PARADISE

It was eleven o'clock at PARADISE; fifteen minutes before the stairwell teams were going to war with MC. Most of the humans on the teams had the *dry-mouth* often associated with soldiers about to go into battle. The androids considered it to be a normal part of their function.

Each team had ten agents and ten androids. The agents were wearing protective vests and were armed with laser pistols. The androids would use their speed, strength and numbers to subdue the maintenance androids after they were down.

At ten minutes after eleven, Cori walked into the open area

within view of both teams. Ten seconds before *GO*, she raised her hands. Both team leaders gave each other a raised clenched fist.

At eleven fifteen, Cori dropped her hands. Twenty lasers fired at the same time. The doors were removed and discarded within thirty seconds. In less time than that, the Main Core issued the orders for the four remaining maintenance androids to prevent intruders from entering the Maintenance Level.

Both teams had assumed that the maintenance androids would make their stand on the Maintenance Level. But, Cori had warned that they were also self-aware and could make decisions independently of the Main Core.

Agent Charles understood Cori's warning when a laser blast blew the ceiling tiles out just above his head, midway between levels two and three. He dropped onto the stairs and started sliding down on his stomach, finally grabbing the handrail support to stop. Looking down, he saw one of the big androids come into view, running up the stairs. It stopped on a landing and aimed its laser at two agents kneeling on the landing above.

Bill yelled up, "COVER ME!" He let go of the post for a two-hand grip on his weapon. With his body sliding down the stairs, his aim was erratic and the shot missed its mark by a few millimeters.

The android, now only ten meters from Bill, turned its powerful laser toward him. Before it could fire, a team-android leaped from the upper level and knocked the maintenance android to the floor. The powerful android recovered quickly and ripped the smaller android in half, throwing the pieces down the stairwell. Simultaneous laser blasts from the two agents above severed the android's left arm at the elbow. It abandoned its attack and retreated down to a lower level.

The teams inside the ductwork had been waiting for the shooting to start before they crawled the final twenty meters to their positions. Now that MC was distracted, they could position themselves for the assault on the Processor Room. They would be coming from different directions, so one of them was sure to make it easily, so they hoped. Joe's team arrived first. Once inside the office Keith looked around at the debris and the charred remains of the large android, partially blocking the door. He and Joe moved the overturned cabinet so Joe could get to the gun safe. Joe handed Keith an antique M-16 Combat Rifle and pointed out the features.

"Ammo, safety switch, sight, trigger. Step one: Aim at its chest. Step two: Pull the trigger for one second; that will put three rounds in him, assuming your aim is accurate. If he moves, repeat Step Two. Got it?"

Keith swallowed hard. "Yeah."

"Dad, are you sure you can do that?"

"Honey, if you can risk going into the room, I can risk making sure you are safe."

Fifty meters away, Adam stuck his head down through the opening and looked around Steve's Backdoor Room. *"The room is safe,"* he said and dropped onto the desk. Steve followed and moved aside for Eric. Eric lost his grip momentarily, allowing his upper body to fall through before he caught himself. He was horrified to see the padded glass nodule dislodge and fall out of the neck of his shirt. An android hand snapped out and caught it just before it hit the edge of the desk.

Adam looked up. *"I prefer not to be neutralized."*

"Good move, Adam, I like your reflexes," Eric said, and lowered himself down.

"You should; you programmed me."

Steve moved to the desk and turned on his computer system; hoping. No luck. The door was locked so Adam twisted the handle until it broke. He opened it slightly to provide a view into the corridor. The sound of occasional weapons fire could be heard in the distance. MC was only thirty meters from their door. Eric suggested that he make a run for it, since they had not yet heard the footsteps of the androids. Steve pointed to the bend in the corridor. "Ten meters from there is a wall-mounted laser. You won't make it past the corner. We have to wait for the teams to neutralize them before we go."

Laser fire from the corridor past Joe's office was intensifying. The Secret Service Team had encountered stiff resistance from two maintenance androids. They had to slow their progress when the battle took out two team-androids and wounded one agent. They were finally able to destroy two wall-mounted lasers and force the big androids to retreat toward the Main Core.

Joe heard the pounding footsteps of the two androids coming toward his office. Everyone took cover. He told Keith that he would take out the last one, after it passed and for him to be ready as a back-up if the first one returned. Keith nodded and clicked the M-16 safety switch to OFF. His swallowed hard.

The first android passed on a dead run, headed toward the Main Core. A few seconds later the second one passed. Joe jumped into the corridor and yelled, "HEY ROBOT!" The machine stopped and turned to take aim. Joe smirked and yelled, "PROCESS THIS!" He pulled the trigger and the android's chest began to disintegrate. The laser was still moving. Keith brought its head into his sights and pulled the trigger. Pieces went everywhere. It got off one laser blast that hit the ceiling and rained pieces of ceiling tile down on them.

Before Keith had time to celebrate, a laser impact on his right shoulder caused him to stagger. During the fight, they had forgotten about the wall-mounted laser. The burning sensation made him drop to one knee and roll onto the floor. The powerful laser was slowly turning downward for a second shot. Allie grabbed a large trash can on rollers and yelled, "JOE!" When he looked back the can was rolling toward him. He caught it and pushed it hard. It rolled between Keith and the laser.

When the laser fired, a shower of paper and other debris from the can created a cloud of trash in the corridor. When the cloud settled, Joe was on his belly by the remnants of the trash can. He pulled the trigger twice. The dislodged laser fell to the floor. He waited in position for the first android to return; it did not. He got up and stomped out the few small paper fires the laser had ignited.

Allie ran to Keith. "DAD; are you okay?!"

"Yes, honey, I think it's just a flesh wound." He sat up and tore his shirt to make a bigger hole to check the wound. It was not as bad as he feared; the laser had cauterized it, reducing the bleeding. Allie and Eve helped him to his feet. He leaned against the wall for a moment. "I'll be fine. We still have work to do."

Agent Charles was more cautious during their advance down the remainder of the stairwell. One landing before the bottom, they passed the upper torso of the android that had been ripped in half earlier. It had lifted its torso into a sitting position. Bill spoke to the damaged android. "What's your designation, soldier?"

"*Papa Alpha 023, sir.*"

"Great job, twenty-three, thanks for saving my life."

"*It's my job, sir; my purpose.*"

"Just the same, I'm grateful. When this is over, I'll see that you get rebuilt." Bill stood and said, "Okay, men, we have more fun waiting below; let's move out!"

They were unimpeded until they opened the corridor door on the Maintenance Level. Bill's Team quickly took out the two closest wall-mounted lasers and the previously damaged one-armed android. In the process, they lost one more team android, who stepped in front of a laser blast to save its human partner. Moving quickly toward the Main Core, they took out the last wall-laser. The other maintenance android was nowhere in sight.

When Steve heard Bill's Team outside, he opened the door. Three weapons were instantly aimed at him and Bill was putting pressure on the trigger. He pulled back and said, "Man, don't do that! You almost got blown away."

Eric stepped into view. "Are we clear to go?"

"Not yet. We can't find the other android. Stay behind until we know for sure." Eric and Adam stayed close to Bill. Steve provided backup with the other agents. When they were within sight of the door to the Processor Room, Bill called a halt and yelled for Joe. Joe responded and asked how many androids they had disabled. "Just one," Bill said.

Joe yelled, "Same here! They gotta be here somewhere!"

Bill yelled back, "We have a clear path to MC! Cover us; we're going in!"

"OK!" Joe and team moved slowly around the corner and saw Bill's Team down the corridor. After a couple of steps, an android burst out of the utility room and slammed Joe against the wall. In such close quarters, it couldn't aim its laser so it raised its massive arm to crush Joe's head.

Keith was too close to shoot without hitting Joe so he raised his rifle to blocked the android's big arm. The rifle was smashed in half and Keith was knocked to the floor.

Allie yelled "DAD!" and crawled up on the android's back. When she grabbed it by the neck it quickly pulled her loose and dropped her in the pile with Joe and Keith.

Bill chose that moment to get Eric into the Processor Room. He yelled for Adam to pull the door off. Adam grabbed the handle but it just swung freely open. When Eric stepped into the open doorway, he could see the seven nested Z-Processors in racks on the far wall. He detected an eerie hum coming from the Main Core.

It took a couple of seconds to get the HDA out of his shirt and remove the padding. He stood in the hallway for a moment, looking at MC. Then, he drew back like a baseball pitcher and threw the nodule straight at the center of the rack. But, in mid-flight, a large android hand appeared from behind the door and caught the nodule.

The android moved from behind the door with the glass-encased antimatter in its hand. Eric and the others started backing up, realizing they could be neutralized at any moment. As it drew back its arm to throw, Adam leaped in and tackled it at waist-level, knocking the big android backwards toward the Main Core. It held onto the nodule. Three rapid nine-millimeter shots hit the right knee of the big android, destroying one of its servos. Steve was on his belly, smoke coming from the barrel of his pistol.

Down the hallway, with the other android hovering over Joe, Keith and Allie, Eve climbed on its back and was twisting its head.

Eric called out, "Allie! I need the other nodule!"

Allie was on top of the pile so she quickly opened the box, grabbed the glass ball and yelled, "EVE!" She tossed the nodule straight up in the air. The enemy android made a grab for it, but missed. As Eve caught it, the big android threw her off its back. But, just before she crashed into a wall, she hurled the nodule toward Eric. The throw was high but he leaped up and caught it.

Adam and the big android were now in a rolling fight on the floor, Adam attempting to relieve it of the nodule. When Eric attempted to run around them, the big android stuck out its foot and tripped him. Before he hit the floor, he swung his arm toward the Main Core and released the nodule. It rolled slowly across the floor toward its target.

Eric yelled, "ADAM, GET OUT OF THERE!"

Adam was on the bottom, so he pulled his feet up under the big android, grabbed it by the shoulders and threw it over his head. The android, with the nodule still in its hand, impacted the Main Core at the same time as Eric's nodule. Both glass balls broke open. There was a brilliant flash of light, followed by the sound of a loud rushing wind. A twelve-meter diameter Black Hole had appeared where the Main Core used to be. The temporary vacuum was sucking Adam across the floor. Eric yelled, "ADAM," and leaped toward him with his hands out. In mid-leap, the room went dark.

Everything went silent when the vacuum was satisfied. In the darkness, the android on top of Joe and Keith, collapsed. Five seconds seemed like an eternity before the emergency power came on. All agents converged on the room to find Eric and Adam lying on the floor, clasping hands, with Adam's feet at the edge of the gaping twelve-meter hole.

Adam looked at Eric. *"Well, Mr. Jennings, I must say, I am very impressed."*

Eric smiled as he and Adam stood. Everyone began cheering and high-fiving. Joe and Keith pushed the inert android off of them and helped Allie to her feet. Eve stood up; she had a broken servo in her right elbow but was otherwise serviceable. The Secret Service agent opened his communicator, dialed the number, and handed it to Eric. When the President answered, Eric said, "Mr. President, I like my steak medium well."

The President gave a thumbs-up to the crowd and hugged the First Lady. There was soon a jubilant celebration for the thousand-plus in the Reception Dome. Harrington stuck his head in the door and pointed to the skylight. "Mr. President, come look!" The thick cloud dome, that had made PARADISE a prison and destroyed so much, was dissipating. In less than a minute, it had evaporated into nothingness. A light rain was now falling on PARADISE, beginning to wash away the physical reminders of the first battle in this New War. The emotional and scientific analysis would last for years.

When the power came back on, all the door locks released, and Evan and Tim rushed into the Hologram Chambers with medical teams. Hundreds of guests came out of the chambers exhausted and emotionally spent. They had been inside their adventures for almost twenty-four hours. Five adventurers had died.

When Brad Smith saw the dome dissolve, he commanded all Homeland Security units to converge on PARADISE. Before they made it to the entrances, people were streaming out into the parking lots. Chief Smith directed his Damage Assessment teams to begin work immediately in the areas the dome had destroyed. He made his way inside to confirm the President was safe.

It wasn't long before the assault teams from the Maintenance Level were getting off the elevators, carrying wounded agents and pieces of damaged androids. Cori was waiting and hugged them all, including Adam and Eve.

Eve asked, *"Does this make us more human?"*

Cori smiled, with a small tear forming. "In my book, it does."

Adam looked puzzled. *"There's no actual BOOK, right? It's just a metaphor for how you feel inside, is it not?"*

Cori smiled at Eve and said, "Men; they'll never get it." She and Eve walked toward Reception.

Adam looked at Steve with the obvious question. Steve shook his head, "Don't ask." Adam followed him out of the corridor.

The news of the rescue took only moments to appear on every view panel on the globe. The celebration at Quantum was more a collective sigh of relief. Zurelle directed Linda to have her team begin intensive damage control. He told his assistant to contact Harrington before the Quantum News Conference that evening, so he could tell the public he had coordinated with PARADISE and had agreed to repair all Z-Processors, free of charge. PARADISE could then reopen in the future, with appropriate safeguards in place.

It didn't take long for the world to discover the truth about the PARADISE crisis and that the rescue of the President was also the rescue of humankind. It was a closer call than most of them would ever imagine. The heroes, those who risked their lives to stop the Main Core, were soon idolized in the news media and around the world. Books and movies about PARADISE were already on the drawing board. The Japanese were quick to claim credit for the technology that rescued the President.

Eric and Allie were the first to be honored. Dr. Lee had been right; they were signing more autographs than they ever imagined. Adam and Eve were usually interviewed along with them. The two heroes revealed the offer to join the Japanese Research Team and work with Dr. Lee on the programming for the deep space ships. They would help change the future of space travel.

President Holloway endorsed the new space travel technology, ensuring that the Tri-American voters knew he planned to purchase the capability to go farther out into the Solar System.

Adam and Eve's processors were first on the list to be upgraded and their programming was enhanced, preparing them to be test pilots for the new ships the Japanese consortium would soon complete.

One interviewer asked Eric and Allie if there was any romance in the future for them. Allie blushed while Eric smiled and said, "Anything is possible." Adam and Eve just looked puzzled.

Some of the older generation of viewers felt it was a little creepy to see such human-acting *robots*. They had no idea how the future would see the blurring of the lines between android and human.

The cancelation of the evacuation order created chaos, in reverse. Residents trying to return to the cities were competing for space with the myriads of news personnel, cleanup crews, construction workers and scientific researchers wanting to analyze what happened at PARADISE.

During his Rose Garden News Conference, the President assured the nation that he had ordered a full investigation into how such a failure could have happened. He also instructed the government's Technology Division to work with other countries to establish standards for future use of computers with artificial intelligence. Doug hoped such aggressive action would result in a dramatic increase in the President's polling numbers.

Within a few days, much to Harrington's surprise, PARADISE was deluged with reservation requests from people who wanted to see the aftermath firsthand. Even with the Adventure Dome closed, the park was fifty percent booked. The PARADISE team had to scramble to get the mess cleaned up and coordinate with the Japanese to have the remaining Z-Processors modified with the HDA upgrades. In the interim, the Main Core was replaced with twenty-five nested Zelon Processors, which could easily run the four domes that remained open.

When the markets opened on Monday, Quantum's stock took the biggest price-drop in its history. Only Daniel Lee's reassurances of a safe fix for the processors kept the stock from tumbling to unrecoverable levels.

Monday afternoon, Quantum released the plan to communicate with the Mars Mission. The high-speed resupply ship would launch Thursday, a day earlier than planned. The emergency message to Ken would be transmitted within a week.

The President ordered a review of ISODS and scheduled a repair mission to upgrade the four orbiting platforms. It would be at least a month before the repair could be done.

To launch his own investigation into Zurelleum, the President called a meeting on Thursday afternoon with Bernard Herrington and the major players from Quantum; Zurelle, Maddox, and Gustav. His first goal was to assess the impact of the PARADISE failure on the overall economy. If necessary, he would spend more tax money on Quantum, but only to save them from bankruptcy. A Quantum failure would be a government failure.

His second goal was to ensure the Mars Mission was a success; Tri-American lives were at stake, along with certain political implications. So, the President put the important question to Zurelle.

"Tony, assuming your emergency transmission helps Mr. Anderson avert a systems failure on the mission ships, will they still be able to safely arrive and begin mining operations on Mars?"

"Well, Mr. President, our message instructs Ken to remove the Zelon computer systems from four shuttles and use them to replace the Z-Processors on the two mission ships. It will slow operations a little, once they get to Mars, but we feel that--"

Doug Clark had entered the conference room and interrupted the briefing. "Mr. President, I have a message."

"Not now, Doug, let's handle it after this meeting."

Doug handed it to him. "No, Mr. President, I think you should read it now."

The President was irritated. "Oh, alright." As he read it, his face turned ashen. He closed his eyes momentarily and then handed it to Zurelle. It was an emergency message from Major Greenlee at the International Space Consortium.

The message simply read:

"THERE HAS BEEN A NEUTRON WARHEAD EXPLOSION IN SPACE. ISODS JUST SHOT DOWN THE MARS RESUPPLY SHIP."

EPILOGUE

10.2 Million Kilometers from Earth

Onboard Mars One

Sandi was about to exit their sleeping quarters when the direct communications circuit to Mars Two activated. The direct line helped Ken and Red coordinate the mission, in private if necessary. As she answered, she looked out the port hole nearby at Mars Two, seemingly motionless in space just a kilometer off the port side of Mars One.

"Hey, Red, it's Sandi. Ken is still in Operations. What's up?"

"Oh, hi Sandi. I just wanted to let Ken know about a glitch in the 3-D Printer. I thought he'd be in bed already."

"Well, he should be. Something must have delayed him in Ops. What's the problem with the printer?"

"It might not be crucial at this point. Maintenance broke the handle on the trash compacter and they are trying to print a new one. But, when they enter the stored schematic, it shuts down before printing it. They tried three times. The system is being driven by the new processors in the Main Core, so there should be plenty of processing power to do the job."

"Hum...maybe the computer guys need to take a look. I'm just heading to Ops to check on Ken. I'll relay your message. I'm sure he'll get right back to you. Just record all the details and you two can discuss it."

"Thanks, Sandi. I entered a Trouble Report in the files. I'll wait to hear from him."

Sandi made her way toward Mars One Operations. The one-half gravity felt good, after a day of training and working in weightlessness. She stopped at a porthole and looked out at the expanse of space, dotted with star clusters and galaxies. *"Wow,"* she thought, *"what could be better than this?"*

She wondered what could have delayed Ken; it was the beginning of the sleep cycle and they should already be in bed. Tomorrow would be a busy day, with the first scheduled Collision Avoidance Drill, using the laser cannons to deflect space debris.

They had only been in space for twelve days, but at 40,000 kilometers-per-hour, they were over 10 million kilometers from Earth. Sandi knew the homesickness she felt must be a little of what explorers throughout history had felt when they headed toward their *unknowns*. *"Not much longer,"* she thought, *"then I can talk to Dad."*

Entering Operations, she heard voices. Ken was recording the Daily Status Report into his personal view panel system, while Albert called out the various readings on the Operations Status Board. The Status Board could download it automatically, but Ken insisted on being in the loop of information.

Sandi watched for a moment and then asked, "Hey handsome, are you coming to bed soon?"

Albert looked up. *"Are you addressing Captain Anderson?"*

Sandi giggled. "Yes, in human terms, he is definitely handsome.

"Yes, ma'am; if you say so, but I wouldn't know anything about that."

Ken still had his nose in his work. "Yeah; whatever." Then he looked up and smiled. "Sorry hon, I'm just trying to resolve this diverse reading on the Main Core Processing Report. My Remote Data Monitor shows that it has processed over two terabytes more data than the Operations Status Board shows. I can't seem to nail down what it did with the extra processing power. It's not a major deal at this point, but anything out of the ordinary is troubling, especially since I got that strange call from Chan just before we lost contact with Earth. He said something about a computer problem."

"Well, Red just called; the 3-D Printer is acting up. He put a report in the Maintenance File for you."

"Okay, let's take a look."

Albert interrupted. "Sir, do you really need to do that tonight? Your sleep time has already begun?"

"It'll just take a second." Ken accessed the Trouble Reports dropdown menu and selected Maintenance. "Huh?...nothing there."

Albert looked at Sandi. *"I tried to convince Captain Anderson that such anomalies are within tolerance for a Main Core with a vast capacity. I can resolve both issues before morning."*

Sandi agreed. "Maybe Albert's right. Why don't you come to bed and let him do his night watchman thing? Maybe the glitches will be more obvious in the morning."

Ken made a few more entries and then turned off the panel. "OK. Maybe a good night's sleep will help. Albert, rerun that last Usage Profile and reboot the maintenance files. Have the results for me in the morning."

"Yes, Captain. Sleep well. Good night to you both."

Albert waited for a few seconds after they left, and then stepped away from the Master Warning Panel he had been blocking from Ken's view. He had disabled the audible warning alarm earlier, just before Ken arrived, but the Master Warning Light had been flashing red for the last five minutes. He gently touched the RESET button. He turned his android eyes to the Communications Status Panel and reactivated the data monitoring circuit. The Main Core was transmitting new instructions to the Mars Two Data Base at a speed of two terabytes.

Albert smiled.

(THE CONTINUATION...of the New War)

ABOUT THE AUTHORS

Max Holt is a retired U.S. Army pilot, having served 22 years on active duty, including two combat tours in Vietnam. He is an avid Science Fiction reader and writer. Max started his publishing company, Max Holt Media, in 2015. This book begins Max's partnership with his brother, Dan Holt, to initiate this new series. Also, they are both also continuing to write additional books in the UNDERNEATH THE MOON saga, expected to continue for several more volumes.

Max and his wife Sandy have two sons and six grandchildren. They enjoy traveling and have collected flags from 37 countries. Other than the USA, their favorites have been Switzerland, Austria, Italy and the UK, where they have established a life-long friendship with a family in Darlington, England. They are now retired and live in Mount Juliet, near Nashville, Tennessee.

Contact Max: www.maxholtmedia.com
                            max@maxholtmedia.com
On Twitter -   @maxholtmedia

Amazon Author's Page: https://www.amazon.com/Max-Holt/e/B012JROY26?ref_=pe_1724030_132998060

Dan Holt is a U.S. Army veteran, having served three years as a Communications Specialist in Germany. He spent the remainder of his civilian career as a self-taught engineer, designing and testing large-scale production equipment for the file folder industry. The efficiency and durability of his designs even garnered interest from some foreign manufacturers.

In retirement, Dan has used his writing skills to express his continuing fascination with science fiction. His variety in sci-fi thought is evident in his other novels, SLEEP MODE and KEEPSAKE. The Underneath the Moon series, Sleep Mode and Keepsake are all now available on audio through www.audible.com. Dan, and his brother Max, are also partnering together to continue writing future books in the Underneath the Moon saga. See all of Dan's books at the publisher's website, www.maxholtmedia.com.

Contact Dan through his Amazon Author's Page: https://www.amazon.com/Dan-Holt/e/B012LRN65K/ref=sr_ntt_srch_lnk_1?qid=1491001715&sr=8-1

www.ingramcontent.com/pod-product-compliance
Lightning Source LLC
Chambersburg PA
CBHW071135170626
46809CB00002B/624